By the same author

The Far Pavilions
Shadow of the Moon
Trade Wind

M. M. Kaye

Death in Zanzibar

Allen Lane

To
the Zanzibar I knew.
With love

ALLEN LANE
Penguin Books Ltd
536 King's Road
London SW10 0UH

First published under the title *The House of Shade* by Longmans 1959
This revised edition published by Allen Lane 1983

Filmset in Monophoto Times by
Northumberland Press Ltd, Gateshead
Printed in Great Britain by
Richard Clay (The Chaucer Press) Ltd, Bungay, Suffolk

Kaye, M. M.
    Death in Zanzibar.
    I. Title
    823'.914[F]   PR6061.H945

    ISBN 0-7139-1521-8

FOREWORD

In the early years of the 1950s there used to be a B.B.C. Radio programme called 'Housewives' Choice', which consisted of popular records — in those days, presumably 78s? — that provided a pleasant accompaniment to tedious and repetitive chores. Any tune in the Top Twenty got played fairly frequently, and one in particular caught my fancy: the first line of the refrain being 'Then I'll go sailing far — off to Zanzibar!'

Since I myself was in the all-too-familiar position of a British Army wife — abandoned, with my two small daughters, in depressing Army quarters in a small garrison town while my husband and his regiment were on active service somewhere on the other side of the world (on this occasion, Korea!) — I would have given a great deal to go 'sailing far', to almost anywhere. But Zanzibar is one of those names that possess a peculiar, singing magic in every syllable; like Samarkand or Rajasthan, or Kilimanjaro; and when the radio was not playing that song I used to sing it to myself, and like Dany in this story, I read anything I could get hold of on the subject of Zanzibar: never dreaming that I would ever see it myself.

Then, when my husband was almost due back in England, his regiment, while *en route* for home, was suddenly diverted to Kenya. And since families were allowed to go out there to join their husbands and fathers, it was not long before the children and I were setting off to Nairobi on a flight that nowadays would only take a few hours, but which in those days, as in this story, took well over twenty-four.

5

It was during our time in Kenya that I got the chance to visit Zanzibar. And I fell in love with it at first sight, for it turned out to be one of those rare places that live up to everything one has hoped and dreamed that they would be. I also had the honour of meeting its greatly respected and much-loved old Sultan, His Highness Seyyid Khalifa bin Harub: grandson of Thuwani of Muscat and Oman — who was a half-brother of the two successive Sultans of Zanzibar, Majid and Bargash, about whom I wrote in a historical novel, *Trade Wind*, which tells the story of Tyson Frost's grandfather, Rory — Emory Tyson Frost of *Kivulimi*.

Since my husband kept being posted to all sorts of novel and entertaining places, I wrote a 'whodunit' set in each of them. Because of this, I made detailed notes of things I was afraid I might forget. So that when, several years later, I got around to writing this story, all I had to do was to hunt up my Zanzibar notebook, and there it all was. An exact description of everything I could possibly need, down to the advertisement painted on looking-glass in the Mombasa Airport, and the millipede crawling across the floor of the tiny, makeshift one on Pemba.

The Zanzibar I knew has gone for ever, and this book is already a 'period piece' — almost a historical novel, so much has changed. But at least I saw it, and lived in it for a brief while, and it is stored away in my mind for ever.

1

The heavy brocade curtains stirred as though they had been blown by a breath of wind, and a billowing fold touched the corner of the dressing-table and overset a small bottle of nail varnish.

It was a very slight sound, but it woke Dany; jerking her out of an uneasy dream in which she had been hurrying down a long lonely country road in the sad fog and drizzle of an early autumn, clutching a small sealed envelope and listening to the drip of rain off the unseen hedges and the footsteps of someone who followed close behind her.

She had caught brief glimpses of this person when she stopped and turned, and once it had been Mr Honeywood with his narrow, dry, solicitor's face and his small dry disapproving cough, and sometimes it had been a large hearty woman in tweeds, striding through the wet mist, or an Oriental; a dark-faced man wearing flowing white robes and a fez — or was it a turban? But none of them had any right to be following her, and she dare not let them overtake her. It was vitally important that they should not over-take her ...

The bottle fell over and Dany awoke.

She sat up in bed shivering in the aftermath of nightmare, and was momentarily surprised to find herself in an unfamiliar room. Then the dream receded, and she remembered that she was no longer in her great-aunt's house, but at the Airlane Hotel in London.

Yesterday, in Market-Lydon, it had been misty and damp; as

though autumn were already far advanced. But here in London on this September morning it still seemed to be high summer, and although it was very early and the city was as yet barely astir, the sky beyond the open window was clear and bright.

The curtains that had been closely drawn last night were now partially open, and the pale light of early morning, filtering into the room, showed a clutter of cardboard boxes, air-weight suitcases, tissue paper, and the new lizard-skin bag that was Great-aunt Harriet's parting present and which contained, among other things, a brand new passport.

Dany had checked over all the impedimenta of foreign travel late last night, and now all she had left to do was to buy a beach hat, a sun-suit and something for air sickness, and to introduce herself to her step-father's sister, Mrs Bingham, whom she had so far never met but who had been staying since yesterday in the same hotel and was also travelling out to Zanzibar on a Zero Zephyr of the Green Zero Line.

London, Naples, Khartoum, Nairobi. Mombasa, Tanga, Pemba, Zanzibar——

Dany shivered again. A shiver of pure delight that ended unexpectedly in a quiver of unease: a sense of disquiet so sharply urgent that she turned quickly, half expecting to find someone standing behind her. But nothing moved except the curtains billowing idly in the dawn wind, and of course there was no one there. And no one watching her! It was only the effect of that silly dream about people following her ...

Dany Ashton had left school almost a year ago, but this was her first taste of freedom, for despite the fact that, as her mother's daughter, she might have been expected to have led an erratic and entertaining existence, her life had hitherto been a remarkably sheltered one. Her mother, currently Lorraine Frost, was a notable beauty who collected and discarded husbands in a manner that would have done credit to a film star, and Dany, her only

8

child, was the daughter of her first husband, Daniel Ashton.

Lorraine had never been maternally minded, and Daniel Ashton, explorer and big-game hunter, had been more interested in such things as the Lesser Kudu and the upper reaches of the Amazon than in fatherhood. He had met his death at the hands of an unenlightened and excitable tribe of South-American Indians when Dany was three years old, and Lorraine had promptly married Dwight Cleethorpe, an affable millionaire from Chicago, and handed her small daughter over to the care of a maiden aunt, Harriet Henderson.

Mr Cleethorpe, whose hobbies were golf and deep-sea fishing, had not lasted, and there had been three more step-fathers in rapid succession, the latest of whom was Tyson Frost, the novelist. But none of them had taken more than a passing interest in their step-daughter, and Lorraine's visits, though exhilarating, were always brief and did little to disturb the even tenor of life at *Glyndarrow*, the large red-brick house in Hampshire where Dany's Great-aunt Harriet lived in cosy Edwardian seclusion while the world passed her by.

Great-aunt Harriet disapproved of Progress and the Post-War World. She had also disapproved strongly of this visit to Zanzibar, but had been unable to prevent it since she was not the child's legal guardian, and moreover her great-niece had suddenly displayed an unsuspected streak of independence.

Dany had been wildly delighted at the prospect of going to this outlandish spot where Tyson Frost owned a house, and she had not only paid no attention at all to her great-aunt's warnings, but had flatly refused to spend the three nights in London under the roof of an elderly relative, or to be accompanied there by Twisdon, Great-aunt Harriet's austere and aged maid.

Chaperones, declared Dany, were as dead as the Dodo, and she was perfectly capable of looking after herself: or if she were not, the sooner she started learning, the better. In any case, Lorraine had advised her to stay at the Airlane, as there would be half a

9

dozen other people there who were also bound for Zanzibar and the house-party at *Kivulimi*, and who would be travelling on the same plane. Her fellow-guests were Tyson's sister, Augusta Bingham and her friend and companion, Miss Bates; the Marchese di Chiago, who raced (but whether horses, dogs, cars or yachts was not disclosed); Amalfi Gordon, a close friend of Lorraine's, and her fiancé Mr Holden — American and something to do with publishing — who intended to get married on the eve of departure and thereby combine business (discussing terms for a new Tyson Frost novel) with pleasure in the form of a honeymoon in Zanzibar. And finally, Mr Holden's secretary, Miss Kitchell. One or any of these people, wrote Lorraine airily, would be sure to keep an eye on Dany.

'If she means Mrs Bingham or Miss Bates, then possibly they will do so,' said Aunt Harriet, frigid with disapproval. 'But what if it should be this Marchese? I cannot think what has come over your mother. It all comes from living abroad: foreigners are notoriously lax. And *no* one could approve of Mrs Gordon! There was an exceedingly unpleasant rumour going round that she had—— Well, never mind. But she is not in my opinion a suitable companion for any young girl. Besides, she has been married and divorced several times already.'

'I don't see that you can hold that against her,' said Dany with a somewhat rueful smile. 'What about Lorraine?'

'That is *quite* different,' said Aunt Harriet firmly. 'She is your mother — and a Henderson. And I do wish you would not refer to her as "Lorraine". You know how much I dislike it.'

'Yes, Aunt. But you know how much she dislikes me calling her anything else.'

Aunt Harriet shifted her ground: 'It's a very complicated journey. I understand that the Green Zero Line only fly as far as Nairobi, and that you would have to spend a night in an hotel there, and take another aeroplane on the following day. Anything might happen. There have been race-riots in Nairobi.'

'Yes, Aunt. But Lorraine — I'm sorry; Mother — says that Tyson's secretary, Nigel Ponting, will be meeting the plane there, so I shall be quite safe.'

'Ponting ... Yes. I have met him. He came here with your step-father two years ago. You were at school. A most affected man. More like a dancing master than a secretary. He minced and giggled. Not at all a reliable type, and I did not take to him.'

'I'm sorry, Aunt.'

Old Miss Henderson had been compelled to give up the unequal struggle, and Dany — naïve, romantic, eager — had left for London unchaperoned, taken a room with a private bath and balcony at the Airlane, and indulged in an orgy of theatres, shopping and freedom.

She had also had a commission to execute for Lorraine, who had asked her to call on Tyson's solicitor, Mr Honeywood, in Market-Lydon in Kent, to collect a document that Tyson would like her to bring out for him. *'This is the address,'* wrote Lorraine. *'It's his house, not his office, as he's more or less retired now. I do hope this won't be an awful bore for you, darling, and of course the person who should really be doing this is Gussie Bingham, or that hearty girl-friend of hers, as they live practically on his doorstep. But Tyson says Gussie is an unreliable gossip with a memory like a sieve, and so he would far rather you did it. I do hope you won't mind, baby? Tyson has written to Mr Honeywood and told him that you'll call for it on the afternoon of the twelfth, between three and four, and that he's to have it ready for you. You won't forget, darling, will you?'*

Dany had duly gone down to Kent, though as she had wanted to fit in a cinema in the afternoon as well as a theatre that night, she had rung up Mr Honeywood and changed the time to eleven-fifteen in the morning instead. That had been yesterday. And now it was the last day: really the last day. Tomorrow she would be flying eastward — to Zanzibar!

Ever since Lorraine had married Tyson Frost, Dany had dreamed of going to Zanzibar. She had ransacked the local library

11

and spent her pocket-money on books about the island: *Princes of Zinj, Isle of Cloves*, and a dozen others. Books that told the saga of the great Seyyid Saïd, Imam of Muscat and first Sultan of Zanzibar. And of such things as the underground wells whose waters were said to come from far inland in Africa, the haunted palace of Dunga and the sacred drums of Zanzibar, the vast legendary treasure buried by Seyyid Saïd in Bet-el-Ras; the horrors of the slave trade and the pirate raids, and the witch-haunted island of Pemba, home of devils, djinns and warlocks.

Europeans were not permitted to hold land in Zanzibar, but long ago Tyson's grandfather — that rowdy, roving, colour-ful adventurer, Emory Frost — had done a service to the great Saïd, and his reward had been the lease of a house, *Kivulimi*, for a period of a hundred and fifty years. Tyson's visits there were irregular and brief, but as this year happened to be the seventieth anniversary of Emory's death, and he intended to write a book based upon the life and times of that fabulous character, he had descended upon *Kivulimi*, complete with wife, private secretary and an assortment of guests. And Dany's dream had at last come true.

'Then I'll go sailing far, off to Zanzibar — though my dream places seem — better than they really are ...' Dany slid out of bed, crooning a snatch from a song that had been popular when she was in the fourth form; and as she did so something moved at the far side of the room and she started violently and bit her tongue. But it was only her own reflection in the looking-glass, and she made a face at it, and going to the dressing-table, picked up the new lizard-skin bag and rummaged through it for a slip of paper on which she had written down the time that the bus for the Airport left the Terminal. It did not seem to be there, and she was about to try one of the drawers when she remembered that it was in the pocket of the camel-hair coat that she had left in the ladies' room on the previous evening, and forgotten to retrieve. She would have to remember to fetch it after breakfast.

Once again something made her jump nervously; a soft slapping sound in the corridor outside that she identified a moment later as the morning papers, dropped by a page-boy whose feet had made no sound on the thick pile of the carpet. She could not understand why she should be so ridiculously on edge this morning; she had never previously been given to nerves. Perhaps this curious feeling of tension was something that everyone experienced when they first realized that they were entirely on their own? If so, she could only hope it did not last long! Giving the page-boy a minute or two to leave the corridor, she crossed to the door. Tea would not be arriving for at least another hour and a half, and she might as well fill in the time by reading the papers.

The corridor was silent and empty, its lushly carpeted length punctuated by white and gold doors, numerous pairs of freshly polished shoes and a varied assortment of daily newspapers. Dany stepped out cautiously and picked up her own selection, the *Daily Dawn*. And as she did so her eye was caught by the heading of a column: *'Man Murdered in Market-Lydon'*.

She opened the paper and stared at it, frowning. Market-Lydon . . .? Why, that was where she had been yesterday! The little town where——

There was a sharp click immediately behind her and she whirled round. But it was too late. The draught had blown the door shut behind her and she was locked out in the corridor.

Dany dropped the paper and pushed futilely at the door. But it possessed a spring lock and remained blandly impervious to her efforts, and she turned from it to stare helplessly up and down the silent corridor. There was, fortunately, no one in sight, but she could see no sign of a bell either; and even if there had been one she could hardly use it when the chances were that it would be answered by a man.

For the first time Dany regretted the purchase of that diaphanous and far too expensive nightgown. Nylon and lace might be enchantingly frivolous, but its purpose appeared to be to reveal

13

rather than conceal, and she was only too well aware that to all intents and purposes she might just as well be naked. Why, oh why had she flung away those sensible, high-necked and sacklike garments of white winceyette that Aunt Harriet had considered to be the only suitable and modest night wear? If only——

It was at this inopportune moment that footsteps sounded on the staircase that led into the corridor some twenty feet from her door.

Despite the heavy pile of the carpet the footsteps were clearly audible and noticeably uneven, and they were accompanied by a male voice singing in a blurred undertone the same song that had recently been running through Dany's head.

' *"I want to go away — be a stowaway,"*' announced the gentleman on the staircase, ' *"Take a trip, on a ship, let my troubles——"* blast!' The singer stumbled noisily on the stairs, and something — possibly a hat? — bounced down them.

Inspiration born of despair descended upon Dany, and snatching up the fallen newspaper she retired hastily behind the front page of the *Daily Dawn* just as the owner of the voice reached the top of the stairs and turned into the corridor.

He proved to be a tall, dishevelled young man in formal evening dress, wearing his white tie several inches off centre, and carrying a gaily coloured balloon and a large and fluffy toy cat with a pink ribbon round its neck. His dark hair was in a state of considerable disorder, and quite apart from his undeniably festive appearance he possessed an indefinable air of what an earlier generation would have termed 'rakishness'.

He stood for a moment or two swaying slightly and looking vaguely about him, and then his gaze alighted upon Dany.

'Well, say!' said the young man, saying it in an unmistakably transatlantic voice: 'what do you know about that!'

He advanced until he was level with her, and then as the full beauty of her situation dawned upon him he gave way to immoderate mirth, and stood before her laughing his head off, while

14

Dany glared back at him like an angry kitten, scarlet cheeked, helpless and infuriated.

'Be quiet!' hissed Dany, 'you'll wake everyone up! Do you know what time it is?'

' *"Three o'clock in the mor ... ning, I've danced the whole night through!"* ' carolled the young man, throwing his head back and giving it everything he had got in a blurred but pleasing baritone.

'And you look like it!' said Dany in a furious whisper. 'But it's nearly six now, and I want to get back into my room. Don't just stand there laughing! *Do* something! Get me a pass key — any-thing! Can't you see I'm locked out?'

'I can,' said the young man. 'And let me tell you that I haven't seen anything better in days. No, sir! It's a pity that your taste in newspapers didn't run to a smaller sized sheet, but who am I to carp and c-cavil? Let's face it, it might have been *The Times*. Not, le' me tell you, that you look like a dame who reads *The Times*. No, I sh'd say——'

'*Will* you be quiet?' demanded Dany frantically. 'And if you aren't going to help, go away! No — no, don't do that! For good-ness sake get me a pass key.'

'Sure,' said the young man cordially. 'Any li'l thing you say. Here, hold the children.'

He handed over the balloon and the white cat, and Dany, mak-ing a rash attempt to accept them, came dangerously near to losing the front page of the *Daily Dawn* in the process. The balloon bounced out of reach and the white cat fell to the floor.

'Now look what you've done!' said the young man reproach-fully. 'You've dropped Asbestos. Have you no compassion on dumb animals? He may be heat-resistant, but he doesn't like being kicked around.'

He retrieved the cat and hunted through his waistcoat pockets with his left hand. 'Don't rush me. I know I had it some place. Ah, here we are! Madam — no. No wedding ring. That's good. Miss — your key.'

He held out a door key with a courtly bow.

'But that *isn't* my key,' said Dany on the verge of shedding tears of sheer exasperation. 'It's yours!'

'Why, so it is! You know something? you're a very intelligent girl. You may even read *The Times*. A pity. Well, I'll tell you what. You can't stand there for everyone to take a look at; 'tisn't decent — besides being darned chilly. I'm parked in that room over there, and I guess you'd better go right in and wait while I fetch some gilded flunkey to batter down your door. O.K.? Don't mention it: my fam'ly motto has always been "Never Give a Sucker an Even Break". Let's go.'

He tacked across the corridor, humming gently, and after a couple of unsuccessful tries succeeded in opening the door of the room opposite Dany's.

'There you are,' he said in the self-congratulatory tone of one who has performed an intricate conjuring trick: 'Move right in. We Holdens are nothing if not hospitable. Make yourself at home. And if there's any little thing you fancy, such as a blanket or a bath towel or a bathrobe, jus' go right ahead and wrap it up. The joint's yours. I'll be right back.'

He bowed again, sweeping the floor in an old-world gesture with the white cat, and removed himself.

Dany did not move until he was out of sight (the *Daily Dawn* did not meet round the back) but as soon as it was safe to do so she crossed the corridor at a run and took refuge in his room.

It was in darkness, for the curtains were still drawn, and she switched on the lights and saw that the bed had been neatly turned down and a pair of maroon-coloured pyjamas laid out upon it. There was also a bottle-green dressing-gown hanging over the back of a chair, and she reached for it thankfully. It was far too large, but all the more welcome for that; for Dany, though slim, was by no means short, and it covered her adequately from throat to ankle, allowing no more than a glimpse of bare feet.

A small travelling-clock on the bedside table informed her that

16

it was already ten minutes to six, and from behind the heavily curtained windows she could hear the muted rumble of the early morning traffic. But there were as yet no sounds of movement from inside the hotel, and Dany sat down on the edge of the bed and prepared to wait.

The room was an almost exact counterpart of her own, though a good deal tidier, and it contained one slightly surprising object: a large photograph of an extraordinarily beautiful woman that stood on the dressing-table, expensively framed in silver and inscribed largely across one corner 'To Lash — with all my love for always — Elf'. It was not, however, the film-star features or the extravagant inscription that was surprising, but the fact that someone had draped the frame in a length of black crêpe, drawn a heavy line through the word 'always' and substituted tersely above it, and in red ink, 'September'.

Dany was engaged in studying these interesting additions when her eye was caught by something else: a familiar coloured label on a suitcase that stood on a chair by the dressing-table. Lashmer J. Holden, Jnr, it would appear, was also intending to fly to Zanzibar via Nairobi.

Holden ... Why, of course! Lorraine had mentioned him. American and something to do with publishing. He was going to see Tyson about some book or other, and to spend his honeymoon in Zanzibar. Although if that photograph was anything to go by ... A cold draught of air blew through the room and billowed the curtains, and a quantity of letters that had been carelessly propped against a china ornament on the writing-table fluttered to the ground and lay strewn across the carpet.

Dany rose and replaced them, noting as she did so that Mr Holden's correspondents appeared to be numerous, but unexciting; the large majority of the envelopes being of the strictly utilitarian variety with the address typewritten on them, and having apparently come from various secretarial agencies.

She stacked them in a neat pile and put them back, and then

17

stopped to retrieve the discarded sheet of newspaper. And as she did so her gaze fell on a word in black type: *'Murder'*.

'Man Murdered in Market-Lydon. Retired Solicitor Found Shot. Mr H. T. Honeywood ...'

But it couldn't be! There must be some mistake. It couldn't possibly be Tyson's Mr Honeywood. That small, dried-up, disapproving solicitor. It must be someone with the same name. People one had met — people one knew — were never murdered. But there was no mistake. Here was his name. And his address: the prim grey-stone house standing back from the road behind a high wall and an ugly screen of wet laurels. Dany sat down slowly on the bed and read the incredible column of close print.

Mr Honeywood had been shot through the heart at close range, presumably by someone whom he had no reason to fear, for there were no signs of a struggle. The safe in his study had been open, and certain sums of money — the funds, apparently, of local societies of which he was treasurer — had vanished, though no one was in a position to say if anything else had been removed. Mr Honeywood had virtually retired from active work and seldom visited the office in the High Street, which was in the charge of a junior partner, Mr John Honeywood, a nephew; but he occasionally saw an old client at his house. It was this scarcity of visitors, allied to the absence of his housekeeper, that accounted for the fact that the crime was not discovered until so late ...

The police were of the opinion that he had been killed some time during the morning, possibly between eleven-thirty and twelve, but his housekeeper, who was elderly and deaf, had asked for the day off to visit a cousin in Tunbridge Wells, and had left the house shortly before 10 a.m. She had not returned until late in the evening, and it was she who had eventually found the body. There was also a charlady who came every morning for two hours and who had left about the same time, but neither lady could say for certain if Mr Honeywood had been expecting a visitor, and the sole entry in his engagement pad for the day read 'D.A.

18

between 3 and 4.' The police were anxious to interview a young woman who had been seen leaving the house shortly after half-past eleven that morning, and whom they thought could give them some information ...

Why — they mean *me*! thought Dany, horrified. But I can't tell them anything! It can't be true——

She let the paper slide to the floor and sat staring down at it. She would have to go round to the nearest police station as soon as she was dressed. Or did one merely reach for a telephone and dial 999? They could not detain her for long, for there was very little that she could tell them. But all the same it would cut badly into her last day, and she had meant to——

Another and far more disturbing thought suddenly struck her. Wouldn't there be an inquest? And if there were, would she have to attend it and lose her seat on the plane? But if she did that she might not be able to get another one for days! Possibly for weeks——! Or even months, if the Nairobi run was a popular one. Tyson and Lorraine might have left Zanzibar and moved on to Spain or Cape Town or New York before she could get another passage, and she could not *bear* it if that were to happen!

Perhaps after all it would be better to say nothing, and do nothing. She had only to wait one more day and then she would be safely aboard the plane. And the police were not in the least likely to fetch her back from Zanzibar for any inquest. It wasn't as if she could give them any help, and anyway she could always write them a letter.

She straightened up with a sigh of relief as though a weight had fallen off her shoulders, and her gaze fell again on the travelling-clock. Twenty-five minutes past six! She had not realized that so much time had slipped by. What on earth was Mr Holden doing? Had he forgotten all about her? It could not possibly have taken him over half an hour to find a valet or a page-boy and collect a pass key.

She jumped up and had started for the door when it opened,

19

and Mr Holden was back, still clutching the cat.

'Relax!' said Mr Holden buoyantly. 'Here come the United States Marines! One of those retired ambassadors in striped pants and ten dollars' worth of whiskers rustled up a spare key. The guy seemed to think he should stand by and personally usher you in, but I urged him to spare your blushes, and he reluctantly handed it over. I guess he fears the worst.'

He held out the key and Dany clutched it gratefully.

'Sorry to have kept you waiting,' pursued Mr Holden cheerfully, 'but I got side-tracked by an Alka-Seltzer. They certainly offer service in this gilded flop-house. Hey! — you're not going, are you? Stick around and be sociable.'

'I don't feel sociable,' said Dany. 'Not at this hour of the morning. Thank you for your help. And for the dressing-gown. I'll return it.'

'So I should hope,' said Mr Holden. 'It has sentimental associations. Say, if I can manage that one I must be in better shape than I thought. "Sentimental Associations". Not bad. Not bad at all. That bathrobe was a present from Elf. Embroidered that flashy great monogram on it with her own fair hands — so she says. But you don't have to believe a word of it. The truth is not in that girl. Jus' between you an' me, honey——'

The door shut with a decisive bang, and he was alone.

'No gratitude,' said Mr Holden sadly, addressing himself to Asbestos. 'That's what's wrong with women. No — bloody — gratitude!'

2

The corridor was still silent and empty, and the entire hotel appeared to be still asleep: a fact for which Dany was profoundly grateful. She fitted the key into the lock, opened the door — and stood wide-eyed and aghast.

The room looked as though a tornado had struck it. Drawers had been pulled out and their contents emptied on to the floor, suitcases had been dragged out and opened, and tissue paper, cardboard boxes and bedclothes strewed the carpet.

'So *that's* what he was doing!' said Dany, breathing stormily. 'I suppose this is his idea of a screamingly funny joke! How dare he — how *dare* he!'

She whirled round and ran back across the corridor, and had reached out her hand to bang on his door when she changed her mind. Mr Holden was undoubtedly under the influence of alcohol — a condition that Dany had not previously encountered — and the chances were that he was at that very moment gleefully waiting for her to burst into his room in a fury so that he could enjoy his silly practical joke to the full. It would therefore be more dignified — and snubbing — to ignore the whole thing.

She went back to her own room and, shutting the door with a commendable lack of noise, spent the next half-hour restoring order, so that by the time the room-maid put in an appearance with a tray of morning tea, the place was tolerably tidy again.

Dany had gone down to breakfast at eight-thirty to find the vast dining-room sparsely populated, and had lost her appetite after one glance at the representative selection of the morning papers that had been thoughtfully placed on her table.

Yes, there it was again. 'Murder at Market-Lydon.' Every paper carried the story, and the accounts did not vary much, except as to detail. One paper mentioned that the 'fatal shot' had been fired from an automatic small enough to be carried easily in a coat pocket or a lady's handbag, and another said that the initials 'D. A.' on Mr Honeywood's engagement pad had been duplicated on a lace and cambric handkerchief that had been found under Mr Honeywood's desk. So that's where I lost it! thought Dany guiltily. It must have been when I was hunting through my bag for Lorraine's letter.

There was one point, however, on which every account agreed. The police wished to interview a young woman who had been seen leaving Mr Honeywood's house 'shortly after half-past eleven', and whom they hoped might be able to assist them in their inquiries.

Well, I won't! decided Dany stubbornly. I'm going to fly to Zanzibar tomorrow, and nothing and no one is going to stop me! I'm not going to help them. I'm not — I'm not!

She pushed the papers aside, and snatching up her bag, almost ran from the room, colliding *en route* with a slim man in a pepper-and-salt suit who had just entered the dining-room. Dany apologized breathlessly, the man said it didn't matter at all, and a stately waiter who, if he were not actually a retired ambassador, might well have been a retired ambassador's gentleman's gentleman, looked so gravely disapproving that Dany flushed hotly and returned to her room at a more decorous pace.

She found that in her absence the room had been swept and tidied and the bed made. And on the bed, laid out with some ostentation on the satin counterpane, was a large and unmistakably masculine dressing-gown.

It managed, somehow, to convey the same austere disapproval that the stately waiter had conveyed with a single cold glance, and Dany's flush deepened as she looked at it. She had meant to return it before going down to breakfast, but she had not trusted herself to be civil to Mr Holden, and it had not occurred to her to put it out of sight in a drawer or cupboard.

He'll have to wait for it, she thought. If he's been up all night he'll be sound asleep by now. I'll wrap it up and hand it in to the hall porter.

She sat down in front of the dressing-table and tried on a small cyclamen velvet hat that had been one of her first purchases in London. Her great-aunt would undoubtedly have disapproved of the colour and swooned at the price, but there was no doubt at all that it did things for her that Aunt Harriet's choice of hats did not.

Lorraine was dark haired and tiny, and Daniel Ashton had been tall and blond; but their daughter had struck out on a line of her own. Dany's hair was light brown: soft, shining and shoulder-length, and curling under in the traditional manner of a medieval page-boy's, while her eyes, a happy medium between Lorraine's blue and Daniel's hazel, were large and grey and lovely.

There was no doubt about it, thought Dany, studying herself in the looking-glass, hats and clothes did make a difference — an astonishing difference. She was never going to wear navy-blue serge again!

She pulled open a drawer that contained gloves, scarves and handkerchiefs — one of the few that had escaped Mr Holden's prankish attentions — and was rummaging through it in search of a pair of gloves that could be worn with a cyclamen velvet hat, when her fingers encountered something that had certainly not been there before. She felt it, frowning, and then took it out; wondering if this was another practical joke and if that was why he had not emptied the contents of this drawer on to the floor as he had the others. It was something hard and cold and heavy that had been rolled in one of her chiffon scarves and hidden at the back of the drawer. Dany unrolled it, and instantly dropped it.

23

It hit the edge of the open drawer and fell with a clatter to the floor, and she sat very still, staring at it, and after a minute or two stooped slowly and stiffly and picked it up. It was a small gun. 'Small enough to be carried in a coat pocket or a lady's handbag ...'

Quite suddenly Dany was frightened. Her knees felt weak and her hands cold, and she seemed to be having some difficulty with her breathing. The looking-glass reflected a movement behind her and she gave a startled gasp and turned swiftly.

She had apparently left the door ajar, and now it swung open and Mr Holden was with her once more: changed, and presumably in his right mind, though still accompanied by the cat.

He did not present the appearance of one who has spent the entire night on the tiles, and except for a slight heaviness about the eyes, no one would have suspected him of having had no sleep in the last twenty-four hours. But the sight of the weapon that Dany held clutched in her hand wiped the amiable smile from his handsome features.

'Hey!' said Mr Holden, considerably startled. 'Put that down! My intentions are strictly Grade A. All I want right now is my bathrobe — it's got a couple of letters I need in the pocket.'

Dany gasped and whipped the gun behind her.

'Tell me,' said Mr Holden, 'do you always hold up visitors in that dramatic fashion? Life in London must have gotten a lot brisker since I was last over.'

Something in Dany's white face and wide eyes suddenly struck him, and his own face changed. He came in quickly and shut the door behind him.

'What's up, kid? In trouble?'

Dany licked her dry lips and swallowed convulsively. She found it astonishingly difficult to speak. 'Yes ... No ... I don't know. Would you ...? There's your dressing-gown. On the bed. Please — take it and go away.'

Mr Holden favoured her with a long, penetrating look and

24

ignored the suggestion. He deposited the cat on the nearest chair and said: 'I thought maybe I'd better bring Asbestos along to play propriety. *"When in Rome ..."* you know. He may not be much of a chaperone, but he's better than none. Makes a third.'

He came across the room and stood in front of Dany, looking down at her, and then turning abruptly away he vanished into the bathroom; to reappear a moment later carrying a tooth-glass which he filled almost a third full from a silver flask that he produced from his pocket.

'Here, drink this,' ordered Mr Holden sharply, handing it to her. 'No, don't sip at it! Knock it back!'

Dany complied, and having done so, choked and coughed, and Mr Holden thumped her on the back and inquired with a trace of impatience if she had never come across rye before, and who the heck had been responsible for her upbringing?

'G-great-aunt Harriet,' gasped Dany, made literal by shock.

'She the one who taught you to tote a gun?' inquired Mr Holden, interested.

'No, of course not! I — it isn't mine.'

'Just borrowed it, I guess. Now, look, I know it's none of my business, but are you in some sort of a jam?'

'N-no,' said Dany uncertainly. 'There isn't anything — I mean ...' She looked down at the gun that she still held clutched in her hand, and said: 'Is this an automatic?'

'Yes,' said Mr Holden.

Dany shuddered suddenly and uncontrollably, and he reached out, and taking it from her, jerked back the cocking-piece. She saw his eyebrows go up in surprise and he said in a startled voice: 'Loaded, by golly!'

He removed the magazine and counted the rounds, and finding these one short, sniffed the barrel. 'And fired! Say, look sister — you haven't by any chance been taking a shot at someone, have you?'

Dany said: '*Has* it been fired? Are you sure?'

25

'Yep. And fairly recently, I'd say.'

He clicked the magazine back into place and, laying the little gun on the dressing-table, thrust his hands into his pockets and stood looking down at her with a crease between his brows. She looked, he thought, very young and scared and helpless, and he wished that his head felt a bit clearer. He had an uncomfortable suspicion that he was about to become involved in something that he would regret, and that were he in full possession of his faculties he would collect his bathrobe and leave the room without loss of time. But he did not go. He picked up the empty tooth-glass instead, and having poured out a second and larger tot from the flask, swallowed it and felt better.

'Now,' said Mr Holden bracingly, drawing up a chair and disposing himself in comfort, 'let's get down to cases. Go ahead — tell me what's the trouble.'

Dany had not previously come into contact with anything stronger than cider cup, and four fingers of rye whisky were beginning to have their effect. The fact that Mr Holden was a stranger to her, and should therefore be treated with proper reserve, did not seem to be of the slightest importance. And anyway he knew her current step-father and was going to marry one of her mother's oldest friends, and perhaps he would be able to tell her what to do.

She said haltingly: 'I — I don't know where to start.'

'Try starting at the beginning,' suggested Mr Holden sensibly.

Dany looked at the gun, and shivered again. She said: 'I found this — the gun — in that drawer just now. Someone must have put it in there while I was at breakfast, or — some time. And I — know it's silly, but I suddenly wondered if it were *the* gun. The papers say it was a small automatic, and though I know it can't possibly be, I thought——'

'Hey, wait a minute,' intervened Mr Holden, pardonably confused. 'What gun, and what papers? You'll have to do better than that, sister. My wits are not all that sharp this morning. And by the way, what's your name? I can't keep calling you "hey" or "you" or "whatsername".'

'Ashton. Dany Ashton.'

'Delighted to meet you, Miss Ashton. I'm Lash Holden, from——'

'I know,' said Dany, cutting him short. 'You're going to *Kivulimi* too, aren't you?'

'What's that?' Lash sat bolt upright, and the movement appeared to be painful, for he screwed up his eyes and winced. 'Say, do you know Tyson?'

'He's my step-father.'

'Well, whatdoyouknow?' demanded Lash in pleased surprise. 'That makes us practically relations. My Pop is a life-long pal of the old reprobate. They used to infest the speakeasies back in the old days when the States were technically dry and Tyson was over on some lend-lease college course. Well, well! It is, if I may coin a phrase, a small world. Yep, I'm off to Zanzibar.'

'On your honeymoon,' said Dany.

Mr Holden winced. 'Who told you that?'

'Lorraine. My mother. She said——'

'The wedding,' said Mr Holden, 'is off. Let's not discuss it, if you don't mind.'

'Oh,' said Dany confused. 'I'm sorry.'

'I'm not. Merciful escape. T'hell with women! Say——' He paused and frowned. 'Haven't we wandered off the point some place? You were telling me something. Yeah; I remember now. That gun. Someone stowed it away among your nylons. Now why would anyone do that?'

'Because of Mr Honeywood,' said Dany.

'Mr Who?'

'Honeywood. I don't suppose you've seen the papers this morning, but he was murdered yesterday, and it says that the police want to — to interview a young woman who was seen leaving his house not very long before it happened. And that was me.'

27

'*You*? Now listen, kid — let's get this straight. Are you trying to tell me that you shot this guy?'

'*No!*' said Dany furiously. 'Oh, what's the good of telling you anything? Of course I didn't shoot him!'

'O.K., O.K.,' said Lash pacifically. 'I just wanted to clear that point up before we went any further. What were you doing in this Honeywood's comb, I mean house?'

'He's Mr Frost's solicitor — the Frosts live near there. Tyson wanted me to bring a letter out with me, and Lorraine, my mother, asked me to call in and fetch it; and I did. I fetched it yesterday morning at eleven o'clock — no, it must have been nearly twenty past, because the train was late; there was some fog about.'

'Well, go on. What happened?'

'Nothing happened. We talked for a bit, and I left.'

'Meet anyone coming away?'

'No. I passed a few people, of course, but I didn't pay much attention. There was a woman with a walking-stick and one with a puppy on a lead, and an African — or an Indian — anyway an Oriental of sorts, in a white — no, that was the dream. In a raincoat: one of those students. I can't remember any more. But it was rather misty, and I wasn't bothering.'

'And why are you bothering now?'

'Because the papers say that the police think Mr Honeywood was — was murdered some time between eleven-thirty and twelve. And I was there until just after half-past eleven, and it seems that someone saw me leave.'

'The murderer, you mean?'

'No, of course not! He wouldn't have told the police. But someone told them; and — now someone else is trying to make it look as though I did it.'

'Baloney!' said Lash impatiently.

'It isn't baloney! It isn't! It was that kind of gun. It said so in the papers. A — a little gun. An automatic. And that horrid thing

28

there isn't mine. I've never even *seen* one before! But it was wrapped up in my scarf, and it wasn't there yesterday because I wore that scarf yesterday——'

'O.K., sister!' said Lash. 'I get you. Yes, it's quite a point. You think someone planted this on you, so that when the police came around asking questions it would be found right here in your room? Well you don't have to worry. It won't have your finger-prints on it, and—— Yes, by God, it will! Mine, too. *Hmm*. That's a fast one.'

He brooded for a few minutes, and then said abruptly: 'Know what I'd do if I were you? I'd drop that damned thing down the elevator shaft and think no more about it. The cops aren't likely to locate you before you get aboard the plane tomorrow, and once you're out of the country they can go ahead with tracing the guy who did the job. Simple.'

'But suppose they do find me?' said Dany, twisting her hands together distressfully. 'Mr Honeywood may have told someone I was coming down. And I telephoned him. I was going down in the afternoon, but I wanted to go to a film, so I telephoned and asked him if I could come in the morning instead. They might trace the call because I telephoned from here. And — and I left a handkerchief in Mr Honeywood's office. It had my initials on it.'

'You *what?*' said Mr Holden, unable to credit it. 'You're telling me that you actually pulled that corny old gag? Good grief! *Women!*'

'You don't suppose I did it on purpose, do you?' retorted Dany hotly. 'And anyway, how was I to know that this sort of — of awful thing was going to happen? How could *anyone* know? People oughtn't to keep valuable things in safes in their houses and then leave their safes open and — and——' Her lips began to tremble.

'Hey!' said Mr Holden, appalled. 'Don't cry. I can handle any-thing else — well, almost anything else. But not tears. Not at this

29

hour of the day, there's a good girl. Here, let me lend you a handkerchief — unmonogrammed!'

He handed one over, and Dany accepted it with a dismal sniff. 'I'm sorry,' she apologized, blowing her nose. 'It was only because I'm so worried, and it's all so — so fantastic and impossible and horrid. Mr Honeywood being murdered, and then finding that gun wrapped up in one of my scarves, and — and not knowing what to do. What *am* I going to do?'

'Nothing!' said Mr Holden firmly. 'Masterly inactivity is my advice. It may be regrettably short on Public Spirit, but right now it looks like saving you a helluva headache. We'll make a nice tidy parcel of that gun, address it to Scotland Yard and drop it in the nearest post box. And you can spend your air trip in writing them a full account of your visit to this guy Honeycomb, and post it in Nairobi: allowing it to be supposed that you missed reading the newspapers today on account of one little thing and another. Not strictly truthful, but a labour-saving device if ever there was one. That should satisfy both your conscience and cops. O.K.?'

'O.K.,' agreed Dany with a breath of relief and a somewhat watery smile.

'Good,' said Mr Holden briskly. 'Then that's fixed.'

He stood up, reached for the gun, and having carefully cleaned off all possible fingerprints with his handkerchief, wrapped it in the crumpled square of linen and stuffed it into his pocket.

'And now I'm afraid I must leave you. I have to go out gunning for a secretary-typist. Mine, believe it or not, has contracted mumps. *Mumps* — I ask you! There ought to be a law against it. See you at the airport, babe.'

He collected his dressing-gown and Asbestos, and departed.

3

Dany sighed and stood up. She still felt badly shaken, but at least she was no longer frightened, for Lash Holden's casual attitude towards the whole horrifying affair had reduced it to manageable proportions.

She was not, she assured herself, obstructing the course of justice by keeping silent. Any information that the gun might convey to the police would be theirs by tomorrow morning. And as far as the details of her visit to Mr Honeywood were concerned, she would tell them that too; but, as Lash Holden had sensibly suggested, by letter. Probably by the time they received it the murderer would have been caught; and if not, at least she would be with Lorraine and Tyson, who could support her story and deal adequately with the police.

Dany closed the drawer in which she had found the gun, and having repaired the ravages caused by tears and Mr Holden's handkerchief, reached for the lizard-skin bag. The unpleasant happenings of the morning had driven the day's programme out of her head, but she had made a list of the few things that she still had to buy, and she took it out of her bag and studied it.

Beach hat, sunsuit, something for air sickness? Ticket for matinee of 'Sun in Your Eye'. *Book for journey?* That should not take long.

It was only when she was replacing the list that she noticed that something was missing from the bag. Surely there ought to be more in it? Money, cheque book, powder compact, lipstick, a crumpled face tissue, a pocket comb, a bunch of keys, a leather

31

pocket-book containing tickets, reservations, permits and certificates, and——

With a sudden sickening sense of shock she realized that her passport was no longer there! The brand new passport that Aunt Harriet had impressed upon her that she must on no account let out of her keeping, and which she had carried about in the new lizard-skin bag for the last three days.

She hunted through the bag with desperate, shaking fingers, and finally emptied the entire contents on to the dressing-table. But there was no passport.

It must be there. It *must* be! thought Dany frantically. I couldn't have lost it. It's never been out of my sight, and it was there last thing last night — I saw it when I was checking the plane tickets. *The tickets!* Had those gone too?

She tore open the pocket-book with hands that were so unsteady that she could barely control them. But the tickets were still there. Everything else was there. And none of it was any use without a passport!

Dany dropped the pocket-book and began a frenzied search through the dressing-table drawers. But the action was purely a panic-stricken one, for she knew quite well that it had been in her bag when she had checked over all her various forms and tickets before turning out the light last night. She had taken the bag down with her to the dining-room at breakfast time, and it had never once been out of her sight except——

Dany straightened up suddenly and stood gripping the edge of the dressing-table. She had been locked out of her room for nearly three-quarters of an hour this morning, and during that time Lash Holden had entered it and turned all her things upside down for a practical joke. Had he taken her passport too, as part of it?

She gathered up the scattered contents of her bag in feverish haste, crammed them back into it, and ran out of the room and across the passage.

Mr Holden's door was shut and she hammered on it, terrified

32

that he might already have left and that she might have to wait the best part of the day before catching him again. But Mr Holden was still at home.

The door opened and he regarded her with a trace of annoyance. 'What, again? Not another lethal weapon, I trust? I've only just finished packing up the first one. Here it is.'

Dany said breathlessly: 'Did you take my passport this morning? When you were ragging my room?'

'Rag——? Sorry; I no speaka-da English.'

'Turning it upside down. Did you? Because if you did I don't think it's in the least funny, and I want it back at once. How *could* you?'

Mr Holden stared, scowled, and then reaching out a hand and grasping her by one arm he jerked her into his room and shut the door behind her.

'Say, what goes on here? I don't get it. No, I have not taken your passport. And just when am I supposed to have roughed up your room?'

'This morning. While I was waiting in here. It *must* have been you. It couldn't have been anyone else! You had the key and——'

Dany stopped: suddenly realizing that someone had got into her room without a key, and hidden a gun there. The balcony——? the fire-escape——?

Lash said: 'Now relax. Just sit right down and have another slug of rye. Looks like you could use one. No? Well I certainly could. You've got me all confused. Chicago was never like this!'

Dany said: 'Then — then it wasn't you. All that mess. I thought it was meant to be a joke, but it was someone looking for my passport. I — I don't understand. Why should anyone want to steal my passport?'

'Probably to use,' said Lash. 'Very useful things, passports. You can't go any place without 'em these days. Some dame may have needed one badly, and thought yours would fill the bill. Or else someone wants to stop you catching this plane.'

He paused for a drink, and then said meditatively. 'You know, that's quite an idea — taking that gun into account. Know what I think? I think someone saw you leave this Honeyball's house, and decided that you'd make a very useful red-herring. Probably saw you coming away as he went in, and—— Say, how did you get back to town yesterday?'

'By train. The 12.5.'

'Well, there you are. Simple! He bumps off this guy, takes what he wants from the safe, and beats it for the station. And who does he see on the platform but a dame who he knows was visiting this solicitor only a few minutes before he was there himself. If he can only play his trump card, it may keep the police dogs baying on the wrong trail for long enough to let him get clear. So he follows you up to town, works out a way of planting that gun among your undies to make the thing foolproof, and—— Has that room of yours got a balcony?'

'Yes. But I don't think——'

'Too easy. The dam' things connect. And there's a fire-escape somewhere. He plants his little time bomb, and then suddenly notices that your bags are lying all over the place covered with air labels — seems you're lighting out for foreign parts. That washes you out as a red-herring, so where does he go from here? Easy: fixes it so you can't leave! No passport, no foreign parts; and there must be a passport around somewhere. He turns the joint upside down until he finds it, pockets the thing and lights out. You are now not only tied by the leg but, what with the newspaper accounts and the fact that you were in this Honeydew's house within the time limit — and that gun and no passport! — it's a cinch you'll panic and start behaving in a manner likely to arouse suspicion in a babe of three: which will be just dandy. How's that for a piece of masterly deduction? Brilliant, if you ask me. The F.B.I. don't know what they missed when father's boy followed him into the business!'

He put down his glass and sat down rather suddenly on the end of his bed, and Dany gazed back at him dazedly. She had taken in very little of what he had said, because her mind was filled with only one distracting thought: she could not catch the plane! She would have to stay here and face the police and questions and inquests and newspaper men, and the scandalized disapproval of Aunt Harriet who would, understandably, feel that all her dire predictions as to the fatal consequences of independence had been fully justified. She was caught!

'No!' said Dany on a sob. 'Oh *no*! I can't stay here. I won't. I *will* go to Zanzibar. They shan't stop me. But — but they can if I haven't got a passport! What am I going to do? Oh *why* did I ever telephone Mr Honeywood? Why did I ever change the times? If I'd only gone in the afternoon instead!'

'And found the body? You wouldn't have liked that.'

'It would have been better than this! Far, *far* better. Can't you do something?'

'Such as what?' demanded Lash reasonably. 'Call up the cops? That would be one helluva help! Now just shut up and let me think for a minute. I don't know how you expect anyone to think while you're carrying on in this uninhibited manner. Hush, now!'

He helped himself to another drink and relapsed into frowning silence while Dany struggled with an overwhelming desire to burst into tears, and was only restrained from this course by a strong suspicion that Mr Lashmer J. Holden, Jnr, was quite capable of boxing her ears should she try it.

She sat down weakly on the nearest chair, her brain feeling as numb and useless as wet cotton wool. The whole thing was impossible and horrible and fantastic: she must be dreaming and she would wake up suddenly and find herself back in her snug, safe bedroom at *Glyndarrow*. This could not be happening . . .

But it was Lashmer J. Holden, Jnr, who woke up.

'I've got it!' he announced. 'By God, what it is to have a brain! Can you type?'

'Yes,' said Dany, bewildered.

'What about shorthand?'

'A — a little.'

'Secretarial college?'

'No. Class at school. Why——'

'Never mind. It'll have to do. O.K. Consider yourself engaged.'

'W-*what!*' gasped Dany.

'Oh — in a purely secretarial capacity. Nothing personal. I'm through with women. Now listen, kid; here's the layout — and is it a lily! If someone thinks they're going to use you as a red-herring to cover up their own get-away, let's wreck the scheme. I've been travelling with a secretary — Miss Kitchell. But Ada has developed mumps, and I haven't so far been able to get hold of a suitable substitute who possesses a valid passport and the necessary visas and forms and whathaveyou to enable her to leave pronto. So what do we do? We take you!'

'Don't be ridiculous,' said Dany crossly. 'You know quite well that I haven't got a passport either! That's the whole point.'

Mr Holden made an impatient noise that is normally rendered in print as *'Tcha!'*

'Use your brain, girl! I'm not taking you as you. I shall take you as Miss Kitchell. You aren't too unlike her. Height about right. Eyes roughly the right colour. Shape a whole lot better, but they don't include that in the photograph. She's older of course, and her hair's red, but she wears glasses and a fringe and about a million curls. The thing's a gift! We dye your hair red — it's a pity, but one must suffer for one's art — get it fringed and frizzed *à la* Ada and buy you a pair of glasses. It's a cinch!'

'But — but ... No! it isn't possible! She won't agree.'

'She won't be asked,' said Mr Holden firmly. 'I have all her documents right here in a brief-case with my own, and all the files and things we need. She sent 'em to me along with the bad news, and forgot to take her own stuff out. So there we are. Masterly, I think. And what's more it will enable me to put a long-cherished theory to the test.'

'What theory?' asked Dany faintly.

'That no one ever yet looked like the photograph on their passport, and that anyway no official ever really glances at the thing. Well, we shall know tomorrow.'

'We can't do it,' protested Dany, though with less conviction. 'We can't possibly do it!'

'Why not?'

'Well — there's this secretary of Tyson's — Nigel Ponting. He's meeting the plane at Nairobi, and he's bound to have seen photographs of me, and——'

'By the time I've finished with you,' said Mr Holden blithely, 'you will have ceased to resemble any photograph ever taken. Except possibly the libel that is pasted to Ada's passport, and that only remotely. And he will not be expecting you, because we will cover that contingency by sending your parents an express cable to say 'Sorry. Delayed — writing.' That'll hold 'em! As for this Ponting, he is an elegant tulip of the precious and scented variety that your great and glorious country has suddenly taken to breeding like rabbits. A pain — no kidding. I met him last time your step-father was in the States, and I can assure you he wouldn't know one girl from the next. One of those. So *phooey* to Ponting. You don't have to worry about him.'

'Well ...' began Dany hesitantly; and was caught in another spasm of panic and doubt. 'No! No, I can't. We couldn't!'

'What's to stop us? They can't give us more than a two-year stretch at Sing Sing — or Borstal, or wherever they send you in this country. And what are two years among so many? Haven't you British any guts?'

There was a sudden angry sparkle in Dany's grey eyes, and her chin lifted. 'All right. I'll do it.'

'That's the girl,' approved Mr Holden, and helped himself to another drink.

'I can't think,' he said, 'why I don't write for a living instead of publishing the puerile efforts of lesser minds. It's all here —

37

brains, dash, fertility of invention and a frank approach to the problems of daily life. What are you just sitting there for? Get going, girl! Jump to it!'

'What am I supposed to do?' inquired Dany, startled.

'Well, pack I guess. You've got to get out of here before the cops catch up on you, so the sooner you check out the better. Get the girl at the desk to call up and cancel your seat on the plane and to send off that cable. That'll help. And tell the room girl and the hall porter and anyone else you meet that you've just heard that your bedridden old grandmother is dangerously ill in Manchester or Aberdeen or some place, and you're having to cancel your trip and rush to her side. Ask the hall porter to get you a taxi to go to whatever station it is where trains leave for the wilds of Caledonia.'

'King's Cross, I think,' said Dany.

'O.K. King's Cross. And when you get there, grab a porter and get him to put your bags in the checkroom, and I'll meet you in the booking hall in an hour and a half's time. Think you can make it?'

'I'll try.'

'Try, nothing! You'll make it or else. If there's one thing that makes me madder than a hornet it's women who keep one waiting around. I've put up with plenty of that in the past, but no more of it for L. J. Holden, Jnr. No sir! Not from now on. Besides, there won't be much time to waste. We have a stiff itinerary before us. Check you in at another hotel, change all your baggage labels, find an intelligent hairdresser and buy a pair of spectacles, for a start. So the sooner you get going the better. See you at King's Cross at 11 a.m. sharp. And mind, I'm not waiting there for ever! Ten minutes is my limit.'

It was, in actual fact, twenty. But he was still there, and in excellent spirits — in every meaning of the words.

'I'm sorry I'm late,' apologized Dany breathlessly, 'but as I was checking out I saw him again — at least it may not have been, but I thought——'

38

'Saw who?' demanded Lash, confused.

'The African — or whatever he is. I told you I passed one when I was leaving Mr Honeywood's. No, it couldn't possibly have been the same one I suppose. I'm being silly. But he was talking to the man at the desk about some letters, and it gave me such a jolt that I forgot I'd left a coat in the ladies' room, and so of course I had to go back and fetch it, and that made me late. I was afraid you would have left.'

'Another two minutes, and your fears would have proved well founded. But a mish ish as good as a — A miss ish — Oh, well; the hell with it! Let's go.'

He hailed a porter, retrieved Dany's suitcases from the left-luggage office where they had been deposited only a few minutes previously, and half an hour later she was sitting in front of a large looking-glass, swathed in a peach-coloured overall, while Mr Holden explained breezily to a giggling blonde hairdresser's assistant the details of Miss Ada Kitchell's coiffure.

'He's a one, isn't he? Your gentleman friend,' said the blonde, dunking Dany's head into a basin. 'In films, are you dear? Must be ever so interesting. Ever been a red-head before? No? Well I expect it'll make a nice change. You won't know yourself.'

'Not bad,' said Lash, viewing the result some time later: 'Not bad at all. Though I can't say that it's an improvement. Definitely a retrograde step. Or is that because I'm seeing two of you? Never mind — you can't have too much of a good thing. Let's eat.'

They had eaten at a small restaurant in a side-street near the hairdresser's shop. Or rather Dany had eaten while Mr Holden had confined himself to drinking. And later that day he had deposited her at a sedate family hotel in Gloucester Road, with instructions to keep to her room and not to panic. He would, he said, call for her on the following morning on his way to the Air Terminal, and he regretted his inability to entertain her further, but he had a date that evening. In fact, several.

'You won't oversleep, or anything dreadful?' said Dany

39

anxiously, suddenly terrified by a vision of being abandoned — alone, red-headed and masquerading as Miss Ada Kitchell — in darkest Gloucester Road.

'Certainly not,' said Mr Holden, shocked. 'You don't suppose that I intend to waste valuable time in going to sleep, do you? In the words of some poet or other, I am going to "cram the unforgiving minute with sixty seconds' worth of drinking done". Or know the reason why!'

'But you didn't have any sleep *last* night,' protested Dany, worried.

'What's that got to do with it? Tomorrow is another day. Be seeing you, sister.'

Dany passed the remainder of the day in solitude and acute anxiety, and crept out at dusk to buy the evening papers. But a fire in a large London store, a train crash in Italy, another revolution in South America and the fifth marriage of a well-known film star, had combined to push the murder of Mr Henry Honeywood off the front pages and into small type.

There were no further details, and with repetition the accounts lost much of their horror for Dany, and became more remote and impersonal. Which soothed her conscience somewhat, though not her fears, for there had been nothing either remote or impersonal about the gun that had been hidden in her room at the Airlane. Or in the fact that someone had stolen her passport! The whole thing might sound like an impossible nightmare, but it had happened. And to her — Dany Ashton. Oh, if only — if *only* she had gone to see Mr Honeywood at the proper time!

She had passed a sleepless night, and was looking white and worn when Lash collected her in a taxi at a comparatively early hour on the following morning. But a glimpse of herself in the large Victorian looking-glass that adorned the hall of the family hotel had at least served to convince her that no one would be likely to recognize her. She had not even recognized herself, and for a fleeting moment had imagined that the wan-faced young woman with the over-dressed red hair and wide-rimmed spectacles was some stranger who was standing in the narrow, chilly hall.

Lash, however, apart from a noticeable pallor and the fact that his eyes were over-bright, showed no signs of fatigue. He exuded high-spirits and was accompanied by a strong smell of whisky and the cat Asbestos, and no one would have suspected for a moment that he had not been to bed or had any sleep at all for two consecutive nights.

He had dismissed with a single short word Dany's trembling assertion that she had changed her mind and couldn't possibly go through with it, and once in the taxi and *en route* to the Air Terminal had made her take several sea-sick pills and swallow them down with rye whisky.

She had been unable to eat any breakfast that morning, panic having deprived her of appetite, and the raw spirit, coming on top of a sleepless night and an empty stomach, had quietened her post-operative nerves and filled her with a pleasant glow of confidence which had lasted until the passengers bound for Nairobi were marshalled in the departure lounge, and she had found herself standing next to a slim, youngish-looking man with a thin, triangular, attractive face, observant brown eyes and a square, obstinate chin.

Catching Dany's eye he had smiled at her; a swift and singularly pleasant smile that she found it impossible to resent, and said: 'I see that we're both bound for Zanzibar. Have you ever been there before?'

His voice was as irresistibly friendly and good-humoured as his smile, and Dany smiled back at him and shook her head.

'No? That's a pity: I'd hoped to pick up a few pointers. This'll be my first visit too. As a matter of fact, I never expected to make it. I've had my name down on half a dozen waiting lists for weeks on end, but all the Nairobi planes seemed to be booked solid. I'd almost given up hope when my luck turned — someone cancelled a seat only yesterday, and I got it.'

41

'Oh,' said Dany, jumping slightly. 'H-how lucky for you.'

'It was that all right! I'm a feature writer. Freelance. My name's Dowling — Larry Dowling.'

'Oh,' said Dany faintly. 'A — reporter.'

Mr Dowling looked pained. 'No. Feature writer. Have you ever heard of a novelist called Frost? Tyson Frost? But of course you have! Well, he's got a house in Zanzibar, and I've been commissioned by a newspaper and a couple of magazines to try and get a feature on him. That is, if he'll see me. He's not an easy man to get at, from all accounts. Still, I ought to be able to get something out of the trip, even if Frost won't play. Might be able to do something on the elections down there. There's a rumour that the local Moscow-Nasser stooges are making an all-out bid for control of the island.'

'Of *Zanzibar*? But it's quite an unimportant little place!' protested Dany, momentarily forgetting her own predicament in a sudden sense of outrage. Was there then no longer any lovely, romantic spot left in all the world that was free from squabbling political parties?

Mr Larry Dowling laughed. 'You know, there was a time when a good many people might have said the same of Sarajevo. But they learnt differently. I'm afraid you'll find that in a world that plays Power Politics there is no such thing any longer as "an unimportant little place".'

'Oh, no!' said Dany involuntarily. 'Why does everything have to be spoiled!'

Mr Dowling lifted a quizzical eyebrow, but his pleasant voice was sympathetic; 'That's Life, that is. I didn't mean to depress you. I'm sure you'll find Zanzibar every bit as attractive as you expect it to be. I believe it's a lovely place. Are you staying with friends there, or are you going to put up at the hotel like me? I hear there is——'

He broke off, his attention sharply arrested by the Vision at that moment entering the crowded lounge. A vision dressed by

42

Dior and draped in mink, preceded, surrounded and followed by a heady waft of glamour and exceedingly expensive scent, and accompanied by a slim, dark Italianate young man and a tall, distinguished-looking gentleman with grey hair and cold pale eyes.

Her entrance created something of a stir, and Mr Holden, also turning to look, lost a considerable portion of his *bonhomie*.

'Here come some of your step-father's guests,' he observed sourly to Dany. 'The Latin type is Eduardo di Chiago. A Roman louse who races his own cars and is a friend of Tyson's — he would be! The one with white whiskers and Foreign Office written all over him (erroneously, he's oil) is Yardley. Sir Ambrose. He's been getting a lot too thick with Elf of late, and she'd better watch her step — there was a rumour around that his Company might be heading for the rocks; and not the kind of rocks she collects, either! It's a pity it isn't true. But at least we don't have to put up with him for long. He's only going as far as Khartoum.'

He did not identify the Vision, but he did not need to. It was, unmistakably, the original of the affectionately inscribed photograph that had adorned his dressing-table at the Airlane. His ex-fiancée and Lorraine's great friend, Amalfi Gordon.

'She's lovely, isn't she?' sighed Dany wistfully, speaking aloud without realizing it.

'Is she?' said Mr Holden coldly.

He directed a brief scowling glance at the Vision, and turned his back on it. But Mrs Gordon had seen him.

'Why — Lash!' Her warm, throaty voice was clearly audible even above the babble of the crowded lounge, but Mr Holden affected to be deaf.

It did him no good. Mrs Gordon descended upon him in a wave of scented sweetness. 'Lash, darling — it's lovely to see you! I was so afraid you'd decide not to come after all.'

'Why?' demanded Lash haughtily. 'This started out as a business trip, and it can stay that way. You surely didn't think that I'd

43

cancel it just because you decided to transfer your affections to some gilded Italian gigolo, did you?'

Mrs Gordon tucked a slender, gloved hand under his arm and gazed up at him from a pair of enormous sea-green eyes; her long soft lashes fluttering appealingly.

No one had ever been able to stay seriously angry with Amalfi Gordon for any length of time. Exasperated, yes. But it was an accepted fact that dear, soft-hearted, feather-headed Elf simply couldn't help it. If she fell into love, or out of it, and hurt people thereby, it wasn't her fault. She never meant to hurt.

Mrs Gordon made a *moue* and said: 'Sweetie, you're not sulking, are you?'

'Of course I'm not!' snapped Lash, descending rapidly from the haughty to the frankly furious. 'What would I have to sulk about? I am, on the contrary, deeply thankful. And now run along back to your Mediterranean bar-fly, there's a good girl.'

Amalfi gave his arm a little coaxing tug. 'Darling, aren't you being just a *tiny* bit kindergarten? Eddie's marvellous!'

'You mean Eddie's a Marchese!' retorted Lash bitterly. 'That's the operative word, isn't it? And you're just another sucker for a title! Apart from that, what's he got that I haven't?'

'Manners,' said Amalfi sweetly. And withdrawing her hand she turned away and rejoined her two cavaliers without having even glanced at Dany.

'How d'you like that?' demanded Lash indignantly. '*Manners!* I suppose if I bowed and scraped and went about kissing women's hands——'

He broke off and subsided into deep gloom, from which he was presently aroused by another clutch at his arm. But this time it was Dany, and he saw that she was staring in wide-eyed alarm at a thin, boney, dark-skinned Oriental in a blue lounge suit, who carried a brief-case, a neatly rolled umbrella and very new burberry.

'It's him!' said Dany in a feverish, ungrammatical whisper.

44

'Who? The one you think you saw in Market-something, or the one you saw in the hotel?'

'In the hotel. But — but perhaps it's both!'

'Nuts! The world is full of Oriental gentlemen — they come in all sizes. And anyway, what of it? He was probably staying at the Airlane. You were. I was. And so, as it happens, were Elf and that slick owner-driver. And we're all flying to Nairobi. Why not him?'

'But suppose he recognizes me? I was standing right next to him!'

Lash turned and surveyed her with a distinctly jaundiced eye, and remarked caustically that it was extremely doubtful if her own mother would recognize her at the moment. To which he added a rider to the effect that if she was going to lose her nerve every twenty minutes she had better give up the whole idea after all and run off back to her Aunt Harriet, as he did not fancy the prospect of being saddled with a spineless and probably inefficient secretary who suffered from frequent attacks of the vapours. A trenchant observation that acted upon Dany's agitated nervous sytem with the bracing effect of a bucketful of cold water, and stiffened her wavering resolution. She cast Mr Lashmer Holden a look of active dislike, and preceded him into the aircraft in chilly silence.

No one had questioned her identity, and if there were any plain-clothes police among the crowds at the airport she did not identify them. The stewardess said: 'Will you please fasten your seat belts,' and then they were taxi-ing down the long runway. The propellors roared and the airport slipped away from them: tilted, levelled out and dwindled to the proportions of a child's toy. They were safely away.

'Well, it seems we made it,' remarked Lash affably, unfastening his seat-belt and lighting a cigarette.

He accepted a cup of coffee from the stewardess and added the remains of his flask to it. He seemed surprised that there was no more.

'Why, hell — I only filled it half an hour ago! No — I guess it must have been earlier than that. Oh well, plenty more where it came from. Happy landings! How are you feeling, by the way?'

'Sleepy,' said Dany.

'That's odd. So'm I. A very good night to you.'

He settled himself comfortably and was instantly asleep, and Dany, looking at him resentfully, was annoyed to find that her own head was nodding. She had no intention of wasting her time in sleep. This was her very first flight, and although the circumstances under which she was making it were, to say the least of it, unusual, she was not going to miss a moment of it. Soon they would be passing over the Channel. France . . . Switzerland. Looking down on the snowy peaks of the Alps. On the Matterhorn and Mont Blanc. Over the mountains to Italy. No, of course she could not sleep . . .

4

Dany awoke with a start to find the stewardess once again urging her to fasten her seat belt. 'We shall be coming in to land in a few minutes.'

'Land? Where?' inquired Dany dazedly.

'Naples. Do you think you could fasten your friend's belt? I don't seem to be able to wake him.'

Dany performed this task with some difficulty, Mr Holden remaining immobile throughout. He did not even wake when the plane touched down, and the stewardess gave up the unequal struggle, and in defiance of regulations, left him there.

Dany climbed over him to join the other passengers who were being ushered out into the dazzling sunlight of the Naples aerodrome, and feeling quite incapable of any conversation, affected not to see Larry Dowling, who had given her a friendly smile as she passed him.

A curious mixture of lunch and tea was served in the dining-room of the airport, but Dany was in no mood to be critical, and she ate everything that was placed before her, surprised to find herself so hungry. Prompted by caution she had selected a table as far as possible from her fellow passengers, and from this vantage point she studied them with interest; realizing that among them, still unidentified, were two more guests bound for *Kivulimi*. Tyson's sister, Augusta Bingham, and her friend Miss — Boots? No. Bates.

It was, she reflected, the greatest piece of luck that she should have been suffering from measles on the only occasion on which

47

this new step-aunt had suggested coming to see her, and that she had selfishly put off calling on Mrs Bingham at the Airlane on Wednesday evening. She had so nearly done so. But there had been the film of *Blue Roses*, and then there had been the choice between doing her duty by introducing herself to her step-aunt, or going to the theatre that evening — and the theatre had won.

Glancing round the dining-room, Dany decided that the two women she was looking for were obviously the two who had seated themselves at Mrs Gordon's table, for the older one bore a distinct resemblance to Tyson. The same blunt nose and determined chin. Yes, that must be Augusta Bingham: a middle-aged woman whose greying hair had been given a deep-blue rinse and cut by an expert, and whose spare figure showed to advantage in an equally well-cut suit of lavender shantung.

Mrs Bingham wore a discreet diamond brooch and two rows of excellent pearls, and looked as though she played a good game of bridge, belonged to several clubs and took an interest in gossip and clothes. Her neighbour, in marked contrast, conveyed an instant impression of Girl Guides, No Nonsense and an efficiently-run parish. Undoubtedly, Miss Bates.

Miss Bates, who despite the heat wore a sensible coat and skirt and an uncompromisingly British felt hat of the pudding-basin variety, provided a most effective foil for Amalfi Gordon, who was sitting opposite her. Mrs Gordon had discarded her mink cape and was looking cool and incredibly lovely in lime-green linen. How does she do it? wondered Dany, studying her with a faintly resentful interest. She's old! She was at school with Mother, and she's been married almost as many times. Yet she can still look like that!

The Italian marquis — or was it marchese? — and Sir Ambrose someone (oil) were giving Mrs Gordon their full attention, and Amalfi was being charming to both of them, as well as to Mrs Bingham and Miss Bates and a couple of openly admiring waiters. Even Larry Dowling was finding it difficult to keep his eyes from straying and his attention on what his table companion was saying.

Mr Dowling was sitting two tables away with the dark-skinned man whom Dany had seen at the hotel, and who was talking earnestly and with much gesticulation. His voice came clearly to Dany's ears: 'You do not understand! You are not Arab. It is the iniquity of it! The flagrant injustice! Why should a suffering minority be exploited for the benefit of cru-el and blood-sucking imperialists of a dying pow-ah, who mercilessly snatch their profits from the very mouths of the starving poo-er? Now I, as an Arab——'

So people really *did* talk like that! And, presumably, others listened. Mr Dowling was certainly listening, though perhaps not quite as earnestly as he should. But then he hoped to write a feature, whatever that was, on the elections in Zanzibar, and——. With a sudden sense of acute alarm Dany remembered something far more important. He wanted to interview Tyson! She would have to warn her step-father, and she would have to keep out of sight. It would be disastrous if this Larry Dowling, who wrote for the newspapers, were to find out that she was Tyson Frost's step-daughter, masquerading as the secretary of a visiting American publisher in order to escape giving evidence at an inquest on murder. It would make an excellent front page story for the newspapers, and Dany shuddered at the thought. Supposing — just supposing — someone were to recognize her? The man whom he was talking to——

Once again panic snatched at Dany. Even if the Arab was not the man she had passed in the mist near Mr Honeywood's house, he was certainly the man who had stood almost at her elbow in the hall of the Airlane, and if he should recognize her, and ask questions, she might be stopped at Nairobi and sent back.

What were the penalties for travelling on a false passport? Why hadn't she thought of that before? Lash Holden had made some

49

flippant reference to it, but she had not stopped to think. She should have thought . . .

Mr Dowling's companion was talking again, even more audibly, but on a more topical subject. 'I feel always sick — most sick — in these aeroplanes. It is my stomach. Everything, I take it. It is no good. The height — I do not know. Yes, we do not move, but still I am feeling bad always. But worse over the sea. I am most bad over the sea. For if the engines fail over the sea, what will happen then? We will all drown! It is terrible!'

He's not airsick, thought Dany. He's only frightened! Well, so am I . . .

Larry Dowling caught her eye and grinned, and unaccountably some of the panic left her. He might be a reporter, and dangerous to know, but he was a dependable sort of person, and she had a sudden, strong conviction that Aunt Harriet would have approved of him. Which was odd . . .

She became aware that passengers for Nairobi were being requested to return to their aircraft, and rising hurriedly she snatched up her coat and bag and hastened out in the wake of her fellow passengers.

Lashmer J. Holden Jnr had not moved, and he did not stir as she squeezed past him to regain her seat. He was, in technical parlance, out for the count; and Dany, vaguely recognizing the fact, was conscious of feeling lost and friendless and very much alone. Until this moment she had felt herself to be a mere member of the crew with Lash in charge and steering the ship, and provided she did what she was told he would bring her safely into port. Now she was not so sure. Viewed dispassionately in the bright Mediterranean sunlight, Lashmer Holden looked a good deal younger. His hair was dishevelled and he looked pallid and unshaven and she studied him with a critical and disapproving eye, and then — her maternal instincts getting the better of her — leant over and loosened his tie, which had worked round somewhere in the neighbourhood of his right ear, and drew down the

50

blind so that his face was shielded from the sun.

The two red-faced gentlemen of unmistakably Colonial appearance who occupied the seats immediately behind her began to snore in gentle and rhythmic chorus, and she wished she were able to follow their example and fall asleep again herself, in order to avoid having to think. But she was by now far too anxious and far too wide awake; and in any case there was that letter to be written. The letter that she must post in Nairobi, explaining herself to the police.

Dany stood up cautiously and removed her attaché case from the rack above her head, noting, with a renewed sense of surprise, the label that proclaimed it to be the property of Miss Ada Kitchell. But with the writing paper in front of her and a Biro in her hand, she found that it was not going to be as easy as she had thought.

Looking back over the last twenty-four hours she wondered if she had temporarily taken leave of her senses. Or had Lash Holden's alcoholic exuberance exerted a hypnotic influence over her? She had been frightened and confused, and stubbornly determined that nothing should cheat her out of this long-looked-forward-to visit to Zanzibar. And in that state of mind she had been only too ready to grasp at the preposterous line of escape that he had offered. But now that she had plenty of time for thought, the folly of her behaviour was becoming increasingly clear.

She had done precisely what someone had hoped that she would do. Panicked and behaved in a foolish and suspicious manner, and allowed herself to be used as a red-herring to confuse the trail of a murderer. She was an 'Accessory After the Fact'; and that, too, was a punishable offence. If she had kept her head and rung up the police at once, even though it meant postponing this visit or perhaps sacrificing it altogether, then it would have been the police who would have found that gun — and without her fingerprints on it. And if she had given them what little information she could,

51

it might have helped them to get on the track of the real criminal at once, instead of wasting time trying to trace her.

She had, thought Dany with bleak honesty, been selfish and cowardly and deplorably gullible. She had obstructed justice and played a murderer's game for him, and she wondered how long it would take the police to find out that Mr Honeywood's visitor had been a Miss Dany Ashton if she did not write and tell them so herself? Perhaps they would never find out. Perhaps, after all, it would be better to say nothing at all — having let things get this far. Could she get a jail sentence for having used someone else's passport, in addition to one for having obstructed justice? Yet she had only wanted to see Zanzibar. Zanzibar and *Kivulimi* ...

Lorraine had sent her some photographs of *Kivulimi* two years ago. They had arrived on a cold, wet, depressing afternoon in November, and brought a breath of magic into Aunt Harriet's stolidly unromantic house. *'There are jacarandas in the garden,'* Lorraine had written, *'and mangoes and frangi-pani and flamboyants, and any amount of orange trees, and they smell heavenly and keep the place nice and cool. I suppose that's where it gets its name from. "Kivulimi" means "The House of Shade".'*

Dany put away the writing paper and pen and returned the attaché case to the rack. It was all too difficult, and she would wait until she could make a clean breast of it to Lorraine and Tyson. Lorraine would think it was all thrilling, and Tyson would probably be furious. But they would take charge of the whole problem, and know what to do.

She sat down again, feeling cold and forlorn and more than a little ashamed of herself. If only Lash would wake up! But Mr Holden did not look as though he intended to wake up for anything short of the Last Trump, and Dany found herself regarding him with increasing hostility.

It was, she decided suddenly, all Lash's fault. If it had not been for him — him and that ridiculous stuffed cat! 'Asbestos' indeed!

52

A fragrant breath of *Diorissimo* competed triumphantly with the smell of cigarette smoke, antiseptics and upholstery, and Dany became aware that Mr Holden's pleasant profile was silhouetted against a background of lime-green linen.

Amalfi Gordon was standing beside him in the aisle, looking down at his unconscious form with a faint frown and an expression that was a curious mixture of speculation, doubt and annoyance. In the shadow of the drawn blind, and with the light behind her, she looked blonder and lovelier than ever, and it was impossible to believe that she must be a good deal nearer forty than thirty, and had been at school with one's own mother.

She lifted a pair of long, gilt-tipped lashes that were undoubtedly genuine, and glanced at Dany with the unseeing and entirely uninterested look that some women bestow on servants, and the majority of beautiful women accord to their plain or unattractive sisters.

It was a look that aroused a sudden sharp antagonism in Dany, and perhaps it showed in her face, for Mrs Gordon's sea-green eyes lost their abstraction and became startlingly observant. She looked Dany up and down, noting her youth and missing no detail of her dress or appearance, and the frown on her white brow deepened. She said without troubling to lower her voice:

'You must be Lash's — Mr Holden's — secretary. I thought he was bringing Ada.'

'She couldn't come,' said Dany shortly, disturbed to find that she was blushing hotly.

'Oh?' It was obvious, and in the circumstances fortunate, that Mrs Gordon was not in the least interested in Lash's secretaries, for she made no further inquiries. But something in Dany's gaze had evidently annoyed her, for she looked down again at the sleeping Lash, and then lightly, but very deliberately, stretched out one slender white hand and smoothed back an errant lock of hair that had fallen across his forehead.

It was a sweetly possessive gesture that spoke volumes — and

53

was intended to. And having made her point, Mrs Gordon smiled charmingly and went on down the aisle to the ladies' room.

Dany subsided, feeling shaken and unreasonably angry, and un-nerved by the narrowness of her escape. What if Mrs Gordon had asked her name, and she had said 'Kitchell'? What would have happened then? *But you aren't Ada Kitchell. I know her.* How would she have answered that? Two redheaded secretaries, both with the same name, would have been difficult to explain away. Un-less they were sisters——? If Mrs Gordon questioned her again she would have to be Ada's sister. Lash should have remembered that Mrs Gordon had met his ex-secretary, and warned her of it.

She turned to look at him again, and apprehension gave place to that entirely illogical anger. She reached out and pushed the lock of hair over his forehead again. That, thought Dany, will show her!

The stewardess dispensed tea, and the two Colonial gentlemen in the seat behind woke up and embarked upon a long and dog-matic discussion of the race problems in Kenya. The thin Arab whom Dany had first seen in the hall of the Airlane — or possibly in Market-Lydon? — passed down the aisle, and one of the men behind her lowered his voice and said: 'See who that was? Salim Abeid — the chap they call "Jembe".'

'Believe you're right. Wonder what he's been doing over in Lon-don?'

'Being made much of by our messy little Pro-Reds and Pink Intellectuals, I suppose. Can't think why we allow that type of chap to go there. They're never up to any good, and they never get any good — the Reds see to that! Swoop down on 'em like vultures the minute they land, and cherish 'em and fill 'em up with spleen, and educate 'em in subversion.'

'I've always heard,' said the other voice, 'that he's an able feller. They say he's getting quite a following in Zanzibar.'

'So I believe. Which is Zanzibar's bad luck! That place has al-ways seemed to me a sort of peaceful oasis in a brawling desert

54

of politicians and power-grabbers. But Jembe and his ilk are out to change all that if they can. Ever noticed how for all their bellowings about "Peace and Brotherly Love" the average Red is eaten up from nose to tail with envy, hatred, malice and all uncharitableness? Their gods and their gospel are hate and destruction, and Jembe is typical of the breed. At the moment his target is the British, because that is a sitting duck these days. But he's a Coast Arab, and if ever he should manage to get us out he'll turn his followers on the Indian community next; or the Parsees — and then the Omani Arabs — and so on. There must always be an enemy to kick, so that he can keep hate alive and profit by it. If Zanzibar is a little Eden, then Jembe is the serpent in it! Did I ever tell you . . .?'

The speaker lowered his voice again as the subject of his remarks passed again on his way back to his seat, and thereafter made no further mention of Zanzibar or of the man he had referred to as 'Jembe'.

The daylight faded, and Dany drew up the blind and found that they were still flying over the sea. She wished that she had something to read. Or someone to talk to. Anything to soothe her jangled nerves and keep her from thinking of Mr Honeywood — and of murder. The couple behind her, having exhausted politics and settled the fate of Kenya, had advanced — loudly — to the unnerving subject of air disasters. A painfully audible anecdote about a settler who, while flying his family in to Nairobi for a week-end, made a forced landing in waterless country where they all died of thirst before help could reach them, was succeeded by another concerning a convivial gentleman called 'Blotto' Coots who 'pancaked' in the sea off Mombasa and was devoured by sharks, and a third relating to one 'Toots' Parbury-Basset who crashed into the crater of an extinct volcano, killing herself, two friends and her African houseboy in the process . . .

'Must have got caught in a down-draught: or else her engine cut out,' trumpeted the narrator light-heartedly. 'We didn't find 'em till the next day. Nasty mess. Bits all over the shop — no idea who was who. Did you hear about that airliner that broke up over the Mediterranean last Tuesday? Come to think of it, must have been just about where we are now. Forty-eight people on board and——'

The Arab, Jembe, rose abruptly and hurried down the aisle once more, casting the speaker a look of virulent dislike as he passed. It was obvious that he too had caught part of the conversation, and Dany remembered his recent assertion that he felt 'always most bad over the sea, for if the engines should fail then, we will all drown: it is terrible!' He had something there, she thought, peering down at the enormous empty leagues of sea so far below them, and wondering if there were sharks in the Mediterranean. She had it on good authority that there were plenty off the Mombasa coast, and it occurred to her that if the timorous Jembe had been tuned in on the fate of the late 'Blotto' Coots, he was likely to feel a lot worse once they left Mombasa on the last lap of their journey.

If he has any sense, thought Dany, he'll take a strong sedative! She was not sure that she couldn't do with one herself.

A star swam palely into the blue immensity above, to be followed by another and another, until at last it was dark. The chairs were tipped back to facilitate sleep, and the lights were dimmed to no more than a faint blue glow; but it was not a restful night — although judging from the stentorian snores, a few people found it so.

In the yellow dawn they came down for breakfast at Khartoum, where the stewardess, assisted by the First Officer, made another unsuccessful attempt to arouse the slumbering Mr Holden. 'We're supposed to turn everyone out at these stops,' explained the First Officer, 'but short of carrying him out, and back in again, there doesn't seem to be much that we can do about this one. He must have been on one hell of a bender. Lucky chap! Oh well — let him lie. Are you with him, Miss — er——?'

56

'Kitchell,' supplied Dany hastily. 'Yes. I'm his secretary.'

'Tough luck! What are you going to do about him when we reach Nairobi?'

'I've no idea,' said Dany truthfully. 'But he's bound to wake up before then.'

'I wouldn't bet on it,' said the First Officer cheerfully, and went away followed by the stewardess.

Dany and the remainder of the passengers, looking heavy-eyed and somewhat creased, had eaten breakfast and exchanged wan, polite smiles as the sun rose over Ethiopia. Sir Ambrose Yardley had left, looking regretful, and his place had been taken by a stout Indian. But otherwise the passenger list was unchanged, and the weary, yawning faces were beginning to look as familiar to Dany as though she had known them all for several years.

Lash had woken shortly after they had taken off again. He had looked at Dany as though he had no idea at all who she was, and having informed his Maker that he felt terrible, had staggered off to the men's washroom where he had apparently drunk several quarts of richly chlorinated water, and returning to his seat had instantly fallen asleep again.

Dany peered anxiously down at Africa and did not think much of it. A vast, flat expanse of orange-brown, broken by splashes of livid green and dotted with clusters of pigmy beehives which she took to be native *kraals*. But at last there arose on the horizon a blue shadow topped by twin snow peaks.

'Mount Kenya,' announced an enthusiastic passenger who had been studying the flight card. 'We should be coming down to land soon. We're due at Nairobi at eleven, and I make it a quarter to.'

'Will passengers please fasten their seat belts,' intoned the stewardess, and Dany turned her attention to the arduous task of rousing her employer.

5

'L'me alone,' mumbled Mr Holden thickly, and without opening his eyes.

'I can't,' said Dany, continuing to shake him. 'Wake up! You can't go on sleeping any longer. At least, not here. We'll be in Nairobi in a few minutes.'

'What of it?'

'We get out there,' explained Dany patiently. 'This particular plane goes no further. Remember? You've got to wake up. Lash, *please* wake up!'

'Go t'hell,' murmured Lash indistinctly.

Dany shook him viciously, and Lash moaned and attempted to sit upright. He forced open his eyes with a palpable effort and shut them again quickly.

'God! I feel terrible!'

'That's what you said before,' snapped Dany unsympathetically. 'And you look it!'

Lash opened his eyes again, but with caution, and scowled at her. 'Do I know you?' he inquired.

Oh dear God, he means it! thought Dany with desperation. He really means it! he doesn't remember—— Panic threatened to rise and engulf her, but she fought it down.

'You should,' she observed briskly. 'I'm your new secretary.'

'Rubbish! What's happened to Ada?'

'Mumps,' said Dany succinctly.

'Then how in hell——? Oh, let it go! Let it go! I'll sort it out later. God——! Have I got a hangover!'

58

The aircraft touched down on the runway with a light bump and Lash clutched his head and groaned aloud.

Dany could never remember afterwards how she had got through the next half hour, but at least she had had no time in which to be frightened. There had been no sign of Tyson's secretary, Nigel Ponting, and somehow or other she had collected her luggage, and Lash Holden's, piloted him through a maze of official procedure, steered him through the customs and shepherded him into a taxi. Her passport — or more correctly, Ada Kitchell's — had received only the most cursory glance, and once in the taxi Lash had roused himself sufficiently to recall the name of the hotel where those passengers who were booked through to Zanzibar were to spend the night.

'Holden?' said the receptionist, peering shortsightedly through rimless glasses. 'Mr L. J. Holden? Oh yes. Yes, of course. We were expecting you.' She beamed on them as though their safe arrival was a matter for congratulation. 'Your rooms are reserved. I hope you had a pleasant flight? There is a message from a Mr Ponting. He had to see the dentist — an emergency stopping, and he could get no other appointment. But he will be calling round later and hopes you will forgive him for not having been at the airport.'

'His loss, our gain,' said Lash sourly. 'Let's hope he gets a gumboil as well, and is hung up at the dentist's indefinitely. Suits me.'

'Er ... um ... quite,' said the receptionist with an uncertain smile. 'The boys will take your luggage along, madam. Sign here please, sir. Now is there anything you would like sent up——?'

'Black coffee,' said Lash. 'A bath of it. And some Alka-Seltzer.'

'Er — certainly. Of course. Will the other lady be arriving later?'

'No,' said Lash shortly. 'There isn't another lady. Where's this room? I can't stand here half the day.'

The receptionist left her desk in charge of an African clerk, and graciously accompanied the procession herself, ushering them at

59

last into a sitting-room lavishly supplied with flowers. There was also, somewhat unexpectedly, a bottle of champagne in a bucket of ice, and two glasses.

'With the management's compliments,' beamed the receptionist, and withdrew.

'Wait a minute!' said Dany. 'What about me? Where do I——?' But the door had closed.

Lashmer Holden Jnr sat down heavily on the sofa, put his head in his hands and gave every indication of taking no further interest in the proceedings, and Dany looked at the flowers and the champagne, and struck by an unpleasant thought, crossed the room quickly and opened the only other door. It led into a bedroom where there were more flowers — orange blossom among them — and an impressive double bed.

'It's the honeymoon suite!' said Dany blankly. 'For heaven's sake——!'

She returned in haste to the sitting-room. 'You'll have to do something. There's been a mistake. They think we're married!'

Lash winced and said very distinctly: 'Would you mind not yelling at me?'

'But this is the Bridal Suite!'

'Yeah. I booked it.'

'You *what*?'

'Don't *shout*!' implored Lash testily.

'You mean to sit there and tell me that——? Is this your idea of a joke?'

'*Joke!*' said Lash bitterly. 'If you think that being jilted on the eve of your wedding, and all for the sake of a grinning, greasy-haired, hand-kissing son of a snake-in-the-grass who—— Oh, go away! Be a good girl and get the hell out of here.'

'*Elf!*' said Dany, enlightened. 'I forgot. Oh, Lash, I *am* sorry. I didn't mean to ... I mean, I ...' She stopped, confused and remorseful.

'I'll take it as read,' said Lash. 'And now, if you don't mind

60

fading away, I think I could do with some sleep. Thanks very much for your help. Good-bye.'

He dropped his head back into his hands again and Dany stood looking down at him with an exasperation that was replaced, suddenly and entirely unexpectedly, by a strong desire to pillow his ruffled, aching head on her breast and whisper consolation and endearments. And this to a man whom she had met only forty-eight hours before, and who, having been instrumental in landing her in this intolerable and probably dangerous situation, could not now even bring himself to remember her!

I must be going out of my mind! thought Dany, astounded at herself. And anyway, he's in love with that Gordon woman, and he's been drinking himself silly because she threw him over. He doesn't care one bit what happens to me. All he wants to do is to get rid of me as soon as possible. He's selfish and stupid and spoiled and egotistical, and he drinks. *And* drinks!

But it was no use. She could not even feel indignant about it, and she still wanted to stroke his hair and comfort him. Oh dear, oh dear, oh *dear*, thought Dany. I suppose this is it!

In common with all young women she had dreamed of the time when she would fall in love. It would be a romantic and rapturous and altogether wonderful moment, and the hero of it would certainly not be a pallid and dishevelled stranger who was suffering from an imperial hangover, and who was himself hopelessly in love with a glamorous widow who had jilted him for an Italian marquis!

Nothing, it seemed, turned out as one had pictured it or planned it. Life was very disappointing. *'Damn!'* said Dany aloud and deliberately.

Lashmer Holden flinched. There was a rap on the door and a white-robed African entered with a tray that bore coffee, a jug of water, a glass, and some Alka-Seltzer. Dany was relieved to find that he both spoke and understood English, and having given him several precise orders she dismissed him and turned her attention to the tray.

The coffee, though not supplied in the quantity originally suggested, was hot and very strong, and she poured out a cup of it and took it over to the sufferer. 'Try some of this,' she suggested. 'It'll probably make you feel a lot better.'

Lash lifted his head and scowled at her, but he took the coffee and drank it. Dany removed his empty cup, refilled it and handed it back, and went into the bedroom. She had already possessed herself of his keys in the Customs shed at the airport, and now she unlocked his dressing-case and dealt efficiently with the contents.

'I've run you a bath,' she announced, returning to the sitting-room. 'You look as though you could do with one. And you need a shave. You'll find your brushes and things in the dressing-room, and the room waiter will be along with something to eat in about twenty minutes. I'm not sure whether it's an early luncheon or a late breakfast, but I don't suppose it matters. Don't be too long, or it will be cold.'

She left him to it, and went away to sort out the room situation with the desk clerk and the receptionist, and returned sometime later looking thoughtful. A room-boy was waiting with a laden tray, and she told him to leave it on the table, and that he need not wait, and after he had gone she stood for several minutes staring thoughtfully at a forlorn white object that was lying upside down on the floor, displaying a neat satin label that guaranteed it to be washable and heat-proof.

'Poor Asbestos!' said Dany, stooping and picking him up. She dusted him off and replaced him, right-side-up, on the sofa: 'I suppose he's lost interest in you too. Never mind. I'll look after you. And him — if it kills me!'

There was a faint sound behind her and she turned to find Lash standing in the doorway.

He was looking exceedingly pale and there were dark circles under his eyes, but he had shaved, and his hair was wet and smooth. He had apparently found the effort to look out a change of clothes too much for him, for he was wearing pyjamas and the bottle-green dressing-gown, and he looked exhausted and ill and bad tempered.

'Do you make a habit of talking to yourself?' he inquired morosely.

Dany flushed, but ignored the question. She said, 'Your food's come. The soup looks rather good, and it's hot. I didn't think you'd like curry, so I ordered steak.'

Lash shuddered, but he drank the soup, and feeling slightly revived by it, managed to eat a reasonable quantity of steak, and topped it off with two more cups of black coffee. After which he lit a cigarette, and said grudgingly: 'Thanks. I feel slightly better. I guess I must have been pretty well plastered. The whole thing is a blur.'

'Including me,' said Dany.

'Yes — no. I seem to remember thinking it was a good idea to bring you along instead of Ada, though God alone knows why.'

Dany told him. At length and in detail.

'I don't believe it,' said Mr Holden hoarsely, breaking the long silence that had followed that recital. 'I — simply — do — not — believe — it!'

'Well it's true!' said Dany hotly. 'And if you think I'd take the trouble to invent such a — a nauseatingly improbable story, I can only say——'

'I *couldn't* be such a brainless, godammed, half-witted moron,' continued Lash as though she had not spoken. 'I couldn't. No one could! Are you giving me a line? No — no, I suppose not. For the love of Mike, why did you pay any attention to me? Couldn't you see I was higher than a kite and not responsible for my actions? Hell! you *must* have known I was drunk!

'I'm sorry,' said Dany, 'but you see I'd never met anyone who was drunk before. Aunt Harriet, you know,' she explained kindly.

'No, I don't know your Aunt Harriet! But—— Now listen — you can't have thought that I was talking sense. You can't!'

63

'I thought you were just — cheerful and optimistic.'

'Cheerful and optimistic! God Almighty!' He pushed his chair back violently, and rising from the table began to pace up and down the room like some caged tiger. 'Look — you must have been able to work it out for yourself. That the whole thing was crazy, I mean. Stark, raving crazy. And that I must have been crazy to suggest it! And anyway, how were you to know that I wasn't? You didn't even know me! For all you knew I might have escaped from the local asylum!'

'But you were a friend of Tyson's,' explained Dany patiently. 'You told me you were. And you were going to stay at *Kivulimi* — like me.'

'What's that got to do with it?' demanded Lash unfairly. 'You can't go two-timing the police and skipping out of the country on a stolen passport — well, a borrowed one, then! — just because I happen to know your step-father. Don't you understand? It's illegal! It's criminal! It's — it's — Good grief, it's sheer, shrieking lunacy! You can probably go to jail for it. And so can I!'

'Well, after all,' said Dany, 'it was your idea.'

Lash stood stock still and glared at her for a full minute in a silence that was loud with unprintable comment, and then he sat down very suddenly on the sofa and shut his eyes.

'I give up,' he said, 'I am just not strong enough to compete with you — or this situation. And to think,' he added bitterly, 'that this was to have been my honeymoon! My romantic, orchids-and-champagne-and-tropical-moonlight honeymoon! Dear God, what have I done to deserve this?'

'Drunk too much,' said Dany unkindly.

Lash opened one inflamed eye and regarded her with strong revulsion. 'One more crack like that out of you,' he said dangerously, '— just one! and I shall ring up the nearest police station and spill the whole dam' story, and let *them* deal with you!'

'And if you do,' said Dany sweetly, 'I shall tell them that you

64

persuaded me into it; and then if anyone goes to jail it will be you. For kidnapping a minor!'

There was a brief silence.

'Why you little——!' said Lash very softly.

. Dany rose briskly. 'I don't think I know what that means,' she said, 'but I can guess. And I'm afraid that calling me names isn't going to be any help. You got me into this, and you're going to get me out.'

'Am I, by God!'

'Yes, you are! So it's no use saying "Am I, by God!" Once we're in Zanzibar, and at *Kivulimi*, you can wash your hands of me, or tell the police, or do anything else you like. But until then I'm your secretary, Miss Kitchell. And I'm going to go on being Miss Kitchell — or else! Do you see?'

'O.K. I get it,' said Lash grimly. 'All right, Miss Kitchell, you win. And now, as I am not in the habit of sharing a bedroom suite with my secretary, will you kindly get the hell out of here?'

Dany studied him with a faint smile. He was looking completely exhausted and exceedingly cross, and once again it occurred to her how pleasant it would be if she were able to put her arms about him and kiss away his tiredness and ill-temper. She felt, suddenly, a good deal older than him, and that it was unkind of her to confront him with any more problems. But it couldn't be helped.

'I'm afraid,' she said carefully, 'that I can't do that either. You see, there are no other rooms.'

'Oh yes there are. There was one booked for Ada.'

'Yes, I know. But they thought I was your wife, and when that receptionist asked you about the "other lady" — meaning your secretary — you said there wasn't one.'

'So what?'

'So I'm afraid they've given the other room to someone else.'

'Then they can dam' well give you another,' snapped Lash.

Dany shook her head regretfully. 'I'm afraid not. There aren't any more rooms. Not even mine! A Mr Dowling's got that. He

65

told them I'd cancelled my passage, and he'd taken it, and could he have my room as well. There isn't a hole or corner to spare anywhere, though the manager was very kind when I explained that I was only the secretary and not the bride, and he rang up at least eight other hotels. But it seems we've chosen a bad time to arrive. There's some special week on at the moment, and the town is packed out. I said I was sure you wouldn't mind.'

Lash looked at her for a long moment, and then he rose and crossed the room, and planted his thumb firmly on the bell.

'What are you ringing for?' inquired Dany, a trifle anxiously.

'Rye,' said Lash grimly. 'I intend to get plastered again. And as quickly as possible!'

6

Dany ate a solitary luncheon in a corner of the cool dining-room, and drank coffee on the hotel verandah with Mr Larry Dowling, whose conversation she found both restful and entertaining. He appeared to be aware that she was feeling worried and distrait, and cheerfully took it upon himself to do all the talking: for which she was profoundly grateful, as it enabled her to relax and enjoy the view, while the necessity for paying some attention to what he was saying prevented her from brooding over her own problems.

'I must get me a suit of white drill and a panama hat,' said Larry Dowling. 'It's obviously that sort of climate. I suppose you wouldn't be really kind and come and help me do a bit of shopping would you, Miss — Miss——?'

'A — Kitchell,' supplied Dany, almost caught off guard. 'Yes. I'd like to very much, thank you. I want to see something of Nairobi, and I have to send off a cable.'

'That's grand,' said Larry gratefully. 'Let's go.'

They set out on foot in the bright African sunlight, and found the Telegraph Office without much difficulty. Dany had dispatched a brief affectionate message by deferred cable to Aunt Harriet, reporting her safe arrival (after first making quite sure that it could not be delivered in England before she herself reached Zanzibar) and Larry Dowling had cabled an even briefer one, express, to an address in Soho. After which they had visited several shops, and Mr Dowling had duly acquired a tropical suit, a panama hat and a pair of beach shoes. He had also bought Dany an outsize box of chocolates, as a small return, he explained, for her invaluable assistance. But Dany was becoming uncomfortably aware of pitfalls.

It was proving no easy matter to talk for any length of time, even to an attractive stranger, without finding oneself mentioning things that belonged to Miss Ashton rather than to Miss Kitchell. And although Larry Dowling had no more than a friendly interest in Miss Kitchell, he was intensely interested in Tyson Frost and anything and everything to do with him, and the indignant Dany found herself being compelled to listen to a candid thumb-nail sketch of her step-father's career and her mother's marriages, with a brief reference to herself.

'I've heard that there's a child somewhere,' said Larry, strolling beside her. 'Kept well in the background, it seems. Not Frost's — hers. But the Lorraine type don't like being bothered by brats: spoils their glamour. Besides, it makes people start doing sums. Difficult to go around looking barely thirty when you've a lumping great deb of eighteen or nineteen summers tagging along in tow. Ever seen her? Mrs Frost, I mean?'

Dany blinked and opened her mouth, and then shut it again, but his question appeared to be purely rhetorical.

'She's a honey!' he said enthusiastically. 'I saw her in London last year at a Press reception for Frost. Tiny, with dark curly hair like a baby's and blue eyes the size of saucers. Looks as though you could pick her up with one hand. Married at least half a dozen times, and when you see her you aren't surprised. Like that friend of hers on the plane — Mrs Gordon. Now there's another charmer! Though for all her looks she's had a pretty tragic life, poor girl. Her last husband fell down their cellar steps in the dark and broke his neck. Tight of course. And as if that wasn't enough, the man she was going to marry last year, Douglas Rhett-Corrington, took a header out of a top-storey window on the eve of the wedding. Seems someone had been writing him anonymous letters, or else she threw him over at the last minute, or something

68

like that. But whichever it was it must have been sheer hell for her, and she deserves a break with the next one. I wish I were in the running!'

'Are you rich?' inquired Dany, startled to find herself feeling so angry and uncharitable.

'Ah! but she's not one of those. They say she only marries for love — even if she doesn't love 'em for long! It just happened that the ones she married had money, because those are the only kind she meets. And if it was only money she was after, she'd have married your boss. A week ago there were rumours that they were going to stage a surprise wedding at Caxton Hall. But now it looks as though it was off. What went wrong.?'

'I've no idea,' said Dany coldly. 'Mr Holden does not discuss his private life with me.'

Mr Dowling's attractive triangular face lit with amusement. 'The perfect, loyal little secretary!' he said, and smiled his swift, disarming smile. 'I'm sorry. I didn't mean to pry. But there's no need for you to clam up on me. I'm not a gossip writer, you know. Young Holden isn't news as far as I'm concerned. It's men like Tyson Frost who are my bread and butter. Him and the Zanzibar elections! That was why I was so dam' pleased about getting on that plane: there were two people on it who might have been very useful to me. An Arab agitator who hopes to become a little Hitler one day, and Tyson Frost's step-daughter — a Miss Ashton. The one I was telling you about.'

'Oh . . . really?' said Dany, swallowing a lump in her throat.

'Yep. And I'd rather hoped I might be able to scrape an acquaintance with the girl,' confided Larry Dowling with rueful candour. 'It shouldn't have been all that difficult, and I might have got a lot of inside information, and even wangled an invitation to stay if I'd played my cards right. I did everything I could to get on that plane, but not a hope. And then at the last minute someone cancels a seat, and I get it. And then you know what?'

'No. I mean — what?' said Dany nervously.

'It's the Ashton girl who's cancelled it! Probably contracted whooping cough or measles or something. A pity. I'd like to have met her. Her step-daddy is news in any language just now.'

'Why just now?' inquired Dany, curiosity getting the better of a strong conviction that she ought to change the subject at once.

'Surely you know? Why, I thought that must be what your boss was after. It's his father who publishes Frost's books in the States, isn't it?'

'Yes. But——'

'Then you can take it from me that's what he's here for. The Emory Frost diaries. They were released this year. Emory was the old rolling stone who was deeded the house in Zanzibar by one of the Sultans. He seems to have been quite a lad by all accounts. There were a lot of curious stories about him — that he was mixed up in the Slave Trade or the smuggling racket, and went in for a bit of piracy on the side, with a spot of wrecking thrown in. He left a whole heap of papers and diaries that he said were not to be read until seventy years after his death, which was June this year. Tyson Frost has had 'em for a couple of months now, so he should have had time to go through them. The betting is that they make pretty racy reading, and that Frost'll publish them in book form. If I can only get him to talk about them I shall be sitting pretty. Is Holden out to get the exclusive rights?'

'Perhaps,' said Dany, trying the effect of a cautious answer.

'Ah!' said Larry Dowling. 'I thought so! It'll go down well in the States. The Yanks had a lot of influence in Zanzibar in the eighteen hundreds, and the first treaty the Sultanate ever made with a foreign country was with America. And then there's some story that Emory ran away with an American girl — rescued her from pirates who attacked Zanzibar, and blockaded the American Consulate in eighteen-sixty something, and ended up by marrying her. What a film that'd make! She must have been Frost's grandmother. They say she was a stunner, and that after she married him Emory become a reformed character and ...'

70

He broke off. 'Wait a minute ... Isn't that one of the women who were on the plane over there? Mrs Bingham? The manager of our hotel told me that she's Tyson Frost's sister. I wonder if——'

He caught Dany's arm, and hurrying her along the crowded pavement, dived into a shop that appeared to sell everything from shoes to saucepans, and went up to a counter piled high with sponges which Mrs Bingham and Miss Bates were prodding speculatively under the bored gaze of an Indian saleslady. Two minutes later Dany realized that she had been quite right when she had decided that Aunt Harriet would have taken to Mr Dowling. Mrs Bingham had instantly done so, and in an astonishingly short space of time he was involved in an animated discussion on the rival merits of natural versus foam-rubber sponges.

Dany had attempted to beat an unobtrusive retreat, having no desire to make her step-aunt's acquaintance before it was absolutely necessary. But she had not been quick enough, and before she could prevent it, Larry was introducing her.

'This is Miss Kitchell, Mrs Bingham. Mr Holden's secretary and a fellow-traveller to Zanzibar. She will be staying with the Frosts. Tyson Frost, the novelist, you know. What's that? ... Your *brother*? Now that really is a coincidence!'

He met Dany's accusing eye with a wicked twinkle in his own, and grinned at her, entirely unabashed. But the remainder of the afternoon proved to be trying in the extreme, for he had not permitted her to separate herself from the company, and her step-father's sister had turned out to be one of those exceedingly talkative women who delight in asking endless personal questions, and handing out endless personal information in exchange.

Mrs Bingham wished to know *all* about America; a country she had not yet visited but hoped to one day. Dany, who had not visited it either, did not come well out of this catechism, and could only pray that Larry Dowling and the brisk Miss Bates were equally ignorant.

71

To Mrs Bingham's loudly expressed surprise at her lack of a transatlantic accent she replied glibly that her parents had only emigrated to America within recent years, and that she herself had been partly educated in England.

'Ah!' said Gussie Bingham with the satisfaction of one who has solved a problem. 'Then that of course is why Mr Holden selected you to come to Europe with him. You would *understand* us. I don't think I ever met this Mr Holden, but his father stayed with me once — let me see, was it in '38 or '39? He is a *great* friend of Tyson's, my brother's. A very pleasant man — for an American. Oh, I beg your pardon, my dear! How very rude that sounds. Do forgive me.'

'It's all right,' said Dany bleakly, wondering how long it was going to be before she was asked something that was so impossible to answer that discovery was inevitable. What a fool she had been to talk to people: any people! She should have kept well out of sight and out of danger. Lash was quite right: she had no sense. All she had thought of was that a stroll round Nairobi with Larry Dowling would be a pleasant way to spend the long afternoon, and that it would be quite easy to keep off dangerous topics. And now look where it had landed her!

Gussie Bingham said: 'Do you suppose this is all there is of Nairobi? Perhaps I should have accepted Mr Ponting's offer to show us round. My brother's secretary, you know. He was here to meet me, and he took us out to luncheon at some club. It was really very pleasant. But as the poor man had spent half the morning in a dentist's chair I insisted that he take a couple of aspirins and lie down this afternoon, and that Millicent and I would look after ourselves. I feel sure he was grateful. You must have met him, of course, when he was in the States with my brother. What did you think of him?'

Dany's heart appeared to jump six inches and then sink at least twice that distance. *Had* Ada Kitchell met this Mr Ponting when Tyson had been over in the States? Certainly Lash had met him,

72

and therefore probably Ada. Why hadn't Lash warned her? Why hadn't she thought of asking him? Why had they both forgotten that angle, and what on earth was she going to do when she did see this man, and he refused to recognize her as Ada Kitchell?

Fortunately Gussie Bingham did not wait for an answer: 'He has been with my brother for several years, but I had not met him before — though he has been to the house, of course. But that was when Tyson was in England a year or two ago and Millicent and I were having a little holiday in Jersey. Still, it was thoughtful of Tyson to arrange for him to meet me. Though I suspect he is really here on Dany Ashton's account — my brother's step-daughter, you know. She was to have been on the plane, but she was not at the airport, and when we made inquiries they told us that she had cancelled her seat. Very odd. Chicken-pox or mumps or something, I suppose.'

It was clear that in this matter Augusta Bingham's mind moved in much the same grooves as Larry Dowling's: school-girl diseases. But fortunately for Dany's nervous system, Mrs Bingham abandoned the subject of the missing Miss Ashton and turned to a less dangerous topic:

'We shall be quite a party at *Kivulimi*, shall we not? You know, I haven't stayed there since Father died. That seems a very long time ago. We spent almost a year there, as children. But Father never really took to the place. Not like his eldest brother, old Uncle Barclay, who was completely besotted with the house. He had a *thing* about it — and about Zanzibar. He loved the place, and hardly ever left it. I suppose that was why he never married.'

'Was he the eldest son of Emory — the first Frost?' inquired Larry Dowling.

'The first Frost to visit *Zanzibar*,' corrected Mrs Bingham gently. 'Yes. The family place is in Kent, of course. I live there now, because Tyson is so seldom in England. Millicent and I keep it warm for him, we say. I don't know what I should do without

73

Millicent. She came to stay with me when my husband died, and she simply runs everything.'

'Does your brother live much in Zanzibar?' asked Larry, steering the conversation firmly back to Tyson Frost.

'Not really. He's such a restless person. Always on the move. He only lives in it by fits and starts. Asks some of his friends there, and then off he goes again. I've always thought it was such a *romantic* thing to have a house in Zanzibar, but Tyson never really stays in it very long.'

'Probably finds it jolly uncivilized,' said Miss Bates. 'Romance is all very well, but give me H. and C. every time! I always say there's absolutely nothing to beat "All Mod. Cons".'

'I'm afraid Millicent doesn't care for foreign travel,' confided Gussie Bingham in an undertone to Dany. 'She detests the East. And she misses the Institute and the Girl Guides and things like that. She has so many interests: a tower of strength. Our vicar often says that he doesn't know how Market-Lydon would get on without her, and I'm sure she agrees with him. Oh! I didn't mean — that sounds unkind of me. What I meant——'

But Dany had ceased to pay attention, for the words 'Market-Lydon' had brought a chill to the hot day. *Man Murdered at Market-Lydon* ... But it wasn't just 'a man'. It was elderly, pedantic, disapproving Mr Honeywood. And since Mr Honeywood had been the Frost family's solicitor for at least two generations, he was almost certainly Mrs Bingham's too. She would have known him well. Did she know he was now dead? Even if she did, the news of his death could not possibly have shocked her half as badly as it had shocked Dany, who had only met him once and very briefly.

Larry Dowling was saying: 'Does your brother often entertain like this when he is in Zanzibar, Mrs Bingham? Or is this a special occasion?'

'Oh, I don't think it was my brother's idea at all. He's not really very sociable when he's writing, and I believe he is supposed to be working on a book just now. But his wife likes to have the house full of guests. I suppose she gets bored when he's writing all day. And then of course ...'

Mrs Bingham's voice went on and on, and Larry Dowling listened with flattering attention, interjecting interested, incredulous or congratulatory noises whenever the flow showed signs of drying up. He was evidently as good a listener as he was a talker thought Dany uneasily. A very likeable man — but a dangerous one ...

She said with forced lightness, breaking into the bubbling stream of confidences: 'Mr Dowling is a newspaper man, you know.'

But if she had intended this as a warning, it missed its mark.

Larry Dowling threw her a brief, quizzical grin that was strangely disconcerting, and although Miss Bates turned sharply and regarded him as though he were something she had unexpectedly turned up with a garden spade, Gussie Bingham, far from being taken aback, was enchanted.

'A *reporter*? But how interesting!'

'Feature writer,' corrected Mr Dowling patiently.

'The same sort of thing, surely?' said Gussie Bingham blithely. 'You must live such an exciting life. Fires and murders and film stars. Paris today and Bangkok tomorrow. How I envy you! Of course Tyson — my brother — knows a great many newspapermen. He says they are the lowest form of human—— Oh, I *am* sorry. That was *very* rude of me. I really didn't mean ... I am quite sure he would like *you*, Mr Dowling.'

Miss Bates sniffed audibly and muttered something about carrion crows and snooping nosey-parkers, and Mrs Bingham frowned repressively at her, and taking Mr Dowling's arm, walked on ahead, chatting energetically and leaving Miss Bates to fall in beside Dany.

'I'm sure I've seen that chap before somewhere,' said Miss Bates, directing a scowl at Mr Dowling's unconscious back. 'I never forget a face. Probably in the papers, being sentenced for libel and defamation, if you ask me. It'll come back to me. I know the type. All charm and good humour, and thoroughly untrustworthy. Only out for what they can get. No better than confidence tricksters. In fact that's probably what he is! We've only his own word for it that he's a feature writer — whatever that is!'

Miss Bates sniffed again, expressively. 'You know,' she confided, 'Gussie's a good sort, and she's got plenty of brains in her head. But there are times when you'd never suspect it. Look at the way she's letting that reporter pump her about Tyson. Anyone could see that he's up to no good. If he's not a crook, then he's after an article — preferably one with a lot of dirty linen involved. Newspapers are a menace. Garbage — that's all they're interested in. Garbage and Murder.'

Murder! ... Yes, murder was only something that you read about in a newspaper. It wasn't real. People one knew died; but they were never murdered ...

Dany had tea on the hotel verandah, still in the company of Augusta Bingham and Millicent Bates, and the Press, as represented by Larry Dowling. Larry had issued an unexpectedly diffident invitation, which she had been about to refuse when the sight of Lash Holden had made her change her mind. For Lash was also taking afternoon tea on the verandah — with Amalfi Gordon. He was wearing a grey suit and showed no signs of a hangover, and Amalfi was looking soft and sweet and appealingly lovely in something that had undoubtedly run someone into three figures in a cheque book, and whose simplicity of line made every other woman within range look (and feel) like a back number of *Home Chat*.

There was no sign of the Marchese Eduardo di Chiago, and Amalfi was talking earnestly and inaudibly, with an expression on her lovely face that admirably combined a sweetly sorrowing archangel and a child begging forgiveness for some minor peccadillo.

76

Lash was looking a little sulky, but at the same time bedazzled, and Dany wondered if the Marchese had been sent off on some errand that would keep him out of the way for an hour or two and allow Mrs Gordon to eat her cake and have it. The anxieties of the afternoon, together with the murder of Mr Honeywood and half a dozen pressing and unpleasant problems, retired abruptly from the forefront of her mind, to be replaced by indignation on the score of the predatory Mrs Gordon and the spinelessness of that gullible, besotted and hypnotized rabbit, Mr Lashmer J. Holden, Jnr.

What can he *see* in her! thought Dany indignantly. And instantly realized just exactly what he saw in her. Amalfi Gordon appeared to have everything.

Well she isn't going to have Lash! decided Dany fiercely, and sat down in a chair from which she could keep an eye upon that feckless and intransigent young man without appearing to do so.

Lash did not become aware of her for at least twenty minutes, but when he did, he reacted promptly; though in a manner that could hardly be termed gratifying. Suddenly catching sight of her, he remained for a moment transfixed, as though he could hardly believe his eyes, and then rising abruptly and excusing himself to Amalfi, he came quickly towards her, threading his way between the intervening tea-drinkers on the crowded verandah.

'I've been looking for you, Miss Kitchell,' said Lash ominously. 'There are several things that need your attention, and I'd be glad if you'd deal with them immediately. And another time, just let me know when you intend to take the afternoon off.'

Dany bit her lip and blushed painfully, but fortified by a sense of humour, and even more by the spectacle of the golden Mrs Gordon left abandoned at the far end of the verandah, she rose meekly.

'I'm so sorry, Mr Holden. I had no idea that you would be needing me this afternoon. Will you excuse me Mrs Bingham? It seems that I have some work to do. Thank you for the tea, Larry.'

77

She introduced Lash to the assembled company, and left. But she had been back in the bridal suite for less than five minutes when the door opened violently to disclose her employer.

He banged it shut behind him and said furiously: 'Say, have you taken leave of your senses? What the heck do you mean by flaunting yourself all over Nairobi and letting yourself get picked up by any Tom, Dick or Harry? Hell! d'you know who you've been getting off with? A newspaperman! Of all people to pick — of *all* people! And that blue-haired dame is Tyson Frost's sister. Your step-aunt, by God! Do you suppose she hasn't recognized you? You'll probably wake up tomorrow to find the whole thing splashed right across the front pages. You ought to have your head examined!'

'Don't worry,' said Dany soothingly. 'I've never met her before, so of course she can't recognize me. And I'm very sorry about Larry Dowling. I didn't think——'

'You never do!' interrupted Lash bitterly. ' *"Larry"* indeed!' Her use of Mr Dowling's Christian name appeared to infuriate him further. 'Has it ever occurred to you to take a look at the passport you are travelling on? No? Well let me tell you that Ada comes from Milwaukee — and they don't talk with a British Broadcasting accent there!'

'Oh dear,' said Dany guiltily, 'that reminds me. Did I ever meet this Mr Ponting? Tyson's secretary? — I mean, did Ada Kitchell ever meet him? Because Mrs Bingham asked me about him, and I didn't know if I should know anything or not.'

Lash raised a couple of clenched fists to heaven while his lips moved soundlessly, and then, lowering them, said in a strictly controlled voice: 'No, by the mercy of Providence you did not meet him. Otherwise we'd have been in a worse jam than we're in right now. What did you tell her?'

'Nothing. Luckily she didn't wait for an answer.'

'Lucky is right! And I hope that's taught you a lesson. Can't you see that your only chance is to lie low and keep out of sight, and not talk to anybody — *anybody!* — until you get to Zanzibar? Once you get there it's your step-father's headache. And if he has any sense, he'll give you six with a slipper where it hurts most!'

Lash went across to the table by the window and helped himself to a drink from a tray that had not been there when she left. But she was relieved to see that the bottle appeared to be far more than three parts full, and that the amount he took was unquestionably modest.

'This,' said Lash, intercepting her look and interpreting it correctly, 'is merely to take the taste of that godammed tea out of my mouth. Much as I should like to duck the whole situation by getting roaring drunk, I shall lay off it until I've got rid of you. Going on a bender is a luxury I can't afford while there are people like you around loose.'

Dany remarked pleasantly that it was kind of him to worry so much about her welfare.

'I'm not,' said Lash shortly. 'You can disabuse yourself of that idea right away. It's myself I'm worrying about. Which is why, Miss Kitchell, you will stay right here in this room and keep your mouth shut until we leave for the airport tomorrow morning. And you will continue to keep your charming trap shut until we are safely inside your unfortunate step-father's front door. After that, I shall, myself, take the first plane out again, with Ada's passport in my pants' pocket, and leave you to it.'

He finished his drink and moved to the door: 'You'll find the draft copies of several letters on that writing table. I guess you may as well fill in the time by typing them. Three carbons. And spell them correctly — in American.'

'Yes, sir,' said Dany meekly.

Lash laughed for the first time in twenty-four hours. 'You know, you're not a bad kid,' he conceded. 'Your I.Q. is probably the lowest on record, and I can't figure out how the Welfare State ever allowed you to go around without a keeper. But you have your moments. Don't let this lick you, honey. I'll see you through.'

Dany was aware of a sudden prickle of tears behind her eyes, and she turned away quickly so that he should not see them. 'Thank you,' she said in a small voice.

Lash said: 'The typewriter is in that square maroon-coloured case. I'm not sure where the paper and carbons are. Look around. Oh, and by the way, just for the look of the thing, you are occupying this suite on your own. I fixed it with the management. Officially, I am down as sleeping in Room 72, during the absence of the owner. Actually, as he's put a padlock on it, I shall be spending the night on this sofa. But as long as no one else knows it, the decencies will be preserved. And there's a lock on that door over there, in case you feel anxious.'

He opened the door into the passage, and added over his shoulder: 'I'll see that they send along some dinner for you. Safer than turning you loose in the dining-room, with wolves like that guy Dowling prowling around.'

'You, I suppose,' said Dany crossly, 'will be dining out. I should have thought you'd have more pride!'

'Take a letter, Miss Kitchell,' said Lash austerely, and shut the door with a bang.

7

It was just on two o'clock in the morning when Dany awoke suddenly and lay still; listening.

She did not know what had awakened her, except that it was a sound. Perhaps it was Lash coming back. No, it could not be that. She had heard Lash come back before she fell asleep; and that was over an hour ago, for she could make out the position of the hands on the luminous dial of the travelling-clock that stood facing her on the dressing-table. Besides, the sound had not come from the next room. It had been nearer than that, she felt sure ...

Dany had slept little and uneasily in the hotel in Gloucester Road, and worse on the plane last night, so she had confidently expected to make up for it here. But sleep had eluded her, and for hour after hour she had tossed and turned in the wide bed, worrying over her parlous predicament and listening for Lash's return.

He had come back at last, shortly before one o'clock. And presumably sober, for he had made so little noise that but for the fact that she was awake and listening for him, she would not have known that he had returned. She had heard a switch click, and a narrow thread of light had appeared under the door between the two rooms, and Dany had sat up in bed hugging her knees and wishing fervently that the conventions did not forbid her going in to the next room to talk to him.

She was feeling lonely and forlorn and frightened, and much in need of comfort, and Lash had not improved matters by starting to whistle very softly between his teeth as he undressed. It was only the ghost of a melody, but the song was familiar. Too familiar. *'Then I'll go sailing far, off to Zanzibar ...'* He sounded light-hearted enough.

He's made it up with her, thought Dany desolately. What fools men are. She's old enough to be his mother! Well, not his mother perhaps — but his aunt. And she doesn't care a button for him. Not really. She'd rather be a *Marchesa* — or a million-airess — or ... Perhaps he *is* a millionaire? No, he can't be! He mustn't be. That Sir Somebody ... Ambrose Something who got off at Khartoum. Oil. *He's* probably a millionaire, and old enough for her. Perhaps she will marry him instead. Or the Italian. But please, not Lash ...

The light under the door vanished, and Dany had fallen asleep at last. To be awakened very suddenly an hour later by a sound that she could not identify.

She listened for it to be repeated, but it did not come again, and presently she relaxed once more and lay staring sleepily into the darkness. An hour earlier there had been a moon: a bright, white, African moon that had shone in at her window and made the room so light that she had got out of bed and pulled the heavy inner curtains over the muslin ones that were intended to keep out such things as flies and dust during the daytime. But now the moon had set and the lights in the hotel had winked out, and the streets of Nairobi were dark and silent. As dark and as silent as her room.

Dany's eyelids had begun to droop when suddenly and horribly she was aware that there was someone in the room with her.

She had been lying looking idly at the faint green dial of the travelling-clock, and she had heard no sound. But she did not need to. Something — someone — had moved between her bed and the dressing-table, and blotted out that small luminous circle. She could still hear the clock ticking quite clearly. But she could no longer see it.

Dany sat up very slowly, inch by terrified inch; moving as noise-lessly as that other presence in the room, until at last she was sitting upright, pressed hard back against the pillows and the padded bed-head. Her hands were clenched on the sheets and every muscle in her body seemed atrophied by fear. She could move no further. She could only sit rigidly and stare into the darkness with dilated eyes, while her breath seemed to fail her and her heartbeats sounded as swift and as audible in the silence as hoof-beats on a hard road.

Nothing moved in the blackness, but there was an odd smell in the room. A queer sickly smell that was somehow familiar and yet very frightening. As frightening as the unseen thing that was in the room with her.

Then all at once the clock face was visible again. The black-ness that had obscured it had moved from left to right, and that meant that it — whatever it was — was moving towards her.

Dany opened her mouth to scream and found that her throat was dry and stiff and so constricted by terror that the only sound that emerged from it was a foolish croaking little gasp. But it had been a mistake to make that sound.

There was a sudden sharp sense of movement in the darkness and something touched the side of the bed. And suddenly, born of a desperate instinct of self-preservation, courage and the power of connected thought returned to her. That foolish croak had only served to guide someone to her; and if she screamed, though she might wake Lash, he could not get to her for she had locked the door. And she might not have time for more than one scream . . .

Dany gathered her strength, and flinging herself suddenly to one side, rolled over to the far side of the bed and was on the floor and on her feet.

The suddenness of the movement evidently took the intruder by surprise, for she heard a sharp intake of breath and a quick movement that was followed by an involuntary gasp of pain. At least it was human, for it had stubbed a bare or a stockinged foot

83

on the leg of the bed. The sound betrayed its position as her own effort to scream had betrayed hers, and that much at least helped her. But only for a moment.

Dany backed away into the darkness, and it was only then that she realized that whoever was in the room with her was not an ordinary thief. A thief, with the window behind him and realizing that she was awake, would have escaped into the night without loss of time. But this was someone who meant to get *her* — Dany Ashton! To kill her . . . For a swift sickening moment the pinched, prim face of Mr Honeywood seemed to float in the air before her.

Murder . . . That was no longer merely an arresting word in a newspaper headline. It was real. It was here in the room with her. Murder. When she moved, it moved. When she stood still, straining to listen, it stood still — listening too. Waiting to pounce . . .

She was shivering so badly that she could hardly stand and she felt as though she would go mad with fear. She had lost her bearings, and though her cold hands were against the wall and she felt along it, she no longer knew in which direction she was moving. Was she going towards the door into the sitting-room or moving away from it? Where was the bed? Where was the window?

And then, for a brief moment, she saw the clock dial again and knew where she was. But in the next instant there was a clatter and the ghost of a chuckle — a horrifying sound in the darkness — and it had vanished. The clock had been deliberately overturned so that it could no longer guide her, or betray a movement.

But she was within a yard of the door now. She must be. Another three steps and she would reach it.

Something struck the wall beside her with a sharp *plop* and almost succeeded in forcing a scream from her. The effort to restrain it and make no sudden movement beaded her forehead with a cold sweat and wet the palms of her hands, but with the next step she knew that she had saved herself: and what had made that sound.

The intruder had thrown one of her heelless velvet slippers at random across the room to trap her into a scream or an audible movement that would betray her position. Her foot touched the slipper and she stooped cautiously and silently, and picking it up threw it in the direction of the bathroom door.

It hit the wall and fell with a soft thump, and once again she heard a harsh, quick-drawn breath, and then a rush of stockinged feet towards the sound. But she had reached the door of the sitting-room and the key was cold between her fingers. She turned it, and twisted the door-handle with hands that were so wet with terror that for a moment the knob slipped sickeningly and would not turn. And then the door was open and she was through; stumbling into unseen furniture and screaming for Lash.

She heard her pursuer cannon into the half open door behind her, but she had reached the sofa and Lash had woken up. 'What the hell——!' he demanded. And at the sound of his voice there came a quick incredulous gasp and a flurry of sound that ended with the slam of a door. And they were alone.

Lash groped his way blasphemously to the nearest switch, his progress grossly impeded by Dany who was clinging to him with the desperate tenacity of a limpet and then the lights snapped on and he blinked dazedly, mechanically patting her shuddering shoulders.

'*Lash . . . Lash . . . Oh, Lash!*' wept Dany, dissolved in tears and terror.

'It's all right,' said Lash awkwardly. 'I'm here. Everything's all right. Was it a real bad nightmare, honey?'

'It wasn't a nightmare,' sobbed Dany. 'It was a m-murderer! A *murderer!*'

'Don't think about it, bambina,' advised Lash kindly. 'It's no use letting all this get you down. Stop crying, honey.'

But Dany merely tightened her terrified clutch on him. 'You don't understand — I wasn't dreaming. It was real. It was *real*——'

'O.K., it was real,' said Lash soothingly. 'But you don't have

85

to strangle me. Look, what about a little drink and a couple of aspirins?'

Getting no response to this suggestion, and finding that Dany had no intention of letting go of him, he picked her up bodily, and returning to the sofa sat down on it, holding her, and reached over her head for the tray of drinks that he had thoughtfully placed within range of his temporary bed.

'Now see here, for Pete's sake sit up and get a grip on yourself. Here, drink this — it's only water ... That's a good child. You know, right now what you need most is a handkerchief. Or let's say six handkerchiefs. Come on, honey. Snap out of it! You're soaking me, and I shall catch one hell of a cold.'

Dany lifted her head from his damp shoulder and sat up, displaying a tear-streaked and terrified face, and gazed helplessly about her.

'What are you looking for?' inquired Lash.

'H-handkerchief, of course.'

'If you'll let go of me, I'll get you one.'

He freed himself from Dany's clutching fingers, and setting her down on one end of the sofa, collected a clean handkerchief from the pocket of his discarded dinner jacket, and handed it over.

'I seem to remember that nightgown,' he remarked, lighting himself a cigarette and smiling at her through the smoke. 'You were wearing that and a sheet of newspaper when we first met. This is quite like old times. I'll admit that right now your face isn't looking up to much, but if it's any consolation to you, the rest is a treat to the eye.'

This observation produced no reaction whatever, and the smile died out of Lash's grey eyes, to be replaced by concern. 'You have had a bad time of it, haven't you, brat? But everything will be all right now. You'll see. Come on, you're awake now.'

Dany dropped the handkerchief and stared up at him with shocked tear-blurred eyes. 'You still think it was a dream, don't you? But it wasn't. There was someone in my room. I heard a noise and woke up, and — and then I ... then I saw the clock. It's — I could see it in the dark. It's luminous. And then ... then suddenly I couldn't see it any more, because someone was standing in front of it——'

The sentence ran out into a violent shudder that made her teeth chatter, and Lash's face changed suddenly and startlingly. He flung his cigarette away and was at the bedroom door in two swift strides, feeling for the light switch. It clicked on, revealing the tumbled bed and the curtains stirring idly in the soft dawn wind. But there was no one there.

The room was empty and the light twinkled on the little pearl and diamond brooch and the narrow gold wristwatch that Dany had worn. She had left them on the dressing-table, and near them, face downwards, lay the gilt travelling-clock.

'Nuts!' said Lash brusquely, relief giving place to irritation. 'You dreamt it. If there'd been a thief in here he'd have taken care of that stuff, and——' He stopped. There was something lying on the floor by the dressing-room door, and the door itself was ajar.

He crossed the room quickly and stooping, picked it up. It was a torch, of a type that is cased in heavy black rubber and capable of being focused.

Lash turned to find Dany at his elbow, white-faced and shivering. 'This yours?'

'No. Of course not.'

'Umm,' said Lash thoughtfully, and vanished into the dressing-room. He did not return for several minutes, and Dany sat down on the edge of the bed, still trembling violently and wondering if she were going to disgrace herself by being sick. It seemed only too likely.

Presently Lash returned, looking puzzled. He said: 'Nothing seems to have gone. It looks screwy to me. Why didn't he grab what he could, and scram?'

'Because he didn't w-want anything like that,' quavered Dany, shivering. 'He didn't come for t-that. He was looking for m-me. He was going to m-murder me.'

'Oh, baloney!' snapped Lash exasperated. 'Will you just lay off carrying on like a character out of a soap-opera? It was obviously only some little African sneak-thief. A town like this is probably full of them! It may even have been one of the hotel staff trying a bit of light burglary.'

'It wasn't,' insisted Dany obstinately. 'It *wasn't*. B-burglars don't want to murder people, and he meant to murder me. I know he did!'

'Now see here,' began Lash patiently. 'You haven't a shred of evidence that he intended to do you any harm at all — beyond relieving you of any cash or jewellery you'd left lying about. He probably hadn't gotten around to that when you woke up, and the chances are that you scared him worse than he scared you: which is plenty! Now why don't you just——'

He broke off and looked about him, wrinkling his nose. 'What's that smell?'

'I d-don't know. It was in here before. *He* brought it——'

'*Chloroform, by God!*' said Lash in a whisper. 'That's what it is! Chloroform——!'

He swept the bedclothes to one side with a single savage jerk, and the smell was suddenly stronger and more clearly identifiable as something fell to the carpet with an almost inaudible plop.

It was an ordinary polythene bag of a size and type frequently used to pack sandwiches in for a picnic, and it appeared to contain nothing more than a pad of cotton wool and gauze.

Lash stooped rather slowly and picked it up, and opening it, jerked his head back sharply with a grimace of distaste as a strong waft of anaesthetic flowed out from it.

He rolled it up again swiftly and pushed it into an empty drawer of the dressing-table, and Dany said, also speaking in a whisper: 'I told you. I *told* you! That was m-meant for me, wasn't it?'

'Maybe,' said Lash curtly.

'Well then why don't you do something? Why are you just s-s-standing there?'

'What do you suggest I do?' inquired Lash coldly.

'Call someone! Wake up the manager. Telephone the police. Something — anything!'

Lash turned away and walked towards the open door into the sitting-room. He said: 'Don't be a fool, Dany. You know damned well that we are in no position to go bawling for the cops.'

He held the door open for her, and having shut it again behind her, went across to the armchair that contained his discarded clothes and picked up his dressing-gown.

'You'd better borrow this again. In fact, if this sort of thing is going to become a part of the daily round, I guess you'd better keep it. Your need would appear to be greater than mine.'

Dany said tonelessly: 'No. You have it. I can use this.'

She wrapped herself in a blanket off his makeshift bed, and sat down in a shivering huddle on the nearest chair, feeling limp and boneless from shock and fatigue and the aftermath of abject panic.

Lash put on his dressing-gown and helped himself to a drink, and sat silent for a time, staring ahead of him in frowning concentration while Dany watched him and did not speak. Presently he stood up abruptly, finished his drink at a gulp, and putting down the empty glass went back into the bedroom.

He was away for perhaps ten minutes, and though Dany would have liked to follow him, merely from terror of being left alone, she found that she was too exhausted to move. She kept her frightened gaze on the open door instead, and presently saw his shadow move once more across the wall.

He came back into the sitting-room, frowning blackly, and mixed another drink which he handed to Dany. 'You'd better take that. You look as though you could do with something stronger than water, and you can't fold up now. I want to talk to you.'

89

He poured out a second and considerably stronger one for himself, and then sat down on the sofa, facing her.

'I'm coming round to the idea,' said Lash, 'that there is more in this than meets the eye. It looks as though that guy in there had gone to quite a bit of trouble. And he wasn't after cash.'

'I *told* you——' began Dany again.

'*Ssh!* Now I'm telling you. He didn't come in by the bedroom window. He broke the one in the bathroom, and came in that way. There was quite a bit of my stuff, and most of yours in the dressing-room, and he's had a darned good look at it. Forced every lock on the ones that weren't open, and gone through every little thing. But as far as I can see he hasn't taken anything. Unless, of course, you were carrying a clutch of diamonds or something? Did you have much money in your bags? Or jewellery?'

'No,' said Dany in a hoarse whisper. 'I haven't much jewellery. Only that brooch and the watch, and a pearl necklace, a diamond bar pin and some costume stuff that were in my dressing-case.'

'And still are,' said Lash. 'They haven't been touched. And neither have my pearl studs and a rather flashy assortment of cuff-links, or a gold and platinum cigarette case and lighter, and one or two more far-from-inexpensive trifles. Not to mention a good few traveller's cheques. All, or any, of those things are just the size to go comfortably into any guy's pants' pocket. Yet he didn't take 'em. Now why?'

'I told you,' said Dany for the fourth time.

'Look, just quit talking will you? This is a soliloquy, not a dialogue. I'm sorting out the facts. That dressing-room and everything in it has had a real going over. The sort of frisking that it would only get if someone were looking for just one thing: one special thing. And it's my guess that if it had been found, your visitor would have got out the way he came in and there'd have been no more trouble. But because he didn't get what he was after, he came into your bedroom; and as you can't search a bedroom thoroughly while the owner is occupying the bed, that's where the

chloroform was going to come in. If you hadn't woken up just
then you wouldn't have known a thing about it: you'd have passed
out cold, and when you woke up you might have felt a little
sickish — but that'd have been all. Except that while you were
out for the count your bedroom would have gotten the same
treatment as the dressing-room. Now am I right, or aren't I?'

Dany merely shivered and drew the blanket more closely about
her, and Lash answered his own question: 'I'll bet I am! But where
do we go from here? that's the six-hundred-thousand-dollar question. Well, I'll tell you. Backwards!'

He drank deeply, and Dany said morosely, her gaze on the glass
in his hands: 'Yes. I can see that!'

Lash grinned at her. 'The point is taken, honey. But you don't
have to worry. I intend to stay strictly sober. This is merely medi-
cinal: an aid to thought. And right now we're going to have to
do some fast and fancy thinking, because I see I was way off the
line in my first assessment of the situation.'

'I don't know what you mean,' said Dany. The whisky Lash
had given her was beginning to make her head swim a little, and
she felt better. But not much.

'You're not concentrating,' said Lash. 'Remember how I met
you? You'd gotten yourself locked out of your room, and while
you were out of it someone took it to bits. But they didn't take
your money or your jewellery, which shows that they were after
something else.'

'My passport,' said Dany impatiently.

'I don't believe it. Not now; though I admit I did once. It
seemed the obvious answer at the time, and that, I guess, is where
we tripped up. Why should anyone take a room to pieces looking
for something that is exactly where they'd expect to find it? in your
handbag and right under their nose. We ought to have seen that
one: it stands out a mile. Those balcony rooms at the Airlane were
a darned sight too easy to get into — always provided one was a
resident. Someone probably meant to try that chloroform trick

91

around six in the morning. Easier than poking about in the dark, and most people are dead asleep at that hour. They were probably already on the balcony or behind a curtain when you saved them a lot of trouble by going to fetch that newspaper, and getting locked out. Taking your passport and planting that gun was probably merely an afterthought, when they couldn't find what they were after. To stop you leaving the country with something that you've got and they want.'

'But I haven't got anything!' protested Dany, beginning to shiver again.

'You must have. And I'm willing to bet you five grand to a stick of bubble-gum that I know what it is! What have you done with the letter that Tyson's solicitor gave you? — that guy who got shot?'

Dany's eyes widened until they were enormous in her white face, and she stood shakily, clutching the blanket about her. 'No! No, it couldn't possibly be that. It was just a letter. It couldn't possibly——'

'Of course it is. It couldn't possibly be anything else! The question is, have you still got it?'

'Yes. I — I think so.' Dany's voice was hoarse and breathless.

'Where?'

'I think it's still in the pocket of my coat. The camel-hair one that's hanging in the cupboard.'

Lash got up and went into the bedroom, and returned carrying a light-coloured loose overcoat. 'This it?'

Dany nodded, and he thrust a hand into one of the deep silk-lined slit pockets and unearthed a crumpled slip of paper, two pink bus tickets, a receipted bill and three ha'-pennies. The other pocket was more productive. It contained, along with a face tissue and a card of bobby pins, a plain envelope addressed to 'Tyson Frost, Esq. By hand'. Lash dropped the coat onto the floor, and slitting open the flap, drew out the contents.

It was another envelope, but of a different variety. This one was a piece of hand-made paper, yellowed with age and folded and sealed in the manner of a day when there were still a few people who did not use manufactured envelopes. There was no address on it. Only the heavy seal bearing the crest of the Frosts over the arrogant motto *'I Tayke Wat I Wyll'*, a number, 74389, and the initials E.T.F. written in faded ink.

'Women!' said Lash. 'And you had it in your pocket the whole time!'

He sat down on the sofa and gazed at her, shaking his head, and then looked down at the sealed envelope again. 'What beats me is why he didn't find it when he went through your things at the Airlane. I guess he can't know anything about women, or you'd have thought—— Say, wait a minute! Didn't you say something about leaving some coat in a powder room? Was this it?'

'Yes,' said Dany, still having some difficulty with her voice. 'I — I forgot it. It was there all night.'

'So that's why. Then it all ties up.'

He stared at the small sealed packet that he held, and was silent for what seemed a very long time.

The room was so quiet that Dany could hear the tiny tick of his wrist-watch and the slow bubbles breaking at the rim of the glass that she still held clutched in one hand. Lash was looking tired and grim and oddly unfamiliar, and as though he had suddenly become a stranger; someone about whom she knew nothing at all.

The silence began to get on her nerves and she found herself watching the bedroom door again, and listening with strained attention for any faint sounds from the night outside. Was the broken window in the bathroom still open? Had Lash thought to lock the door between it and the dressing-room. Suppose the man were to come back — and with a gun or a knife instead of a pad soaked in chloroform?

Lash spoke at last: slowly and in an undertone, as though he were talking to himself rather than to Dany.

'Yes ... that would be it, of course. It's the only way it fits. I remember now. You said something about telephoning. You phoned this solicitor of Tyson's and asked if you could see him in the morning instead of that afternoon. Which means that you should have gone there in the afternoon, and someone who knew that, but not that you had changed the time, meant to get there first — to get their hands on this!' He tossed the small envelope in the air and caught it again. 'That's why the safe was opened, of course.'

'But Mr Honeywood ... Why should anyone murder Mr Honeywood?'

'Because you can't open a safe without keys. Unless you're a professional cracksman. And whoever was after this, and didn't realize that you'd got in ahead of him, expected to find it in the safe.'

'But — but he had a gun. He could have *made* Mr Honeywood open it. He didn't have to kill him!'

'Suppose your Mr Honeywood knew the guy? I'd sure like to know what's in this bit of paper.' Lash balanced it in his hand thoughtfully and said: 'I'm not sure we oughtn't to take a look at it.'

'But you can't. It's Tyson's! And it's sealed. You can't go breaking the seal.'

'Can't I? What makes you think that? There's something inside this that was worth a man's life. Someone was prepared to murder Honeywood in cold blood in order to get it, and you don't get many people risking the death penalty for peanuts.'

'It's Tyson's letter,' said Dany stubbornly, and held out her hand for it.

Lash shrugged his shoulders and passed it over. 'I won't say "Take better care of it this time", because it seems to me that in your own cock-eyed fashion you haven't done too badly. But for Pete's sake don't leave it lying around, because whoever was after it has got a shrewd idea who's got it.'

Dany gazed at him appalled. 'I — I didn't think of that. That means——' Her voice trailed away and she shuddered uncontrollably.

'Exactly!' said Lash dryly. 'It's someone who followed you from London and must have been on the plane with us. And what is more, it's someone who knows quite well that you are not Miss Ada Kitchell from Milwaukee!'

8

The alarm clock rang shrilly, notifying the fact that it was now 5 a.m., and Dany awoke for the second time that morning; to find herself in possession of a bad headache and sharing not only the bridal suite but the bridal bed.

The proprieties had been observed by the slenderest of margins, and one which would hardly have been recognized as such by even the most broad-minded: Miss Ashton being inside the bedclothes while Mr Lashmer J. Holden Jnr, still wearing his dressing-gown, was disposed gracefully outside them.

Blinking at him in the pale light of early morning Dany recalled with painful clarity that it had been her own hysterical and unmaidenly insistence that was responsible for this scandalous state of affairs. She had, she recalled, refused frantically and flatly to be left alone. A combination of panic and whisky had drastically altered her sense of values, and the ethics involved had ceased to have any meaning for her when compared with the terrifying prospect of being left alone once more in that darkened bedroom.

Lash yawned and stretched, and having propped himself on one elbow, regarded her flushed cheeks and appalled eyes with comprehension and some amusement.

'All in all, a very cosy and domestic scene,' he remarked pleasantly: 'I can't think what the younger generation is coming to. Or what your dear Aunt Harriet would say if she could see you now!'

'Or your dear "Elf"!' snapped Dany. And instantly regretted the retort.

'Puss, Puss, Puss!' said Lash, unruffled; and rolled off the bed.

He stood up yawning largely and rubbing his unshaven chin, and announced that she had better stay where she was while he had the first bath and shaved: 'And don't go ringing for the room-waiter until I'm out of the way. The less publicity we get, the better.'

Dany occupied the time in wrapping the sealed envelope in a chiffon head scarf and then putting it back into her coat pocket as far down as it would go, and pinning the chiffon wrapping firmly to the lining with a large safety pin. That at least would ensure that no one could possibly pick her pocket without her knowledge.

Time being short, she took over the bathroom while Lash dressed, and as soon as she was in a fit state to answer any knock on the door he went away, leaving her to pack.

He had finished breakfast by the time Dany appeared in the dining-room, and had gone out into the verandah, where she could see him through an open door talking to Mrs Bingham, Millicent Bates and a pallid willowy man whose face was vaguely familiar to her. Amalfi, the Marchese, Larry Dowling and the Arab, Salim Abeid, were also on the verandah, standing together in a bored group just beyond them, yawning at intervals and making desultory conversation, while presumably waiting for a taxi, or taxis.

The sight of Salim Abeid was a shock to Dany. She had not realized that he too had been staying at the hotel, and she was digesting this fact, and its possible implications, when Lash came quickly back into the dining-room and over to her table.

'That out there,' said Lash without preamble, 'is your dear step-father's secretary, Ponting. So just watch your step, will you, and keep your mouth shut. He may look like the popular idea of an underdone Interior Decorator — and choose to talk like one — but there's nothing much the matter with his little grey cells, and don't you forget it!'

'So *that's* who it is!' said Dany, relieved. 'I knew I'd seen him somewhere.'

'Holy Mackerel——! Say, I thought you said——'

'Oh, I haven't ever met him before,' said Dany hastily. 'I've only seen his photograph. He was in some snapshots that Lorraine sent me.'

Lash exhaled noisily. 'Thank God for that! For a moment I thought we were going to run into more trouble. Well, if you've seen photographs of him, it's an even bet he's seen plenty of you, so for Pete's sake be careful. His hobby is ferreting out information and gossiping about it, and in that line he can give points to any women ever born! He was being infernally inquisitive last night. It seems that there should have been a Miss Ashton on that plane, and he can't figure out why she hasn't come.'

'Oh dear!' said Dany guiltily. 'He hasn't done anything about it, has he?'

'Nothing much he *can* do, is there? Apart from ringing the Green Zero office, and he did that yesterday. They came right through with it and said that Miss Ashton had cancelled her passage only twenty-four hours before the flight, so he had to be satisfied with that. But he's still making quite a song and dance about it, and but for that providential goddam tooth of his he'd have fetched up at the airport yesterday when I was in no condition to deal with the situation. It's a pity his dentist didn't give him an overdose of gas while he was at it, and save us his company this morning as well. But I suppose one can't have everything. Don't be too long over that coffee. We leave in ten minutes.'

They drove through Nairobi in the cool of the early morning, and once again there was the ordeal of passports and officials to be faced. But at last they were in the departure lounge, and the worst was over. The last lap——

Larry Dowling appeared at Dany's elbow, and relieving her of her typewriter, asked with some concern if she were feeling all

98

right. Larry's eyes, thought Dany, were like a Kentish trout stream with the sun on it. Clear and cool — and friendly. Looking at them, she felt again that he was a dependable person — in a way that Lash was not. And yet . . .

Gussie Bingham, smart in a suit of lilac-blue linen that toned admirably with her blue-rinsed hair, said briskly: 'You look tired, my dear. I hope you don't allow Mr Holden to keep you working too late. Personally, I had an excellent night. But then I am thankful to say that I always sleep well wherever I am. It's all a matter of *control*. I don't think you have met Mr Ponting yet, my brother's secretary? Mr Ponting——!'

'Dear lady?' said Mr Ponting, hastening to obey that imperious beckoning finger.

Dany turned quickly so that her back was to the light, and shook hands with Mr Ponting. His hand felt limp and boneless and as soft as a woman's, and his voice was high and light and affected.

'Ah!' said Nigel Ponting gaily. 'A fellow wage-slave! A toiler at the oar! You and I, Miss Kitchell — mere downtrodden secretaries: hard-working honey-gatherers among this decorative swarm of holidaying drones. They toil not, neither do they spin, while we are compelled to do both. Gross injustice, is it not? We must form ourselves into a Trades Union. Ah——! Eduardo. *Buon giorno!* I didn't see you at the hotel. How are you? You look *deliriously* fit. I suppose you all know each other madly well by now—— No? Oh dear! I'm so sorry. Miss Kitchell, this is the Signor Marchese di Chiago, a fellow guest bound for *Kivulimi*. Miss Kitchell is Holden's confidential secretary, Eduardo, so we are Birds of a Feather.'

The Marchese bowed over Dany's hand and gave her a long observant look that tabulated her admirable physical assets, added the spectacles, fringe and curls, and subtracted the number he had first thought of.

He was a slim, dark man, handsome in a typically Italianate

99

manner, and although he was not much taller than Nigel Ponting, he gave the impression of being twice the size. The willowy Mr Ponting, thought Dany, would have made quite a pretty girl. And possibly he thought so himself, for he wore his butter-coloured hair far too long, and allowed a single artistic lock to fall carelessly across his white forehead — apparently as an excuse for a frequent graceful tossing of the head that would temporarily return it to place. His eyes were a limpid and unblinking blue like the china eyes of a Victorian doll, but nevertheless they conveyed a disturbing impression that very little escaped them, and Dany was more than relieved when he took the Marchese affectionately by the arm and walked away, talking animatedly of mutual friends in Rome.

Gussie Bingham, hailed by Miss Bates, hurried off to see to some question of luggage, taking Larry Dowling with her, and Dany retired to a seat near the window and struggled with another attack of panic. Officials came and went, appearing suddenly in doorways and glancing keenly about the room, and each time she was sure that she was the one they were looking for. Every stranger was, or might be, a plain-clothes detective, and every idle glance that came her way turned her cold with apprehension. They *could* not stop her now! Not now, when she was almost within reach of safety. Her head ached and she felt chilled and sick and taut with the strain of trying not to think of the happenings of the last few days, or the dreadful thing that Lash had said last night: 'It's someone who must have been on the plane with us.'

But that was absurd and impossible. It was out of the question that it could be anyone who had travelled out from London with them. Dany turned restlessly to look out across the vast, dun, dusty expanse of the aerodrome, and as she did so a man passed by on the other side of the window. It was the Arab, 'Jembe' — Salim Abeid — who had been on the plane from London. She saw him stop not far away in the shadow of an adjoining building

100

to speak to a man who seemed to have been waiting there. An olive-skinned Arab in a well-cut white suit.

Salim Abeid seemed to be speaking with the same fervour that he had displayed at Naples, and Dany wondered if his conversation was still confined to politics. His hands waved, his shoulders shrugged and his eyes flashed, but his companion showed little interest, and apart from an occasional surreptitious glance at his wrist-watch, remained gravely impassive.

Salim Abeid turned and gestured in the direction of the glass-fronted departure lounge, and for a moment it seemed to Dany as though the Arab in the white suit looked straight at her, and once again panic attacked her. Perhaps he was a policeman. An Arab policeman. Perhaps this man 'Jembe' was telling him about her: that he had seen her in the hall of the Airlane in London. Or worse — far worse! — was *he* the one who had murdered Mr Honeywood, and searched her room at the Airlane — and meant to chloroform her last night?

Dany felt her heart begin to pound and race again, and she looked wildly round for Lash — or for Larry. But Lash was at the far side of the room being monopolized by Amalfi Gordon, and Larry, looking faintly resigned, was collecting a cup of coffee for Mrs Bingham. He smiled at her across the crowded room, and her panic unexpectedly diminished. She was imagining things and behaving, as Lash had said, like some hysterical heroine in a soap opera. Surely her situation was parlous enough without her manufacturing turnip-lanterns with which to scare herself further. And yet . . .

'Will passengers on flight zero three four, proceeding to Mombasa, Tanga, Pemba, Zanzibar and Dar-es-Salaam, please take their seats in the plane,' announced a sepulchral and disembodied voice.

The orange earth of Africa slid away beneath them. A waste of sun-baked earth and flat-topped thorn trees, dotted with slow-

101

moving specks that were giraffe and zebra, wilde-beeste, lion, and drifting, grazing herds of antelope — for this was the Nairobi Game Park.

A lone white cloud, faintly tinged with pink, lay in the cool blue of the early morning sky, and as they neared it Dany saw that it was not a cloud, but a mountain. A solitary snow-capped mountain faintly reminiscent of a Japanese print of Fuji-Yama. Kilimanjaro, the 'Mountain of Cold Devils', looming lonely above the enormous, dust brown plains: a gaunt, burnt-out volcano whose snows defied the burning African sun.

A voice from the seat behind Dany's, a man's voice, fluting, high-pitched and seemingly a deliberate parody of an announcer on the B.B.C.'s Third Programme, said: 'Yes — *rather* spectacular, isn't it? And they say that there is the corpse of a leopard in the crater, frozen into the ice. No one knows how it got there, or why. Deliciously intriguing, don't you think? I *adore* mysteries!'

Dany made a movement as though she would have turned to look at the speaker, but Lash's hand shot out and closed warningly on her wrist. *'Ponting,'* he said soundlessly and Dany turned hurriedly back to her contemplation of the view.

Nigel Ponting's neighbour was apparently Mrs Bingham, and with the object of instructing the ignorant — or possibly because he was addicted to the sound of his own voice — he embarked on a lengthy verbal tour of Kenya.

'And you have simply no idea how primitive those up-country roads are,' fluted Mr Ponting. 'Mere tracks, I assure you. *Torture* to the tyres! Not, of course, to mention one's *spine*! Though actually, when one gets there, it is quite deliciously stark. The natives — the animals — the scenery! Intoxicatingly primitive. Such an improvement on down-country Kenya and the Settler Belt, which is so *painfully* Pre-World-War-One, I always think. *Too* Poona, don't you agree? But the Northern Frontier now ...'

His voice tinkled on and on like water trickling from a faulty tap, interspersed at intervals by vague noises from Gussie Bing-

102

ham (herself no mean monologist but at present patently out-classed) and it would have been a soothing enough sound had he not changed to the subject of Dany.

'I can't understand it,' said Nigel Ponting fretfully. 'I simply *cannot* understand it. No word at the hotel, and her room reservation not even cancelled. One hopes that the Frosts have had a cable, but really — one didn't know whether to go or stay! I suppose the wretched girl has been smitten with some form of spots. Measles, or some similar schoolgirl affliction.'

Lash turned his head and grinned maliciously at Dany, but she did not share his amusement. She was getting tired of hearing herself referred to as though she were a school-age adolescent, and in any case she could see nothing comic, in the present circumstances, in having to listen to this particular form of conversation.

'*Actually,*' said Nigel, 'it was on Miss Ashton's account that I was over here at all. Your brother thought that it would be a graceful gesture to have her met at Nairobi, and probably save you trouble if I could see to her and show her the town. So he kindly arranged for me to take a little holiday at about this time to fit in with the date, and now the wretched girl has not arrived! *Too* tiresome of her, as I fully expect to be sent back to meet her when she finally does so. And I *detest* air travel. I may not show it, but I'm always simply terrified in a plane. Aren't you?'

'No,' said Gussie Bingham, firmly seizing her chance. 'I can't say I am. But then I am a fatalist. I feel that if fate intends me to die in an air-crash, I shall die in an air-crash: and that is all there is to it. And if it does not then there is nothing to worry about. Everything, dear Mr Ponting, is pre-destined. Everything! There is no such thing as chance. Once one has grasped that simple but essential truth, life becomes far less complicated. One ceases to worry.'

Mr Ponting uttered a sharp cry of disagreement. 'Oh no, no, no, no *No*, Mrs Bingham! I cannot agree with you. The doctrine of pre-destination, even if it were proved right, *must* be wrong.

So spineless. Surely one should grasp opportunity and *mould* it to one's will?'

'That's what Millicent says. We have *such* arguments. But it is my contention that when we think we are grasping an opportunity we are merely doing something that we were ordained to do, and cannot avoid doing. For instance, when we left Lydon Gables for London we were half-way to the station when I remembered that I had taken my passport out of Millicent's bag to show to a friend (a really laughable photograph!) and left it on the piano. So of course we had to hurry back, and what do you think! We found that a live coal had fallen out of the drawing-room fire, and the carpet was already smouldering! Mrs Hagby might not have had occasion to come in for several hours, and had we not returned the house might well have burned down!'

'Very lucky,' conceded Nigel Ponting.

'Lucky? No such thing. We were *meant* to return. I was meant to leave that passport behind, and so could not have avoided doing so.'

Nigel gave a little tittering laugh. 'And supposing you had missed your train and had not been able to reach London, and the airport, in time? Would that also have been *meant*?'

'Oh, but we were not meant to miss it! It was fortunately running late. Though even if it had not been we should not have missed the plane, because we came up to London two days early, on the afternoon of the twelfth, and stayed at the Airlane, as Millicent had some shopping to do and——'

Dany was aware of a slight movement beside her, and she saw that Lash's hands had tightened suddenly on the newspaper he held so that it's outer columns were crumpled and unreadable. But surely he had known that Mrs Bingham and Miss Bates had been at the Airlane? And surely he could not think — *Someone on the plane* ... Gussie Bingham ... No, that at least was not possible!

Nigel was saying pettishly: 'But really, Mrs Bingham, one cannot bring oneself to believe that Providence is interested in such

104

matters as a coal falling out of your drawing-room fire or a fog to delay your train, or the fact that passport photographs always make one look so painfully improbable that you were impelled to share the joke with some friend. Now I myself am more interested in psychology, and it is my contention that when you left that passport on the piano——'

Dany rose abruptly. She did not want to listen to any more talk of passports, or the Airlane, or anything else that forced her to think of frightening and horrible things, and she handed her folded coat to Lash and said briefly: 'I'll be back in a minute.'

'Feeling all right?' inquired Lash, half standing to let her pass. 'You're looking a bit green.'

'No. I'm quite all right, thank you.'

She went quickly down the aisle and took refuge in the ladies' room, where she stood staring out of the window at the wide blue sky and the little idling clouds. But her thoughts had only come with her, and she could not hold them at bay.

Gussie Bingham ... Millicent Bates ... Jembe ... Mr Honeywood. *Murder in Market-Lydon* ...

Dany gave it up and returned to her seat.

The tiny, dragon-fly shadow of the aeroplane flitted across muddy green water, mangrove swamps and forests of palm trees ... Mombasa. 'May I have your attention please? The indicator will tell you when to fasten your seat belts. In a few minutes we shall be coming in to land——'

The passengers trooped out dutifully into hard sunlight and a salty smell of the sea, and among them Dany noticed the slim Arab in the white suit whom she had seen Salim Abeid talking to so excitedly at Nairobi that morning.

Apparently there were others on the plane who also knew him, for Nigel Ponting, catching sight of him, left Mrs Bingham's side and hurried after him. They shook hands and stood talking together for a few minutes on the hot, sandy tarmac, and Dany, passing them, heard Tyson's secretary say: 'I do hope you had a

105

lovely time? Frankly, Nairobi is *not* my cup of tea. But of course it's different for you — you've friends there. Now *I* went up to the Northern Frontier with Bunny, and——' The words 'deliciously stark' pursued her as she reached the shade of the airport entrance.

Salim Abeid — 'Jembe', pushed past her, looking far from well, and making for the opposite side of the room he sat down at a small table, ordered himself a cup of black coffee, and began to read an Arabic newspaper which he held in noticeably trembling hands.

The waiting-room of the airport was hot and crowded, and Lash having left her to her own devices, Dany bought a magazine at random off the bookstall and retired with it to a comparatively secluded seat near a pillar. But she did not read it. She sat staring unseeingly at the printed page and listening absently to the medley of accents about her, until her attention was attracted by a large framed advertisement for a local air-line that hung on one side of the pillar a little to her left.

The advertisement, she discovered, was painted on looking-glass, and in it she could see the reflection of Gussie Bingham's blue curls, Millicent Bates' pudding-basin hat, and Amalfi Gordon's flower-like face.

Amalfi, thought Dany, was not looking her best this morning. She looked as though she were hot and rather cross, and the conversation of Eduardo di Chiago, whose handsome hawk-like profile was just visible at the extreme edge of the looking-glass, appeared to be boring her, for she was replying to it in monosyllables and allowing her gaze to wander. Mrs Bingham, on the other hand, seemed to be enjoying herself. She was laughing at something that someone had said, and all at once the wild idea that she might have had anything to do with the murder of Mr Honeywood was exposed as utterly ridiculous.

Perhaps it had been the Arab, Jembe, after all. Or else it was some stranger on the London plane whom she had taken no note of. Or even Sir Ambrose Yardley! The complete absurdity of that last thought drew a wan smile from Dany: she was letting her imagination run away with her with a vengeance! And anyway, Sir Ambrose had not been in Nairobi last night. It *must* be some stranger . . .

The group in the looking-glass broke up and moved away, and she could no longer see the reflection of anyone she knew. Passengers on other flights arrived and left again, and the waiting-room became noisier and more crowded. Dany's head began to ache intolerably, and every separate sound in the medley of sounds became an added irritation: a fretful Indian child wailing with dismal persistence, the crash of an overturned cup and the trickle of spilt liquid, the shrill giggling chatter of a covey of Arab matrons, and the loud laughter of a group of young planters round the bar.

'You never told me you could read Arabic,' remarked Lash's voice behind her.

Dany started violently and bit her tongue, and focusing for the first time on the magazine that she held, discovered that it was indeed printed in a totally unfamiliar script.

Lash reached across her shoulder, and twitching the magazine out of her hands, reversed it and handed it back. He said: 'You'll forgive me for mentioning it, Miss Kitchell, but there's nothing quite so conspicuous as someone pretending to read a paper that they're holding upside down. And that fresh boy-friend of yours, the newspaper guy, has been watching your reflection in that slice of glass with considerable interest. It's a game that two can play. Maybe he just likes red-heads — but then again he might have other ideas.'

Dany said breathlessly: 'Larry Dowling? What ideas? He — he couldn't know anything. And anyway he's only interested in people like Tyson. And politics.'

'That's a buyer's estimate,' said Lash dryly. 'Murder is news any place. So just try and stop acting like you had a ton-load of guilt on your conscience. It shows.'

'I'm sorry,' said Dany in a small voice.

'That's O.K. It's not much longer. We're almost there.'

'But not quite,' said Dany unsteadily.

'Where's your fighting spirit?'

'I haven't any — Not at present.'

Lash said: 'Poor baby.' But without sarcasm. And then once again a quacking, disembodied voice from the amplifier cut through the fog of babel in the crowded room:

'Passengers on flight zero three four, proceeding to Tanga, Pemba, Zanzibar and Dar-es-Salaam ...'

9

They walked out into the glaring sunlight and a sea wind that sang through the casuarinas and whipped hot grains of sand against their legs, and took their places in the waiting plane; dutifully fastening their seat belts and stubbing out cigarettes. Larry Dowling, from a seat just behind Dany and across the aisle, called out: 'Hi—— Stewardess! we're one short. Don't shut that door. My neighbour isn't here yet. Mr Salim Abeid.'

The stewardess smiled in the tolerant manner of a school teacher coping with a backward new boy, and said sweetly: 'Thank you, I have the list. There is no need to worry. He will be along in a minute.'

But five minutes ticked by, and then ten, and though the plane vibrated to the roar of the engines it did not move, and the passengers began to fidget restlessly, turning to peer over their shoulders at the open door or to look anxiously at their watches.

'What's holding us up?' demanded a stout man from a seat near the front. He rose and looked down the aisle, his red face purpling with indignation. 'We shall be late at this rate, and I've got a conference on at Tanga at 10.15. Hey! Stewardess — Miss!'

The stewardess turned and smiled a bright official smile. 'Just a moment, sir.' She leaned out and spoke to someone through the open door, and then came quickly down the aisle and vanished into the pilot's cabin. Two more minutes passed, and then she re-appeared accompanied by the captain and the First Officer, and all three left the plane.

'*Now* what?' demanded the gentleman who had a conference in Tanga. 'This is the ruddy limit! How much longer do they intend to keep us hanging about?' He lumbered wrathfully down the aisle and peered out into the sunlight, and they could hear him shouting down to someone on the tarmac.

'*Really*,' said Nigel Ponting in a fading voice, 'these business types and their *hustle*! As if half an hour one way or another *mattered*!'

'There I don't agree at all,' said Gussie Bingham tartly. 'Delay is always maddening. And it will probably be most inconvenient for Tyson, who is sure to be meeting us. What do you suppose is holding us up?'

'Whatever it is, dear lady, it is surely a comfort to know that it is *Meant*,' said Nigel with malice. 'But let us trust that it is not some vital fault in the engines, or we shall be pre-destined to wait here for *hours*!'

Mrs Bingham was saved the necessity of finding an adequate retort to this shrewd shot by the return of the Tanga-bound passenger. 'Seems that one of the Zanzibar passengers has been taken ill,' he announced, and went angrily back to his seat. 'Can't think why we should all be held up for a thing like that. Do they expect us to wait until he feels better?'

At this point the stewardess returned, looking flushed and put out, and made a brief announcement: 'May I have your attention, please? I am afraid that we shall be delayed for a further — er — few minutes. We are so sorry that you should be put to this inconvenience, but we hope it will not be too long before we — er — take off. You may smoke if you wish, but will you all please keep your seats.'

Once again a buzz of conversation broke out; to die away as two airport officials and a young European police officer in a starched khaki uniform entered the plane. One of the officials spoke politely and briefly into the microphone: 'Sorry to trouble you,

110

but we have to make another passport check. Will you have your passports ready, please?'

Dany threw a wild, terrified glance at Lash, but he did not return it. He drew out his own passport and held out a hand for hers, still without looking at her, and his complete lack of emotion brought her some measure of reassurance. She could hear the voices and footsteps and the rustle of paper as the officials passed up the aisle, examining every passport, checking it against a list and jotting down brief notes on a loose-leaf pad.

'Holden,' said Lash laconically, handing over his passport as they stopped beside him. 'My secretary, Miss Kitchell.'

Dany forced herself to meet the man's gaze and hold it calmly, and although it seemed to her that he stood there for an appalling length of time, it was, in fact, all over in under three minutes. They had only asked one question: the same question that they had put to everyone on the plane. 'Where can you be reached during the next ten days?'

Even the young police officer had heard of Tyson Frost, and had read his books. 'Another of you,' he said jotting down the address. 'Mr Frost seems to be throwing quite a party. He's a wonderful chap, isn't he? I saw him when he came through here a few months ago. Got his autograph, too!'

The boy grinned and passed on to the next passenger, and Dany relaxed again. It was all just some routine check after all. She turned to smile her relief at Lash, but Lash was not smiling. He was looking, on the contrary, remarkably grim and there was a curious suggestion of alertness about him: as though his nerves and muscles were tensed. It was the same look that he had worn during the previous night, and it frightened Dany.

The three men came back down the aisle, their check completed, and Larry Dowling said: 'How is he, officer? — Mr Abeid? Nothing infectious, I hope? He seemed all right when he got off just now. Is he really bad?'

'He's dead,' said the police officer shortly, and departed.

There was a brief shocked silence. The silence that must always greet such an announcement, whether it refers to a friend or a stranger. The ending of a life.

It was broken by Millicent Bates, who said loudly and incredulously: '*Dead?* D'you mean that Arab chap who was on the London plane with us? What rubbish! They must have made a mistake. Why, he was chatting away to Mr Dowling, on and off, all the way from Nairobi. I heard him. He can't possibly be dead!'

'Heart, I expect,' said Larry Dowling uncomfortably. 'He said he always felt bad in a plane. He looked a bit green. But he can't have been air-sick. We haven't bumped about at all. I think it was just nerves.'

'As long as it's not plague or cholera or one of those beastly Eastern diseases!' said Millicent with an audible shudder. 'I told you we should regret coming out East, Gussie!'

Dany heard Mrs Bingham turn sharply in her seat. 'Don't talk nonsense, Millicent! Of course it can't be anything infectious. If it were they'd quarantine the lot of us!'

'How do we know they haven't?' inquired Miss Bates. 'We're still here!'

The entire plane was silent again, digesting this. Presently the silence was broken by the return of the captain and the First Officer, and five minutes later Mombasa Airport was behind them — a dwindling speck among toy trees.

Dany turned to look at Lash again, and said in an anxious undertone: 'Would they really quarantine us if it was something infectious?'

'If it had been anything infectious they'd never have let us leave.'

'Oh. Yes. I didn't think of that. I suppose it must have been a heart attack. Or a heat stroke.'

'I doubt it,' said Lash curtly.

112

'Why?'

'They wouldn't have taken all that trouble to check up on the lot of us, and make certain of being able to get in touch with us again, if it were anything as simple as that. They think it's something else.'

Once again Dany was conscious of feeling oddly breathless. She said: 'I don't know what you mean.'

'Then you're lucky,' said Lash briefly, and put a stop to any further conversation by lying back and closing his eyes with deliberation.

Small puff-ball clouds lazed in the hot blue air and trailed their shadows far below across acres of pineapple plantations spiked with sisal, and thick, pale, leafless baobab trees ...

Tanga, and another wait: shorter this time. An agonizing wait: but there were no police officers to meet the plane. The voice of the stewardess again: 'May I have your attention, please. The indicator will tell you when to fasten your seat belts ...'

Now they were over the sea. A glassy sea that merged into a glassy sky with no line anywhere to show where one ended and the other began: blue and green, violet and amethyst, streaked with the pale ribbons of wandering currents; the colours shifting and changing as the shadow of the plane swept across deep water, coral beds, rock bottom or sandy shallows.

Pemba: the Green Island. Rich in cloves and dark with the legends of witches, demons and warlocks. A long, sandy runway and the sea wind rustling the palm-leaf thatch and matting sides of the little hut that did duty for airport office and waiting-room. Amalfi Gordon, looking as out of place as a diamond tiara in the one-and-ninepennies, and gazing in horrified disbelief at an enormous slow-moving millepede that was crawling placidly across the dusty floor. Millicent Bates, her worst fears realized and 'What Did I Tell You?' written all over her. Gussie Bingham, seated on the extreme edge of a wooden bench upon which she had first thoughtfully spread a clean handkerchief, and also

113

watching the millepede with an expression of acute apprehension. Eduardo di Chiago, Nigel Ponting and the Arab in the white suit standing together in the open doorway, silhouetted against the hot empty expanse of sand and sky, talking together in Italian. And Larry Dowling fanning himself with his new panama hat and gazing absently at a framed poster that urged prospective travellers to 'Fly BOAC.'

There were eight other passengers of assorted nationalities in the hot little hut. A stout German business man, a Swedish tourist hung about with expensive cameras, two British army officers on leave, a Parsee, an elderly Indian couple and a citizen of the United States of America — Mr Lashmer J. Holden Jnr, who once again appeared to have fallen asleep.

How *can* he just doze off like that, thought Dany indignantly, when we shall be arriving in Zanzibar in no time at all, and if they've heard anything there we may find police waiting for us at the airport? And if Mother is there to meet us she'll know me at once, even in spectacles and with this hideous hair-fixing, and suppose she says something in front of the passport and customs people before we can stop her, and—— Oh, I wish it were all over! How *can* he go to sleep!

Lash opened one eye, winked at her solemnly, and shut it again, and Dany blushed as hotly as though she had been caught speaking her thoughts aloud. She turned her back on him with deliberation as Nigel Ponting drifted in and introduced the Arab:

'Here's someone you simply *must* meet. Seyyid Omar-bin-Sultan. He has a simply heavenly, *heavenly* house in Zanzibar. In fact two — or is it three? Anyway, if you want to see the island you must lure him into taking you on a conducted tour. No one can tell you as much about it as he can. He practically *is* Zanzibar!'

Seyyid Omar smiled and bowed. His English was as fluent as his Italian had been and he spoke it with barely a trace of an

114

accent. He in no way resembled his compatriot, the late Mr Salim Abeid, for his complexion was no darker than the Marchese di Chiago's, and he was a charming and entertaining conversationalist.

Lash did not open his eyes again until the passengers were summoned once more to take their seats in the plane, but as they left the little palm-thatched hut he took Dany's arm and delayed her, walking slowly until the others had drawn ahead.

'Now get this,' said Lash, speaking quickly and in an undertone. 'When we get there, waste as much time as you can before you leave the plane. Fuss over the baggage — anything. But get right at the end of the line. I've got to see your mother first — if she's at the airport. Or your step-father. Or both. Otherwise we're going to find ourselves in the can before we can blink twice. Got that?'

Dany nodded. And then they were back once more in their seats, facing an illuminated sign that was saying 'No Smoking. Fasten Seat Belts.'

Pemba dwindled in its turn to a little dark dot in a waste of blue, and ahead of them lay something that at first seemed no more substantial than the shadow of a cloud on the glittering sea. Zanzibar . . .

The blue of deep water gave place to the gorgeous greens of sandbars and shallows, and they were losing height and swooping in over acres of clove trees and groves of palms. Above orange orchards and the clustered roofs of houses.

Lash reached out a hand and closed it over one of Dany's, gripping it hard and encouragingly, and then there was a bump and a jolt and they were taxi-ing up the runway to stop at last before a long white building backed by innumerable trees.

Lash unfastened his seat belt for the last time and said 'Here we go!' And went.

Dany never knew what he had said to her mother and Tyson,

both of whom were at the airport to meet the plane. He had had less than five clear minutes; certainly not more; but he had apparently made good use of them.

'*Darlings!*' called Lorraine, greeting her guests as they emerged from behind a barrier where they had queued to have their passports and permits inspected and stamped. 'How lovely to see you all. Elf——! What heaven to see you, darling. And Gussie! Gussie, you look *marvellous*. And madly smart. Hullo, Millicent. Eddie! — *years* since we saw you last! Oh well, months then, but it seems like years; and isn't that a lovely compliment?'

Lorraine never seemed to change, thought Dany, regarding her mother with indulgent affection. She was not beautiful in the way that Amalfi Gordon was beautiful, but she managed none the less to convey an impression of beauty, and that did equally well. Part of her appeal, thought her daughter dispassionately, undoubtedly lay in her lack of inches and that entirely deceptive appearance of fragility. It made even undersized men feel large and strong and protective.

Lorraine was wearing white linen and pearls, and she did not look like anyone's mother. Or, for that matter, like the wife of the burly, loud-voiced, bearded man in the salt-stained fisherman's slacks and faded blue T-shirt, who seemed slightly larger than life and was clearly recognizable to any reader of the Press of any country in the world as Tyson Frost, author of *Last Service for Lloyd*, *Clothe Them All in Green O*, *The Sacred Swine* and at least half a dozen other novels that had been filmed, televised, analysed, attacked, imitated, selected by Book Societies and Literary Guilds and sold by the million.

Lash said briefly: 'My secretary, Ada Kitchell; Mrs Frost,' and Dany, demurely shaking hands with her own mother, was seized with a sudden hysterical desire to burst into helpless giggles.

Lorraine had not blinked, but her small face had paled a little and her blue eyes had widened in dismay. She said faintly: 'So

116

pleased——' And then in an anguished whisper: 'Darling — why *red?* and that *appalling* fringe!'

Tyson's large, sinewy hand descended on Dany's shoulder blades with a smack that made her stagger: 'Well, Miss Kitchell — delighted to meet you. Perhaps you and Bates won't mind going in the station wagon with the luggage. No, Lorrie! you'd better take Elf and Eddie and Nigel. Hiyah, Eddie? Back again like a bad lira? Didn't think we'd see you down this way again after giving you sandfly fever or whatever it was you caught last time you were here. No, by cripes — it was dysentery, wasn't it? Gussie, I'll take you and young Lash. Go on, pile in.'

He opened the door of the car, and suddenly caught sight of Seyyid Omar-bin-Sultan. 'Hullo, you old wolf. Didn't know you'd be back so soon. How was the night-life of Nairobi?'

He took Seyyid Omar by the arm and said: 'Gussie, this is a friend of mine. I'd like you to meet Seyyid — Oh, you've met? Good. Well get on into the car then. We don't want to hang around here all day.'

Gussie got in, followed by Lash. 'Come round and look us up as soon as you can,' bellowed Tyson as Seyyid Omar moved off towards a large white car bearing a Zanzibar number plate. 'Who the hell are you?' He turned to glare at Larry Dowling, who removed his hat and smiled amiably.

'Merely a fellow-traveller — in a strictly non-political sense,' said Mr Dowling. 'As a matter of fact, I came here hoping to meet you, Mr Frost. If I may call sometime——'

'In what capacity? As a member of my public or the Press?'

'Both,' said Mr Dowling promptly.

'Then let me break it to you right away,' boomed Tyson, 'that I despise my public wholeheartedly, and I never talk to the Press. Good day.'

He dived into his car, slammed the door and drove off in a cloud of dust, followed by his wife in a second car, and Dany, Millicent and the luggage in a station wagon. Larry Dowling, who was not

117

unused to this sort of thing, bestowed a brief, good-humoured grin on Dany, shrugged philosophically and hailed a taxi.

At any other time or in any other circumstances, Dany would have found her first sight of Zanzibar fascinating and exciting. But now that she was here at last, all that she could feel was not so much relief as overwhelming exhaustion. She had, as Lash would have said, made it. But it did not seem to matter.

The station wagon, piled high with assorted suitcases and driven by a smiling African in a smart white uniform and a red tarboosh, whirled them along white, shadow-splashed roads, tree-lined or palm fringed. Past pastel-coloured houses and sudden glimpses of a sea that glittered blue as a broken sapphire.

Hibiscus, oleander, bignonia and wild coffee starred the road-side, and brilliant masses of bougainvillaea spilled over garden walls in an extravagant riot of colour. And then they had reached the town and were threading their way at a foot pace through streets so narrow that neighbours living on opposite sides of them could surely shake hands with each other from their upper windows. Tall, whitewashed houses, so high that the streets were deep canyons and crevasses. Hot white walls, hot black shadows, and white-robed black-faced men. Huge, elaborately ornamental doors decorated with fantastic carving and great metal spikes. The smell of strange Eastern spices and hot dust; the scent of sandal-wood and frangi-pani and cloves. A sound of laughter and music and drums ...

On the far side of the town they passed through a fringe of squalid slums: an ugly shanty-town of rusty tin, corrugated iron, crumbling mud walls and decaying thatch, which gave Miss Bates an excuse for a dissertation on the subject of Oriental inefficiency and the inexcusable stupidity of Eastern races who were critical of the benign blessings of British rule.

The road crossed a bridge over a malodorous creek and skirted a shallow bay full of mud flats where the rotting hulks of ancient dhows lay stranded beyond the reach of the tide. And then they were among trees again: forests of coconut palms, thick groves of mango and orderly plantations of clove.

'How much farther do you suppose this place is?' inquired Millicent Bates restlessly. 'I should have thought Tyson would have had the sense to live nearer the airport.'

'There wasn't any airport a hundred years ago,' said Dany.

'What's that? Oh — Oh, I see. Well it's a bally nuisance all the same. I don't mind telling you that I could do with a strong cup of tea. Gussie and I always have one about eleven o'clock, and it's one of the things I miss. But at this rate it will be jolly nearly lunch-time by the time we get to this shady house of Tyson's. Shady house . . .'

Millicent threw back her head and laughed uproariously at her own joke. 'Not bad, that, you know. I must remember to tell Gussie. And I bet it's not far out, either! From all one hears about old Rory Frost, I'd say there'd been a good few shady goings-on in that house. And I wouldn't put much beyond Tyson, either! He's the kind who'd watch his grandmother carved up if he happened to need some first-hand information on dissection for a chapter in one of his books. All the Frosts have been hard nuts; or else crazy, like old Barclay. I can't think how Gussie—— Ah, this looks like it at last.'

The car turned left off the main road and into a narrow side lane that was barely more than a track, and presently they were skirting a long, high wall of whitewashed stone. Bougainvillaea, flowering jasmine and orange trumpet flowers draped it with scent and colour, and from behind it rose the tops of many trees.

'Yes, this must be it,' said Millicent with relief. 'The road seems to end here. There's the sea.'

The station wagon had been the last to leave the airport, and the two other cars, having easily outpaced it, were already back in the garage. The road was empty as they drew up before an ancient, iron-studded door set deeply into the long wall, where a stately Somali servant in white robes and a wide, welcoming grin awaited their arrival.

A scent of orange blossom, frangi-pani and warm damp earth drifted out to meet them, and through the open doorway Dany could see a garden full of flowers and winding paths and freckled shadows, and a tall, square, three-storied Arab-style house whose windows looked out across the massed green of trees and a blaze of flowers towards the sparkling sea and the long blue horizon. *Kivulimi*, at last!

10

'And now,' said Tyson, closing the door of the guest-house behind him and depositing a bottle and a handful of glasses on the nearest table, 'for the love of Allah, let's get this sorted out. Have a drink, Junior. In fact, have several. You look as though you needed 'em — and by God, I do! What in the name of hell's delight is all this about?'

Lash had been allotted the small, three-roomed guest-house that was built on the seaward wall of the garden overlooking a curving bay which was part of the domain: a wall that had once been part of the outer defences of a small fort, and dated from the days of Portuguese domination. Half a dozen armed men could have walked abreast along its crenelated top, and Tyson's father, Aubrey Frost, had reinforced the crumbling stone, and converted a look-out and two guard rooms into a small but pleasant guest-house, shaded by a gigantic rain tree and overhung by a profusion of purple and crimson bougainvillaea.

Tyson had led the way there, followed by his wife, his step-daughter and Lashmer Holden, after first seeing to it that his other guests were safely in their several rooms, unpacking suitcases and preparing for luncheon.

Lash accepted a drink and disposed of half of it before replying.

'You may well ask,' he said. 'And you aren't going to like the answer. We are, not to put too fine a point on it, in one helluva jam.'

'It was like this——' began Dany.

121

Lash said: 'Now look——! you keep out of it. Right now I'm doing the talking. You can take over when I'm through.'

He turned back to Tyson: 'There's just one question I'd like to ask before we get down to cases. Why did you send this kid here tracking all the way down to the country to fetch you a letter from a guy called Honeywood, when your sister's living right plunk on his doorstep? Don't think I'm inquisitive, but I'm interested. How is it you didn't ask Mrs Bingham to collect it for you?'

Tyson stared. 'What the hell's that got to do with this? Or you?'

'Plenty,' said Lash. 'How come?'

'I don't see that it's any affair of yours. But if you've travelled out in the company of my sister without learning that she is talkative, untrustworthy and bloody inquisitive, you must have brought lack of observation to a fine art!'

'Tyson, *darling*!' protested Lorraine faintly. 'Gussie isn't——'

'Yes, she is. And well you know it! And don't interrupt. Well, boy, having answered your question, let's have an answer to mine. What the hell is all this fantastic fandango about?'

'Have you,' said Lash, asking another one, 'by any chance heard that Honeywood was murdered a few days back?'

'*Honeywood!* Good God! When — how——' He turned sharply to face his step-daughter. 'Then you didn't see him after all? Does this mean that you didn't get that letter?'

'Yes, she did,' said Lash brusquely. 'That's the trouble. And it makes a long and screwy story.'

He finished his drink, and having replenished his glass sat down on the window seat and supplied the salient points of that story with terseness and economy.

'Is that all?' said Tyson Frost with dangerous restraint, breathing heavily.

'It'll do to go on with,' said Lash laconically.

'Then all I can say,' said Tyson, saying it, 'is that there must

122

be insanity in your family! And, by heck, I always knew it! Were you out of your mind?'

Lash winced. 'To be frank with you, yes. I happened to be plastered at the time.'

'My God! So I should think! Why — it's sheer lunacy. It's criminal. It's——'

'I know, I know,' said Lash wryly. 'You aren't telling me anything. I seem to remember saying all that myself when I surfaced yesterday. And more! There isn't any angle you can put to me that I have not already come up against — hard. The point is, what do we do now?'

'Cut her hair,' said Lorraine in a fading voice. 'And wash it. Darling, *really*——! It's quite *hideous*. Not the colour so much; I could bear that. But that awful fringe! The sort of thing film stars used to wear in the ghastly twenties. Too frightful. And darling, those spectacles! For goodness sake take them off at once. They make you look too dreadfully intelligent.'

'It's an illusion,' said Lash sourly.

Lorraine ignored him: 'That's right, darling. And don't put them on again. You look so much nicer without them.'

Tyson said: 'Your mother, thank the Lord, is utterly incapable of intelligent thought or of grasping the essential guts of any situation.'

'It would appear to run in the family,' commented Lash caustically. And added as a gloomy afterthought: 'And maybe they've got something there, at that. An inability to grasp the essential guts of this set-up is something I wouldn't mind having myself right now. And you're dead right about that hair-style. It's a pain. I never did go for red-heads, anyway.'

'No. You prefer blondes, don't you?' said Dany with a sudden flash of waspishness.

'Hell, who doesn't? Is there any more of that Scotch around?'

Tyson pushed across the bottle and said angrily: 'You're all mad! The whole lot of you! What the blue-asterisk-blank does

123

it matter what Dany's hair looks like? It seems to me, young Lash, that you're taking a ruddy casual view of all this. What do *you* propose to do about it?'

'I?' Lash looked mildly surprised. 'Oh, that's dead easy. I propose to eat a hearty meal at your expense, and then I'm catching the next available plane out of here. And I don't give a damn which way it's headed! From now on this is your headache, brother!'

'*Lash!*' Dany's voice had a sudden break in it.

Lash got up quickly and going to her, took her face between his hands. 'Listen, babe, I know I got you into this, but you'll be all right now. All you've got to do is to make a clean breast of it. Lay all your cards on the table. I can't help you. You know that. All I've done is to give you a wrong steer, and make bad worse. I——'

Dany said in an imploring whisper: 'Lash, please don't go — please!'

'Look, honey; it isn't going to help one bit if I — Oh, hell!'

He released her abruptly and turned suddenly on Tyson Frost: 'What I want to know,' said Lash furiously, 'is why you ever let her get mixed up in this sort of thing in the first place! Couldn't you have got someone else to do your dirty work for you? You must have known darned well that there was dynamite in that letter. What was it?'

'Yes, dear,' said Lorraine, sitting suddenly upright. 'What was in it? Why should anyone else want it?'

Tyson said: 'Why does anyone want three million?'

'*W-what!*' Lorraine sprang to her feet. 'Tyson, darling! What are you talking about? You can't mean——'

'Sit down,' said Tyson. 'All of you. That's better.'

He crossed the room with a step that was curiously light for so big a man, and reaching the door, jerked it open and peered out; looking along the broad open top of the wall and down into the green shade of the garden below, as though to assure himself

that there was no one within earshot. After a minute he closed it
again carefully, and went over to the window to lean out and
look down on the sun-baked slope of rock thirty feet below. At
last, satisfied with the result of his survey, he came back to the low
cushion-strewn divan that stood against one wall of the sitting-
room and sat down on it; the wood creaking protestingly under
his weight.

'I shall have to go back a bit,' said Tyson Frost, lighting
himself a cigarette and inhaling deeply: 'As you probably know
— it seems to be common property! — my revered grandfather,
Rory — Emory Frost, who died way back in the eighteen-eighties
— left a stack of papers and diaries with the family solicitors,
Honeywood & Honeywood, with instructions that they were not
to be opened or their contents made public for seventy years,
which is reckoned to be man's permitted span. That time limit
expired a few months ago, and the stuff duly arrived out here.
And good ripe stuff it is! Roaring Rory must have been a hell-
raiser and a half in his day, and ... But that's neither here nor
there. The point is that it took me some time to go through it,
and it wasn't until about three weeks ago that I came across a
folded piece of paper that had been pushed in between the leather
and the backing of one of the covers. And I wouldn't have found
it at all if the backing hadn't split. It was interesting. It was very
interesting ...'

Tyson reached for the glass he had left on the floor and took
a long pull at it.

'You know,' he said thoughtfully, 'it's astonishing how often
life can give points to the movies. Have any of you ever heard
the legend of the lost treasure buried by Seyyid Saïd?'

'Yes!' said Dany.

'No, *really*, darling,' protested Lorraine. 'You can't believe that
story! I mean, it's *too* ridiculous. I know it's in one of the guide
books, but——'

'"But me no buts",' said Tyson flapping an impatient hand,

125

'I too thought I was too old to fall for that one. But there was something mightily convincing about that bit of paper. If no one else believed in the treasure, Grandfather Emory certainly did. And for a very good reason.'

'I suppose he helped to bury it?' commented Lash with sarcasm.

'In a way,' said Tyson. 'And you can take that damned impertinent superior sneer off your face, young Holden!'

He glowered for a moment, refreshed himself from his glass, and then said: 'No. According to old Rory, when Seyyid Saïd died he left the secret with a witch doctor of Pemba, who promptly and rather meanly put a curse on it to the effect that anyone finding it could only use it to bring evil — something of that description. It was intended, one supposes, to discourage people from hunting around for it, but Saïd's successor, Majid, wasn't going to be put off by a thing like that. According to Grandfather Emory, he tortured the witch, collared the information, dug the stuff up with the enthusiastic assistance of my unregenerate ancestor, and generously went halves with him. Emory's share, if I have worked out its present-day value correctly, must have been close on three million sterling.'

There was a brief silence, and then Lash rose to replenish his glass. 'All this,' he said, 'if you will forgive my saying so, is the ripest slice of pure Gorgonzola that I have come across in an ill-spent life. Me, I don't believe a word of it! But it's obvious that someone else does. And I don't mean you or your grandfather, either!'

Lorraine's eyes were enormous and she spoke in little gasps: 'But Tyson! ... but darling ... three *million*! He can't have ... What did he *do* with it?'

'Buried it,' said Tyson blandly. 'Or so he says.'

'But *where*?'

'Ah! that's the catch. He doesn't say. All he says is that he has deposited the key in a sealed envelope with old Honeywood (that would probably be our Honeywood's grandfather, or else

126

his great-uncle) and that it is only to be handed over if and when someone asks for it, quoting, correctly, a number and some initials that were on the envelope. The number being seven four three eight nine, and the initials being his own, E.T.F.'

'I'll be damned!' ejaculated Lash, startled.

'I don't doubt it: not if this is your usual form,' commented Tyson unkindly. 'Well — there you are. It seemed a damned sight too good to be true, and I didn't believe a word of it. Life isn't *that* much like the movies! But it was worth investigating, and as a first step I wrote old Honeywood, asking if he had such a letter in his possession. He had — which shook me. Deposited with Honeywood & Honeywood in eighteen sixty one. I thought it was well worth looking at, and I didn't want to trust it to the post. *Or* to Gussie! Between you and me, I don't ... Oh, well, let it go. The point is that as Dany was coming out, it seemed a good idea to ask her to call and collect it and bring it out with her. And that's all there is to it.'

'Except that you gave him a date and a time for that call,' said Lash.

'And why not? The thing was almost certainly in a safe deposit box in some bank, and he'd have to get it out and have it ready to hand over. It wouldn't have been at his house, and as I still correspond with him and not his junior partner, I said I'd send Dany to get it from him; which meant to his house. And if I know anything of old Honeywood, he wouldn't have had it there very much before he needed it. He's a careful guy. Or rather, he was, poor brute.'

'So that was it!' said Lash. 'Then I was right.' He got up and stood looking out of the window, his hands in his pockets. 'Someone knew, and meant to get there first. But Dany spoilt the game by going down in the morning instead of the afternoon.'

He turned abruptly: 'Who else knew?'

'No one,' said Tyson shortly.

'Oh, nuts! Of course someone else knew.'

127

'I apologize,' snarled Tyson. 'I should have said: "I myself did not tell anyone." Not even my wife.'

'What about Ponting?'

'Or my secretary!'

'But he could have found out.'

'Oh no, he couldn't. I took dam' good care of that! Curiosity is Nigel's besetting sin, and I had no intention of letting him get a look at the Frost papers — or my letters to Honeywood! I keep those papers in a locked box, and the key to it is round my neck. Some of that stuff could touch off quite a few explosions even now, and I'm taking no chances. Besides there's money in 'em.'

'And murder!' amended Lash grimly.

'So it would seem. All the same, I don't believe——'

'Belief is no good,' said Lash impatiently. 'Could you swear on oath that neither your secretary nor any servant or guest in this house, nor your wife, could possibly, under any circumstances, have seen that paper of Emory's?'

Lorraine gave a faint indignant cry: 'Well, *really* Lash! Why *me*? I mean, even if I had (and I didn't, I hadn't an idea) *would* I have been likely to tell anyone?'

'I don't know,' said Lash. 'Would you?'

Lorraine made a helpless fluttering gesture with her little hands and gazed appealingly at her husband.

'Of course she would,' said Tyson brutally. 'That's why I didn't tell her. I never tell any woman a secret unless I want it given the widest possible publicity in the shortest possible time.'

Lorraine gave a small sigh. 'You know, Tyson darling, I can't understand how it is that you write so well when you so often talk in clichés. Schizophrenia, I suppose. Not that you aren't quite right about me, as it happens. Whenever anyone tells me a secret I always think "Now who shall I tell first?" '

Tyson gave a short bark of laughter. 'I know. But to revert to your question, young Lash, the answer is "No". The key of that box has never been out of my possession, and just in case you are

128

going to suggest that Lorrie might have removed it one night while I was asleep, I will add that I am a remarkably light sleeper. And anyway, I don't believe for one moment that anyone in this house was even aware of the existence of that paper.'

'And what about the letters you wrote this guy Honeywood? They must have contained quite a few relevant details. Enough, anyway, to arouse a considerable slice of curiosity as to the contents of that sealed envelope! The number and the initials, and roughly the date when it was deposited with the firm. Who mails your letters?'

'Abdurahman, when he goes into town. And he can't read English.'

'But he could have shown 'em to some of the local boys who could.'

'Why? My purely personal correspondence is pretty voluminous — quite apart from the stuff that Nigel deals with for me, which is vast. Any house-servant or local snooper who was interested in it would have had his work cut out for months, steaming open envelopes in the hope of stumbling across something of interest. So you can wash that one right out.'

But Tyson had forgotten, thought Dany, that there was at least one other person who had not only read his letters, but who possibly knew something — perhaps not much, but enough — of the contents of that time-yellowed envelope.

She said: 'Mr Honeywood knew something, I think. He didn't seem to approve of my taking the letter. He said something about letting sleeping dogs lie, and that no good would come of it. Perhaps he knew what was in it. His grandfather may have told him.'

'Of course! And *he* may have talked!' said Lorraine.

Tyson let out another crack of laughter. 'What, old Henry Honeywood? That desiccated clam? You didn't know him like Gussie and I did!'

'Perhaps not; but I do know that it isn't only women who

129

talk,' retorted Lorraine. 'Any dried-up old-maid bachelor can usually leave them at the post when it comes to gossip. And he had a housekeeper: that stout old lady with the hearing-aid. She was probably eaten up with curiosity. It's an occupational disease with housekeepers. I expect she read all his letters and gossiped over the contents with all her friends at the Women's Institute!'

'Not Mrs Broughty,' said Tyson, looking thoughtful. 'She's another clam. But that char of his, Mrs Porson, is quite a different proposition. She often does odd jobs for Gussie, and she talks her head off. Why, once when Elf was staying down there she told her the most staggering details of a case that———. Oh well, that's neither here nor there. But as she could only have got hold of them by taking an unauthorized interest in old Henry's correspondence, I suppose we shall have to take it that there may have been a leak. In fact there must have been! So I think that our next move is to notify Scotland Yard — and see that the letter goes by hand. I'll write it first thing after luncheon, and take it round myself to the Residency and ask the Resident as a personal favour to send it in the next diplomatic bag — they must have one. Thank God I happen to know the Commissioner of Metropolitan Police. That may help. I'll write direct to him, and if he wants to set the local cops on to us, he can. But as it will be at least three days, and possibly four, before he can get a letter, it'll give us time to see if there's anything in this fantastic Buried Treasure yarn. Where's the key, Dany? Let's have it.'

'But it isn't a key,' said Dany. 'At least, not an ordinary key — a metal one. I would have felt it if it was. I think it's only a folded piece of paper.'

'Probably a map,' said Tyson.

'Or clues, like a crossword!' Lorraine's face flushed as charmingly as an excited child's.

Lash said dampingly: 'Far more likely to be one of those rambling bits of abracadabra that say *Walk fifty paces due south*

130

from the back porch of Ali Baba's house, and when you reach the blasted fig tree, wait until the sun be overhead, and dig where the shadow of the fig tree joins the ditch. A fascinating document that fails to take into account that by this time Ali Baba's house has been pulled down and replaced by a fish-glue factory, the blasted fig passed out of the picture seventy years back and someone's drained the ditch in the course of an irrigation scheme! That's all we need yet!'

But Lorraine refused to be damped. 'But the treasure would still be there — *somewhere*! Oh, Tyson, just think if it should turn out to be true! It's the most thrilling thing. Will there be jewels? There ought to be. Carved emeralds and pigeon's blood rubies and diamond hilted daggers and ropes and ropes of pearls. *Marvellous!*'

'It depends on how Emory and his Sultan pal split the loot,' said Tyson, finishing his drink. 'But being a citizen on whom remarkably few flies appear to have rested, I bet he played safe and took the gold. Anyway, that's what it sounds like — if, of course, he took anything, and this isn't the old reprobate's idea of a belly-laugh at the expense of his posterity. I wouldn't put it past him!'

'Oh *no*, darling!' protested Lorraine. 'I won't believe it. It's got to be true. I *want* it to be true. We shall solve the crossword, and creep out at night with spades and dig up buckets and buckets full of gold.'

'And find ourselves in the local lock-up for attempting to steal what is undoubtedly the property of the Sultan of Zanzibar,' said Lash morosely.

'Ah, that's just where you're wrong, boy,' said Tyson, heaving himself up and fetching another drink. 'There was no green in Grandfather Emory's eye. His half was a gift, for services rendered. Duly attested, too. There is a document to prove it. It was inside the opposite cover; and there's a nice clear thumb print attached, as well as the donor's seal and signature. It would

131

probably stand in a court of law even today. However, we haven't got the stuff yet. Where's old Honeywood's letter, Dany?'

'In my coat pocket,' said Dany, and smiled a little wanly. 'It seemed the safest place, and I did fix it so that it couldn't be pickpocketed!'

She reached for the camel-hair coat that she had carried over to the guest-house with her and hung over the back of her chair, and after struggling with the safety-pin, drew out a soft square of chiffon that was folded about a small yellow envelope with five numerals and three initials written on it in faded ink.

She stood staring at it wide-eyed, feeling it: horror and incredulity dawning in her face. Then she turned it over quickly.

The heavy seal that had closed the flap was broken, and the envelope was empty.

11

'It's preposterous!' bellowed Tyson for the fourth if not the fifth time. 'It's just plain bloody impossible!'

'Oh, darling,' moaned Lorraine, 'don't go on and on and *on* saying that. Besides, it's so *silly*! How can it be impossible when it's *happened*?'

'It can't have happened; that's why! Not the way she said, anyway. You can see for yourself the way that bit of stuff was folded and pinned. I tell you it was humanly impossible for anyone — anyone outside of an astral body! — to do the job unless that coat was out of Dany's possession for at least five minutes. Great suffering snakes — I've tried it! You saw me. No one could unpin it from the lining, take it out, get at the envelope and remove the letter, and then put the whole shooting-match back again just exactly as it was, at the bottom of a deep slit pocket. Not even Houdini! She must have left the coat lying about.'

'But I didn't,' protested Dany, on the verge of tears. 'I had it under my pillow for the rest of the night, and it was perfectly all right when I wrapped it in the scarf this morning. The seal wasn't touched. I tell you, I *know*! I would have felt at once if it was empty. Like I did just now.'

Tyson said: 'You must have washed, I suppose? Or had a bath!'

'Of course I did, but——'

'And you took it with you?'

'No, but——'

'Well, there you are! Someone must have got into the room.'

133

Lorraine said plaintively: 'Tyson darling, don't keep on interrupting the child. Do let her finish a sentence.'

'Lash was there,' said Dany. 'He was dressing while I had a bath.'

'It all sounds very intimate and domestic,' growled Tyson.

Lash said pleasantly: 'It was. Though quite unavoidable, as I have already explained. But if you make any further cracks like that you are going to find that life is even more like the movies than you had supposed.'

'Meaning that you'll knock me down?' inquired Tyson. 'You couldn't do it, boy.'

'It would give me the greatest pleasure to try,' snapped Lash.

'I daresay it would. But I do not intend to let the sons of my college friends use me as a punching-bag to work off their spleen.'

'Then stop bullying the kid!' said Lash. 'Can't you see that she's had just about all she can take? Lay off her, will you?'

Tyson cocked an eye at him, and said meditatively: 'I well remember your Aunt Maimie describing you once — accurately I have no doubt — as a rakish heel who could hook the average woman with the ease of a confidence trickster getting to work on a frustrated small-town spinster. That was when you were getting into trouble over the Van Hoyden girl — or was it girls? So let us have less of the Galahad attitude from you, boy, and fewer back-answers! Were you really in that suite the entire time that Dany was in the bathroom?'

'I was.'

'Did you know where the letter was?'

'I did. Are you by any chance suggesting that I took it?'

'*Bah!* Don't be tedious,' said Tyson crossly. 'Can you be quite certain that no one else came into the room during that time? No hotel servant, for instance?'

'No one. Repeat — no one.'

Tyson turned back to Dany. 'I presume he didn't stick around while you were dressing?'

Dany flushed pinkly. 'No, he didn't. He went off to have breakfast.'

'And no one else came in?'

'No. I locked both doors. And I took the coat with me when I went in to breakfast, and I've never let go of it since, until I came in here and put it on that chair. No one could have taken that letter. No one but myself or Lash. It isn't possible!'

'Did you take it?'

Lash took a swift step forward and Tyson said: 'Let her answer for herself, boy! Well, Dany?'

Dany looked at him; her cheeks flushed and her eyes wide and sparkling. 'I think,' she said stormily, 'that you are the most odious, selfish, egotistical, *impossible* man I have ever met, and I'm sorry I ever came here!'

'Yes, isn't he?' said Lorraine, giving her husband a fond glance. 'I remember saying just the same thing to him the first day I ever met him. And he gets worse. But baby, you didn't really take it, did you?'

Dany rounded on her, anger giving away to exasperation. 'Mother, you cannot really think——'

'*Darling,*' protested Lorraine plaintively, '*how* many times have I asked you not to call me that? It makes me feel a *hundred*. No, of course I don't think you stole it or anything like that — nor does Tyson. Just that you may have thought that — what with the murder, and everything being so foul for you — that it would be better if you simply tore the horrid thing up and got rid of it.'

'Well I didn't!' said Dany tersely. 'And perhaps it's a pity I didn't think of it — now that someone else has got it.'

'Meaning me?' inquired Lash gently.

'Why do you have to say that?' demanded Dany resentfully. 'You know quite well I don't mean anything of the sort!'

'But you've just said that only you or I could possibly have taken it. And if *you* didn't, that leaves me, doesn't it? Or is there something wrong with my arithmetic?'

135

'Don't bully the girl!' boomed Tyson. 'Can't you see she's had all she can take? Lay off her, will you?'

Lash laughed and threw up a hand in the gesture of a fencer acknowledging a hit. '*Touché!* I'm sorry, Dany. Well, what do you suggest we do now?'

'Eat,' said Lorraine firmly, and rose to her feet. 'It must be nearly one o'clock, and everyone else will be wondering what on earth has happened to us, and getting hungrier and hungrier. Come on, darling, let's go and see what they're doing. And Dany will want to wash.'

'Just a minute,' said Tyson. 'Let's get this straight. If we are to subscribe to this theory that whoever was after that letter was also on the London to Nairobi plane, it follows that whoever has got it now was on the Nairobi to Zanzibar one this morning. Am I right?'

Lash said: 'It certainly looks that way, doesn't it? If it weren't for one outstanding snag, on which the whole thing snarls up.'

'And what would that be?'

'What the hell is the use of three million — or three hundred million if it comes to that — if you can't get it out of the island? O.K. for you perhaps, or for anyone who lives right here. But how would anyone else start in shifting it? Me, for the sake of argument?'

'I, boy. *I!* Don't be so sloppy with your grammar!'

'Okay; I. Me, Lashmer J. Holden, Jnr. What do I do with a coupla hundredweight of bullion? Load it into my bags and smuggle it through the Customs just like that, I suppose?'

'Then you suppose wrong,' snapped Tyson. 'Use your head! Do you *really* imagine that anyone who is after that much money, and prepared to kill in order to get it, hasn't worked that one out? Good God, boy, there are literally dozens of ways of getting in and out of countries illegally in these days, if you've money behind you — or the prospect of money. And don't start yapping that "It isn't possible!" Of course it is! A bloody sight too possible! What do you suppose there is to prevent you going for a sail or out fishing one fine evening, and being picked up a mile or so offshore by a dhow or a motor-boat? Or a private yacht? — damn it all, your own father's got one of those! There are hundreds of miles of empty coast-line and little creeks or beaches where you could be landed on a dark night, and be picked up by a plane. Good grief, this is the Air Age! There are any amount of privately owned planes around — and any amount of empty Africa for 'em to land on! You wouldn't be your father's son if you couldn't work out that one, and we can take it someone else has. The problem is, who?'

Lash shrugged his shoulders: 'Someone who was on both plane rides, I guess. I checked up on that, and apart from your personal guests there were only two. That newspaper guy you were so charming to outside the airport——'

'What newspaper guy?' interrupted Tyson, sitting up sharply. 'I don't remember any—— Yes, by God, I do! Some blasted squirt in a panama hat who asked if he could call. Was he on the London plane?'

'I just told you so. And staying at the same hotel in Nairobi.'

'He was, was he?' said Tyson meditating. 'Perhaps I shouldn't have been so hasty. Well we can fix that. As there's only one hotel in this salubrious spot, we know where he is. Lorrie darling, ring up the hotel will you, and ask for—— What's his blasted name?'

'Dowling,' supplied Dany. 'Larry Dowling.'

'Mr Dowling; and when you get him on the line, tell him I'll be delighted to give him an interview, and would he like to come and stay here. Run along and do it now.'

'But Tyson——!' Lorraine's gentian-blue eyes were wide with dismay. 'We can't. Darling — a reporter!'

'He isn't a reporter,' said Dany, but was ignored.

'Everything will be all over the front page of every newspaper before we know where we are,' wailed Lorraine. 'Think of Dany — and all of us. Just *think*!'

'I am,' said Tyson impatiently. 'And I appear to be the only

137

one who is capable of doing so. It's a dam' sight safer to have all the suspects under one roof.'

'With an eye, of course,' said Lash, 'to the cash deposit.'

'If that was meant for sarcasm, boy, you'll have to do better. Naturally with an eye to the cash deposit. What do you take me for?'

Lorraine's hands made their familiar fluttering gesture, and she said: 'I don't understand. I don't understand anything.'

'He means,' translated Lash, 'that one of a reasonably narrow field of suspects has just got hold of the key to grandpop's bank vault. It is therefore quite an idea to keep 'em all right here, where he can watch 'em, and the first guy who is caught borrowing a spade and sneaking out to do a bit of digging is it. See?'

'But of *course!*' exclaimed Lorraine happily. 'Tyson darling, how clever of you. I'll ring up this Mr — Mr Dowling at once.'

'You do that,' said Tyson. 'Get going. No — wait a minute. There were two of them. Didn't you say there were two?'

'Were,' said Lash, 'is right. There's only one now.'

'I don't get you.'

'The other one,' said Lash, 'was an Arab. A shining light in the local Zanzibar-for-Mother-Russia movement, I gather. One Salim Abeid.'

'Oh, Jembe — *"the thin man".*'

'That's the guy. Or to be accurate, that was the guy.'

'What do you mean by that?' demanded Tyson sharply.

'I mean he's dead. He died rather suddenly this morning at Mombasa Airport, which is why our plane was held up. I thought maybe they'd have told you that one: you must have had to wait quite a while for us.'

'*Dead?*' said Tyson, his bull voice almost a whisper. 'You don't mean ... What did he die of?'

'They didn't say. He walked off the plane and into the airport with the rest of us, apparently a sound insurance risk, and when

138

we were herded back on, he failed to turn up. There was a certain amount of delay and flurry, and first the stewardess told us he'd been taken ill, and then a squad of cops and officials turned up and took another look at our passports and re-checked our visas — and for all I know got our fingerprints as well. They seemed anxious to know where they could get in touch with us during the next few days.'

'What do you suppose they'd want to do that for?'

'Your guess,' said Lash dryly, 'is as good as mine.'

Lorraine looked anxiously from Lash's face to her husband's, and came back from the door to clutch at Tyson's arm. There was a sudden trace of panic in her light, lilting voice: 'What guess, Tyson? What does he mean? What are you both hinting at?'

'Nothing,' said Tyson brusquely. 'Only that Jembe had a lot of political enemies. There's no need for us to start visualizing burglars under every blasted bed in the island. And anyway he probably died of heart failure.'

'Almost certainly,' said Lash pleasantly. 'Few of us die from anything else.'

'Be quiet, boy!' blared Tyson. 'The young should be seen and not heard! It's all right, Lorrie. You run along now and phone that infernal reporter. And be nice to him.'

Lorraine sighed and relaxed. 'I'm always nice to people, darling.'

She turned from him and directed an appealing smile at Lash. 'I do hope you don't mind being in the guest-house by yourself, Lash?'

'Why should I mind? It's charming.'

'Now that *is* sweet of you! I was afraid you might feel sore about it. Being put up in a sort of honeymoon cottage when——'

'Oh, not again!' groaned Lash. 'Once was enough. I get you — you mean this was the cosy little hideaway that you'd gotten all fixed up for the newly-weds, was it? Well, it was a swell idea and I shall not feel any qualms about occupying it — provided I'm allowed to do so strictly solo. You don't have to worry about it. It wasn't your fault.'

'But it *was*. That's what's so *awful*,' Lorraine's voice was tragic. 'I feel that it's so much my fault: Elf wrote to me, you know. You see it was I who asked Eddie — Eduardo — to look her up when he was in London, because he'd suggested that he might come down here again, so I thought it would be nice for them to know each other, and of course I never dreamed—— But I don't expect it will come to anything: so much that Elf starts doesn't, you know. She's so vague and soft-hearted and irresponsible, and she never means any harm. She's like a sweet, spoilt child who just picks things up and then drops them.'

Lorraine illustrated with a graceful, expressive gesture, and Lash winced. 'I get you.'

'Oh, but I didn't mean *you*, Lash!' Lorraine's eyes were wide with dismay. 'I meant Eddie. He's only a new toy. And rather a novel one. But when that's over, everything will be all right again, won't it?'

'Sure. Just dandy,' said Lash bitterly. 'And now if you don't mind, could we just cut the whole question of my love-life off the agenda? I prefer murder.'

'Yes of course, dear,' said Lorraine hastily. 'I *do* feel for you. And I'm sure it will all come out right in the end. Come on, Dany darling, let's go and get tidy. And you *will* get rid of that awful fringe, won't you sweetie?'

'No she won't!' declared Tyson unexpectedly. 'Here, Dany——' he picked up the discarded spectacles and replaced them firmly on her nose. 'I'm sorry if it worries your mother and fails to please the United States Marines, but it seems to me that you'd better stick to that fancy dress and go on being Miss Kitchell for the next few days. It'll save a lot of explaining. And the less explaining we have to do once that scribbling journalist is on the premises, the better.'

'Are you really going to ask him over?' inquired Lash.

'Certainly,' said Tyson, bristling. 'Any objections?'

'None at all. It's your funeral. But it seems to me that your sense of proportion has slipped a disc. If you import this Dowling guy you can watch to see that he doesn't start in digging up grand-pop's dollars, but if he starts digging any of this dirt instead, how are you going to stop him splashing it all over the tabloids?'

'Murder him!' said Tyson succinctly. 'Now let's get on up to the house and have some food.'

12

The House of Shade stood three storeys high on a wide stone terrace that was approached from the garden by short flights of steps set at regular intervals about it. Each of its storeys was of a different height, for the ground floor had once been a colonnade surrounding an open central courtyard about which the house was built, and the rooms on the first floor had been large and long, and were abnormally high. It had been Tyson's father — who had a mania for improvements — who had divided them into bedrooms, bathrooms and dressing-rooms.

The top storey, by comparison, appeared unduly low, and the rooms were hotter than those on the floor below, for the sun beat down strongly on the flat Eastern roof and the shade of the trees did not reach them. But the breeze did, and by night they were cool.

There was a lily pool in the courtyard, where lethargic goldfish idled in the shade of the flat green leaves, and on each floor the rooms led out on to pillared verandahs that faced each other across it, in a manner vaguely reminiscent of a courtyard in Seville.

Curious, curving stone staircases with shallow, disproportionally wide treads, their heavy banisters of hammered iron wrought in an odd geometrical design and barely a foot and a half in height, rose from each corner of the courtyard, inside the verandahs and leading up on to the next. Dangerous looking things, depending for their support only on the stout metal and the proportion of stone that had been built into the thickness of the wall, and proof that some long-dead Arab builder had known his trade as well as Adams or John Nash.

At the edge of each verandah, stone jars filled with sweet-scented creepers and flowering shrubs stood between the tall supporting pillars, and gave an entrancing impression of hanging gardens. But from the outside the house looked far less decorative and unusual: a square, white, very high building with a flat crenelated roof and rows of green-painted shutters.

It was sometime during the afternoon, and shortly before Tyson left to take a letter in to the Residency, that Mr Cardew, the Police Superintendent of the Zanzibar Division, called briefly at the House of Shade.

His car came and went again, making so little sound on the white coral dust of the palm-shaded road that no member of the house-party heard it, and apart from Tyson, only a Somali servant, a somnolent gardener's boy, and a drowsing cat on the wall above the main gate, had seen him.

He had stayed less than a quarter of an hour, and it was not until much later in the day, when night had fallen and the house-party were seated at the dining-room table in a glow of candle-light, that Tyson had chosen to bring up the subject of his visit.

The dining-room at *Kivulimi* was a long narrow room, with a row of arches along one side that had once been open, but which Tyson's father, Aubrey, had converted into french windows. They stood wide tonight, letting in a heady scent of flowers and luring moths and other nocturnal insects to a fiery death in the candle flames, and from her seat between Nigel and Larry Dowling, Dany could see out into the garden where the tree shadows and the moonlight formed a complicated mosaic patched with gold from the lighted windows.

She had plenty of leisure to enjoy the sight, for Lorraine, in the interests of playing safe, was keeping Larry Dowling engaged in conversation, while Nigel was hotly defending a modern masterpiece, recently purchased for the nation, in the face of

143

Gussie Bingham's assertion that it was a shocking waste of the taxpayers' money (by which she meant her own) and indistinguishable from a pool of spilt ink and a squashed tomato — which would have come cheaper.

Larry Dowling had arrived in a taxi shortly after luncheon, and much to her surprise Dany had found herself not only pleased, but more than a little relieved to see him. Which was foolish of her, she knew, since Larry's profession made him a danger to all of them. But for some indefinable reason she felt a greater sense of safety and a lessening of tension while he was within reach. Larry, she thought, would not let one down.

Lash Holden had greeted Mr Dowling with a marked lack of enthusiasm, and having commandeered his taxi had returned in it to the airport to inquire into the possibility of reserving a seat for himself in a Nairobi-bound plane on the following day. He had not been back by four-thirty, when Lorraine's guests had assembled for tea on the shaded terrace outside the drawing-room windows, but he had joined them later when they had gone down to explore the sea shore and exclaim over the weird, wind-worn shapes of the coral rocks, and watch the sun go down in a blaze of rose-tinted splendour.

He had not spoken to Dany, and had in fact appeared to avoid her, and she looked at him now across the width of the wide table in the glow of the candles, and wondered if she would ever see him again. I suppose I could always get a job in America, she thought. Tyson or Lorraine could fix that; they've got loads of friends there, and Lash's father is Tyson's best friend. I'd be able to see him. But if Mrs Gordon decides that she likes him better than Eduardo after all . . .

Dany turned to look at Amalfi, who was being charming to Tyson and prettily petulant to Eduardo, and her heart sank. She knew that she herself had little to complain of in the way of looks, for she had inherited them from her father who had been an outstandingly handsome man. But Ada Kitchell's unfortunate

144

hair-style did not suit her, and neither did Ada Kitchell's spectacles. They combined to reduce her from a pretty girl to a nondescript one, and even the dress she had chosen to wear did not help, though once she had thought it entrancing — a short, smoke-grey dress whose wide skirt, ornamented with two enormous patch pockets appliquéd with white magnolias, reduced her slim waist to hand-span proportions. She had been charmed with it when she bought it; but now it only appeared rather ordinary, and what Aunt Harriet would have termed 'suitable for a young girl'.

Amalfi, looking anything but ordinary, was wearing pale gold chiffon that exactly matched her pale gold hair, and her jewels were an antique set of topazes set in gold filigree. It was a colour that did charming and complimentary things to her sea-green, mermaid's eyes, and she was using them now with dazzling effect on Tyson.

I don't know how Mother stands it! thought Dany resentfully: and turning to look at Lorraine was instantly answered.

Lorraine, wearing a fragile confection of black spider-lace, with diamonds that were a magnificent reminder of the brief reign of Dwight P. Cleethorpe, was, in her own and entirely different way, as entrancing as Amalfi, and she was engaged in employing all her charms on Larry Dowling; who was looking equally dazzled.

They can't help it, thought Dany, feeling depressed and deplorably gauche. They were born with charm. They just turn it on like a tap, and half the time it doesn't mean a thing. They can't help having it, or using it, any more than Millicent Bates can help being — Millicent Bates!

Millicent was sitting opposite her between Lash and Eduardo di Chiago, and 'Dressing for Dinner' meant only one thing to Miss Bates. A long dress, and she was wearing one. An undatable garment in solid blue marocain that made no concessions to frivolity and did nothing for her flat-chested, square-shouldered

145

figure. She was engaged in giving Lash, as an unenlightened Colonial, a lecture on the advantages of a National Health system, when she was interrupted by Tyson who at last elected to broach the subject of the Superintendent of the Zanzibar Division's afternoon call. His voice boomed down the lengh of the table and successfully terminated an anecdote concerning scheming foreigners in search of free false teeth.

'By the way, Lash, about that plane reservation you wanted for tomorrow, I'm afraid you'll——'

Amalfi turned sharply: 'What plane reservation? Lash, you aren't leaving? Not when you've only just arrived! Darling, don't be silly!'

Nigel gave his little giggling laugh. 'It's all this American passion for hustle. Here today and gone tomorrow! So enervating.'

'On the contrary,' snapped Lash, 'it's a strong instinct for self-preservation.'

'Darling, I'm not all *that* dangerous,' cooed Amalfi dulcetly. 'Are you frightened?'

'Terrified!' said Lash promptly. 'But apart from that, as I find that the business side of this trip can be dealt with in half an hour — provided our host will sit still that long — I don't feel justified in wasting too much time idling; however pleasantly. I have a lot of commitments.'

Mrs Bingham said: 'Poor Miss Kitchell! And I feel sure that you were so looking forward to seeing something of Zanzibar. What a slave-driver your Mr Holden is!'

She beamed sympathetically at Dany, and Lash looked startled. It was a point that had somehow escaped him. If Dany had to continue masquerading as his secretary he could hardly leave without her. Or with her.

Blast! thought Mr Holden with quiet and concentrated bitterness. And was visited by inspiration. He half rose and bowed at Mrs Bingham. 'Ma'am, you put me to shame. You're dead right. I'm a slave-driver, and Miss Kitchell certainly needs a rest. But she's going to get one. I don't happen to need her for the next week or so, and she's going to stay right here, grab herself a nice long vacation, and join me later when I'm due back in the States.'

And now, thought Lash with some satisfaction, just try and gum up that one!

Tyson did so.

'It looks,' he said blandly, 'as though you will be spending it right here with her, my boy.'

'Oh no, I shan't,' began Lash firmly. 'I intend——'

Tyson said crossly: 'If you will all have the goodness to lay off interrupting me every time I open my mouth, perhaps I can get on with what I was saying? ... Thanks! About that plane reservation. I'm afraid you'll have to cancel it, boy. In fact, I have already done so on your behalf. The police have requested that you all remain *in situ* for a day or two.'

'The *police*?' Amalfi dropped the glass she was holding, and it fell with a little splintering crash, sending a red stream of claret across the table. 'What police? Why?'

'Josh Cardew. He was over this afternoon. He says it's just a routine matter, but that they've been asked to check up on everyone who was on the Nairobi–Zanzibar plane this morning, and more particularly, on the London–Nairobi one. So it would help if you'd all stay around for a bit. It's that chap Jembe.'

'Salim Abeid?' inquired Larry Dowling. 'You mean the man who died in the airport at Mombasa this morning?'

'I mean the man who was murdered in the airport at Mombasa this morning,' corrected Tyson. 'It would appear that someone added a good-sized slug of cyanide to his coffee, and they somehow don't think he did it himself.'

Gussie gave her glass of wine a horrified look and put it down hurriedly. 'But how dreadful, Tyson! I remember him quite well. He was on the London plane too. But why on earth should the

147

police want to question any of us? Too ridiculous, when it must have been someone in the airport. The barman who gave him the coffee, I expect.'

'They're checking up on all that. Needle-in-a-haystack job, I'd say. I gather the airport was pretty crowded.'

'Packed,' said Gussie Bingham, and shuddered. 'Besides being abominably hot, in spite of all those fans and things.'

Larry Dowling said reflectively: 'It can't have been all that easy to drop something in a man's drink without being spotted; even in a crowded room. Bit of a risk. It must have been someone he knew.'

'I don't see why,' said Nigel, mopping up claret with a clean handkerchief. 'Anyone — simply *anyone* — could have jogged his elbow or distracted his attention as they went past. *Too* simple. You knock the man's newspaper on to the floor, or stumble over his briefcase, and while he's picking them up and you're apologizing — *plop!*'

He dropped an imaginary pellet into an imaginary glass, and Eduardo di Chiago said: '*Brr — !* this is a most unpleasant conversation. For myself, I do not like to talk of death. It is unlucky.'

'Oh, I do so agree with you,' said Lorraine earnestly. '*Dreadfully* unlucky. And now I suppose there's *bound* to be a third.'

'A third what?' demanded Gussie Bingham, startled.

'Murder of course, darling. Things always go in threes. Haven't you noticed that?'

'But there's only been one murder so far,' objected Millicent Bates.

'My dear — but haven't you *heard*? Why, I thought we only hadn't because we don't get the English papers for days, but I thought you two must have seen all about it.'

Tyson cast his eyes up to heaven, and thereafter, realizing it was too late to intervene, shrugged his shoulders and circulated the port.

'Seen all about what?' demanded Millicent sharply.

'Why, about Mr Honeywood. Tyson's solicitor. He's been murdered.'

'*Honeywood* — old Henry Honeywood?' The thin stem of Gussie Bingham's wine-glass snapped between her fingers, and once more there was a dark pool of wine winking in the candle-light. But she did not appear to have noticed it. She leant forward to stare down the table at Lorraine, and her voice was suddenly strident: 'Where did you get that story?'

But Lorraine was not paying attention. She reached out, and picking up an empty tumbler, lifted it and dropped it deliberately on to the floor, where it shivered into fragments.

'That's the third one,' she said reassuringly. 'And it was an odd one anyway, so it means we needn't bother about losing any more of the set. I do apologize, Gussie darling — what were you saying?'

Gussie turned towards her brother with a rustle of lilac satin and a clash of bracelets.

'Tyson, what is this preposterous nonsense that Lorraine has got hold of?'

'It isn't nonsense,' said Tyson, helping himself liberally to port. 'Only heard it myself today. The poor old boy's been murdered. Shot in his study on the morning of the day you left for London. I daresay you missed seeing it in the papers because of the move — last minute shopping and all that sort of flap. And it wouldn't have been front page stuff.'

'No, I didn't see it. And I still can't believe—— What would anyone want to murder old Henry for?'

Tyson shrugged. 'Ask me another. Theft, I suppose. The safe was opened. I don't really know any details.'

'And where,' demanded Millicent, 'did you get all this from? If you've got the home papers, I'd like to see them.'

Tyson looked disconcerted, and Lash thought with a trace of malice: That'll teach him to watch his step!

'They'll be around somewhere,' said Tyson, rallying. 'But as

149

a matter of fact, I had a letter by the afternoon post. Have some port, Gussie.'

'Who from?' inquired Millicent Bates.

'Oh — a man you wouldn't know,' said Tyson hastily.

'What did he say? When did it happen? How ...'

Tyson rolled a wild eye in the direction of Lash, who refused to meet it, and found himself enduring a lengthy catechism which he replied to as well as he could.

'Why are you so interested anyway?' he inquired irritably. 'He wasn't *your* family solicitor.'

'He happened to be both honorary treasurer of our Wednesday Women's Guild and treasurer to the Market-Lydon Lads of Britain League, and as such was a personal friend of mine,' snapped Millicent. 'What time did you say it happened?'

'For Pete's sake, how am I expected to know? It'll be in the papers.'

'Eleven forty-eight, precisely,' put in Larry Dowling gently. 'They know the time because the murderer evidently pressed the muzzle of the gun against the victim's body — it would have helped to muffle the shot — and the shock of the explosion damaged a repeater watch the old gentleman carried in his breast pocket, and stopped it.'

'Good God,' said Tyson heavily. 'The Press! I'd forgotten we had a newshound in our midst.' He glared at Larry Dowling as though he had found a slug in his salad. 'Did you by any chance cover this case, Mr Dowling? You appear to know a hell of a lot about it.'

'No. Not in my line. But I read the papers. It was in most of them on the 13th. I must have seen five accounts of it at least.'

'Umm,' grunted Tyson, and returned to the port.

'Eleven forty-eight,' said Millicent Bates, and repeated it slowly. 'Eleven ... forty ... eight.'

'And what exactly does that mean?' inquired Nigel of the table

150

at large. 'It sounds *just* like the Girl with the Golden Voice *"On the third stroke it will be eleven forty-eight and twelve seconds precisely".*'

Millicent Bates scowled at him across the table. 'If you really want to know,' she said tartly, 'I happened to pay a rush visit to a friend of mine on the morning of the 12th. I'd forgotten to give her the key of the Wolf Cubs' hut, and we were leaving that afternoon. She lives at the end of Mr Honeywood's road — it's a *cul de sac* — and I was wondering if I might not actually have passed the murderer. He must have come down that road.'

Nigel smiled with maddening tolerance. 'Do you know, I *hardly* think so, dear Miss Bates.'

'And why not?' demanded Millicent Bates, bristling.

'But surely it stands to reason that a murderer would not go *prancing* along a public highway and in at the front door by daylight? He'd be far more likely to *creep* in by a shrubbery or something.'

'Which just goes to show,' said Miss Bates, 'how little you know what you're talking about. You could possibly creep *out* of Mr Honeywood's house through a shrubbery, because you could use the kitchen-garden door. But it has a slip lock and you can't open it from the outside. And as there is a high wall around the house, the only way in, for anyone who didn't want to do some jolly conspicuous climbing, is through the front gate. And I *do* know what I'm talking about, because I happen to know the house well.'

'So well,' said Nigel gaily, 'that you will soon have us shivering in our little shoes, wondering if you couldn't have done it yourself!'

Millicent Bates' weather-beaten countenance flushed an unbecoming shade of puce, and Gussie rushed angrily to her defence.

'You appear to look upon murder as a joke, Mr Ponting. But the death of an old acquaintance is hardly a joking matter to us.'

151

'Oh dear! Oh-dear-oh-dear-oh-dear!' wailed Nigel. 'What can I say? I *do* apologize. *Dear* Miss Bates, you must know that I didn't mean it! My wretched, *distorted* sense of humour. *Do* say that you forgive me?'

Millicent made a flapping gesture with one large and capable hand, in the manner of one waving away an irritating insect, and said gruffly: 'Don't talk rot! My fault for harpin' on it. But I couldn't help being interested — realizing that I might well have passed the man.'

'Or woman,' put in Larry Dowling softly.

Millicent Bates turned swiftly to face him. 'Why do you say that?' she demanded sharply.

'No reason. Just that it may have been a woman. Nothing to show it wasn't — if the papers were anything to go by. You didn't read them, or you'd have seen that he had a female visitor that day. She even took the precaution of leaving a handkerchief behind her — complete with monogram.'

'Oh,' said Miss Bates doubtfully. 'I didn't think of that. Yes, I suppose . . . it could be.'

'Some winsome ornament of the Wednesday Women's Guild, stealing through the mist on the track of the funds!' tittered Nigel. 'Oh dear — there I go again! My *wretched* sense of humour. I won't say another *word*!'

Millicent made no retort, beyond staring at him long and male-volently. But there was suddenly something in her face — in her frown and her narrowed eyes, that suggested that his words had reminded her of something. Or suggested something. Something quite impossible, and yet . . .

No one spoke, and for the space of a full minute there was a curious, strained silence in the room; and then Millicent nodded at Mr Ponting. The brief, brisk nod of someone who has been presented with a fresh viewpoint and accepted it.

On the opposite side of the table Larry Dowling leant forward with a small, swift movement that somehow had the effect of

152

a pounce, and said sharply: 'So you *do* think it might have been a woman — a woman he knew!'

But if he had expected to startle Miss Bates into any admission he was disappointed. Millicent turned to look at him, and having successfully conveyed the impression of not liking what she saw, inquired blandly: 'What did you say, Mr Dowling?'

Larry Dowling flushed and sat back. 'Er — nothing.'

'For which relief, much thanks!' boomed Tyson. 'I am getting bored with this murder. Let us talk about something else.'

'Yes, *do* let's,' said Nigel. 'Murders are *not* precisely one's idea of sparkling dinner-table chit-chat. So gruesomely proletarian. I can never *think* why anyone should want to hear about them.'

Amalfi laughed her lovely throaty laugh, and said: 'Don't be so affected, Nigel darling. Everyone *adores* a good murder. Look at the way they always get into all the headlines and fill the Sunday papers. And what about the way you've been going on about this one? No one else has had a chance to get a word in edgeways!'

She turned to her host and said: 'Tyson, you ought to be entertaining us. If you don't like murders, talk about something else. Anything. Tell us about this house.'

'What about it?' inquired Tyson. 'It was allegedly built about a century and a half ago by a harassed husband whose second wife couldn't get along with the first. But if you want to swot up on it, my late Uncle Barclay wrote an exceptionally tedious book about it which he published at his own expense in the late 1890s and inflicted on his friends. You probably saw one at Gussie's — she has it bound in red morocco and displayed on the piano, to atone for the fact that she's never read it. You'll find several copies lying around here. All the historical and architectural dope down to the last deadly detail. I do not advise it for light reading. But don't let that stop you if you're really interested.'

'I'm not,' said Amalfi. 'Not to that extent, anyway. You are

153

all being very dull tonight, and I want to be flattered and entertained.'

She turned and smiled meltingly at Eduardo, who accepted the invitation with alacrity, and not long afterwards they had all left the dining-room and gone out to drink Turkish coffee on the terrace in front of the drawing-room windows, where Gussie had again demanded the home papers.

Tyson had departed in search of them, and had returned saying that he could not find them, but a few minutes later Nigel had drifted languidly across the terrace with a wrapped package in his hand which he had handed to his employer with an eloquent lift of the eyebrows that had not been lost on at least one member of the party.

The London newspapers had arrived on the same aircraft that had brought the Frosts' guests from Nairobi that morning, and had not been delivered at *Kivulimi* until the late afternoon. The wrapping was still unbroken. 'I thought you said you'd read them?' said Gussie Bingham accusingly.

Tyson affected not to hear her, and removed himself hurriedly to the far side of the terrace where Amalfi Gordon, temporarily deserted, was leaning on the stone balustrade and looking out between the trees to where the moon had laid a shimmering golden carpet across the quiet sea.

'Pleasant, isn't it?' said Tyson, coming to anchor beside her. 'And peaceful. There can't be many places like it left in the world. Or there won't be soon. Progress can be a loutish thing.'

'Don't be pompous and gloomy, darling,' chided Amalfi. 'There are thousands of places just as lovely as this. And as peaceful.'

'That's where you're wrong,' said Tyson, leaning his elbows on the warm stone. 'I've seen a lot of the world. A hell of a lot of it! But there's something special about this island. Something that I haven't met anywhere else. Do you know what is the most familiar sound in Zanzibar? — laughter! Walk through

154

the streets of the little city almost any time of the day or night, and you'll hear it. People laughing. There is a gaiety and good humour about them that is strangely warming to even such a corrugated, corroded and eroded heart as mine, and this is the only place I have yet hit upon where black and white and every shade in between 'em appear to be able to live together in complete friendliness and harmony, with no colour bar. It's a living proof and a practical demonstration that it can be done. They are all, whatever their race or caste or religion, loyal subjects of His Highness the Sultan — may he live for ever! — and they get on together. But it won't last. In the end one of the Jembe kind will manage to destroy it. Yes — there are times when I am prepared to agree with that bigoted old bore, my late Uncle Barclay, that Progress is a lout!'

Amalfi had been picking jasmine buds and smelling them absently, wearing the abstracted smile of one who is not in the least interested in the conversation, but the name 'Jembe' caught her attention, and she dropped the flowers and turned quickly:

'Tyson darling, that reminds me. I'm sorry to go on about this sort of thing, but did you *really* mean that we can none of us leave this house until the police find out who gave that tedious little Arab agitator a dose of poison in Mombasa?'

'God forbid!' said Tyson piously. 'If that were so I might find myself permanently stuck with the lot of you, and I'm not sure that my constitution could stand it. Or yours! No, it's only a question of a day or two, while they make a few inquiries. They might want to ask if any of you by any chance remember seeing someone speaking to him at the airport. Or standing near him. Something like that. Why? Were you thinking of cutting short your visit? I thought you were supposed to be staying with us for at least three weeks.'

Amalfi smiled at him, and reaching up to pull his greying blond beard said: 'But you know quite well that I never do what 'I'm supposed to do, and I never know how long I shall stay

155

anywhere. If I'm enjoying myself madly, I stay, and if I'm not, I move on. It's as simple as that!'

'It must come expensive,' said Tyson.

'Oh, frantically. But I don't *always* have to pay for it myself.'

Tyson bellowed with sudden laughter. 'That's what I like about you, Elf. No deception, is there?'

'*Masses*, darling. You've no idea how much! But not in that way. After all, money *is* rather madly important. Don't you agree?'

'I work for mine,' said Tyson dryly.

'Oh, but so do I. One has to sing for one's supper, you know; and I sing — charmingly!'

'I'll grant you that,' said Tyson with a grin. 'But hasn't it been a bit trying at times? Johnnie Leigh, for instance.'

Amalfi's mermaid eyes clouded. 'Oh but darling — I never can think of money when I marry them. It's always *love*. And it's only later that one—— Oh ... wakes up to reality.'

'And in the wrong bedroom, with a private inquiry agent hired by your husband taking notes through the transom,' said Tyson cynically. 'Still, you've been lucky in one way. The co-respondent was always noticeably solvent and well able — and more than willing! — to keep you in the mink.'

'Darling!' said Amalfi reproachfully. 'You make it sound as though I were a gold-digger. But I'm not. I'd have married Johnnie even if he hadn't a *soul*!'

'And Robin Gratton? And Chubby?'

'But of *course*! I'm like that. I suddenly feel I *must* have something — that it's the only thing in the world worth having and that once I've got it I shall be happy ever after. And then I'm not. But I adored Chubby. My heart broke when he was killed. It did, really Tyson!'

'Nonsense! You were hardly on speaking terms that last year. And you haven't got a heart, darling. Only a soft mass of emotions. Though I'm not so sure about your head!'

156

'I'm afraid that's just as soft,' sighed Amalfi regretfully.

'I wonder? Still, you seem to have had your fair share of romance during the last year or two, despite that alleged broken heart. Why don't you bite on the bullet and marry one of them?'

Amalfi laughed. 'What, again? It doesn't seem to take with me, does it?'

'It will one day.'

'Like it has for Lorrie? Perhaps. But how is one to know? I always think I know; and then I find I don't.'

'Try marrying a poor one for a change. You ought to be able to afford it.'

'I don't think I could. One can never really have enough money, can one? All the really heavenly things cost so much. Diamonds and Dior models and holidays in Bermuda.'

'But Chubby must have left you a packet.'

'Not a packet, darling. Unfortunately there turned out to be platoons of dreary aunts and other dim relations that I had never even *heard* of, and it seemed that Chubby was depressingly Clan-minded — worse luck. And then the death duties were *iniquitous*. And anyway, I'm hopeless over money. I always have been. It seems to melt!'

'I'm not surprised; what with diamonds and Dior models and holidays in Bermuda!'

'Yes,' said Amalfi, and sighed deeply. 'That's why it's simpler to fall in love with someone rich. But then I like them to be handsome and charming too, and there's no getting away from it, that kind are limited in number and dreadfully spoilt. They know that they aren't a drug on the market, and they can be difficult.'

'What you mean is that they bite back and won't let themselves be trampled on by any woman for long. And more power to 'em. You know, Elf, I propose to give you some sage advice. You won't be able to go on looking like a luscious slice of peach for ever, and it's time you settled down with a different type.

157

The kind that'll let you play your favourite game of eating your cake and having it.'

'I don't think I know what you mean, darling.'

'Cut out these playboys with plenty of cash, like young Lash or that slick-smoothie, Eddie. They may be fun, but they'd be hell as husbands for a woman like you. They aren't good at turning the other cheek — or a blind eye! You ought to have learnt that at least by this time. What you need now is a nice kind sugar-daddy of the adoring door-mat type, who will let you get away with murder.'

Amalfi shivered suddenly. '*Ugh!* Darling! What a simile to choose after all that gruesome chatter at dinner!'

'Well, "Make a monkey out of him with impunity", if you like it put that way.'

'Is that what Lorraine did? I wouldn't have said that you were exactly a door-mat type. Or a sugar-daddy!'

'Lorrie,' said Tyson, 'isn't in the least your type. Or only superficially. She's merely incurably romantic. That's her trouble. She'd be perfectly happy married to someone who could offer her a semi-detached and a "daily" — as long as she loved him. You wouldn't be. Now, would you?'

Amalfi gave him a narrowed, slanting look under her long lashes, and there was, all at once, a trace of scorn in her lovely face and a shade of contempt in her voice. 'Darling Tyson. You read us all like a book! So clever.'

'Sarcasm doesn't suit you, Elf. Am I to take it that you are going to take a brief whirl at being a Marchesa? If so, I ought to warn you that Eddie is even more susceptible than you are, and the only reason that he has not totted up a long list of ex-wives, all drawing heavy alimony, is because his grandmother holds the purse strings, and can not only cut off supplies when she chooses, but frequently does. It's a great trial to him; though it doesn't seem to have persuaded him to try work yet. He—— What's the matter? Surely you knew that?'

'No,' said Amalfi shortly. 'I thought——' she stopped and bit her lip, and Tyson laughed.

'Well, don't say later that no one ever warned you! If you've really reached the fatal stage of marrying them younger than yourself, you'd better take Lash Holden. American men put up with a lot more rough stuff from their wives than less idealistic races, and when it comes to the parting of the ways they'll break out into a rash of Old World chivalry and allow themselves to be sued as the erring partner, and milked like goats for iniquitous alimony with never a bleat. But with Eduardo you'd be the one who'd do the paying, if anyone did. His family might have accepted Chubby's widow — though considering the circumstances, I doubt it — but they're likely to kick like cows at those two divorces. And as for that unfortunate business of Douglas—— Well if you'll take my advice, Elf, you'll scrub Eddie and settle for young Lash. That is, if it's not too late.'

Amalfi drew back and regarded him with sudden hostility. 'I don't think,' she said slowly, 'that I am amused any longer. In fact I'm quite sure that I'm not.'

'Because I've told you the truth about yourself and a couple of gilded playboys?'

'No. Because you begin to bore me, darling. And I cannot endure being bored.'

She smiled sweetly at him, her eyes cold, and turned and walked back across the terrace to join the others. And presently Nigel had gone in to switch on the radio-gramophone and turn back the carpet of the drawing-room, and they had all danced: with the exception of Tyson, who could not be bothered, and Millicent Bates, who could not.

Tyson and Millicent had sat side by side on the stone balustrade of the terrace, watching the dancers through the open doors, and Millicent had said moodily: 'I wish you would tell me where you got that secretary of yours, and why. I don't know how a man of your type can stand all that affectation and giggling.'

'He's good at his job,' said Tyson lazily, 'and don't let that affectation fool you. It's fooled a lot of hard-headed businessmen in the publishing line and film racket into thinking that they can pull a fast one, and they've all wound up with headaches, having paid over far more than their original top figure. He deals with all my contracts, and behind that tittering facade he's as cunning and inquisitive as a barrelful of monkeys, and as shrewd as a weasel.'

'I don't doubt it,' said Millicent grimly. 'A nasty type. We had an assistant cashier like that in Market-Lydon. An absolute rotter. I always said that there'd be an ugly scandal one day, and of course there was. You can't trust 'em a yard!'

Tyson chose to be amused, and letting out a roar of laughter he clapped Millicent on the back with a large and hairy hand.

'Bates, you're perfect! You're a collector's piece. But so is Nigel; and I like collector's pieces. From all pale, pink-blooded, pure-souled people, Good Lord, deliver me!'

'That's *your* pose!' snapped Millicent Bates.

'Maybe,' said Tyson, unruffled. 'We all have one. Smoke screens to fool people with. Gussie's is good-nature.'

Millicent stiffened indignantly: 'Pose my foot! Gussie's the kindest creature alive!'

Tyson laughed again, and drained his glass. 'Bates, my Bonnie Brown Owl, I applaud your loyalty while deploring your dis-honesty. You cannot have lived with Gussie all these years without knowing that there is nothing she enjoys more than planting a feline barb where she hopes it will hurt most, and then, covered with pretty confusion, pretending that it was just an unfortunate slip of the tongue. It's her favourite parlour sport. You must have found out long ago that Gussie only loves herself. And to forestall you saying "So do you!" I will hasten to say it myself — "And so do I." That may be selfish, but by golly it's sense! Let's face it, Bates, we're not a really pleasant lot, we Frosts. The only one of us who doesn't appear to have had any vices was old Uncle Barclay, and he was a crank! Let's drink confusion to his ghost.'

He got up and walked over to the table with the drinks, and Millicent Bates, following him, put down her empty glass and shook her head. 'No thanks. No more for me. I think I shall go to bed.'

She turned to stare once more at the dancers revolving in the lighted drawing-room: Gussie and Nigel, Dany and Larry Dowling, Amalfi and Lash Holden, Eduardo and Lorraine . . .

She stood there for perhaps five minutes, watching them with a curious intentness.

'It's very odd,' mused Millicent Bates.

'What is?' inquired Tyson.

'Everything!' said Millicent, and left him.

13

Dany leant wearily against the window-sill of her bedroom and looked out across the treetops to the silver stretch of the sea.

She had come up to her room over an hour ago, intending to go to bed. But once there she found that she was not sleepy. Merely too tired to go to the trouble of undressing, and too dispirited to take any pleasure in the beauty of the night. For it had been neither a pleasant nor a peaceful evening.

Tyson and Millicent Bates had both vanished shortly after ten, and Gussie had quarrelled with Nigel, who had withdrawn in a huff, leaving Dany to deal with the radiogram. Gussie had flounced off in search of her brother, presumably to complain, and Lash, having danced a particularly soulful waltz with Amalfi, had taken her down into the garden — ostensibly to look at the nocturnal flowering Lady-of-the-Night which grew in profusion in a bed some distance from the house.

They had stayed away for so long that Eduardo's southern blood had obviously begun to rise dangerously, and although they had returned separately it was perhaps unfortunate that Lash had been the first to reappear. For there was, unmistakably, a distinct trace of lipstick on his chin.

The Marchese's jealous gaze had not missed it, and his eyes had flashed in a manner that would undoubtedly have brought the house down in the days of the late Rudolph Valentino — a gentleman whom he much resembled. He had spoken a short, hissing phrase in Italian, to which Lash had replied with an even

162

shorter one of strictly Anglo-Saxon origin, and only the agitated intervention of Lorraine had prevented a stirring scene.

Amalfi had not reappeared for some time — part of which, at least, she must have devoted to repairing her make-up. She had pointedly ignored Lash and devoted her attention to soothing Eduardo's lacerated feelings, but she did not appear to be in a good temper.

The only person present who had shown no sign of nerves or temperament was Larry Dowling, and Dany, whose own nerves were uncomfortably taut, was not only duly grateful for it, but despite the fact that there was something about Larry's lazily observant gaze that suggested very little escaped him, even more grateful for the impulse that had made her step-father add him to the house-party. She tried to remind herself that as a journalist — feature writer or no — news was his business, and that the present complicated situation would make entertaining reading for a sensation-hungry public. But it did not seem to weigh against the undoubted fact that she felt safer when Larry was in the room, and more insecure whenever he left it.

She wished that she could bring herself to take the sensible course of retiring to bed, but a raw recollection of the terror of the previous night had made her disinclined for sleep or solitude, and the lights and music, and Larry's strangely reassuring presence, at least provided an illusion of safety. But the long hours spent in an aeroplane had begun to tell on all of them, and by eleven o'clock lethargy had descended on the dancers, and with it a spirit of tolerance.

Nigel came out of his huff and apologized to Gussie, who yawned and informed him that of course she wasn't annoyed with him. She was never annoyed with anyone: even with people who pretended to a knowledge of subjects with which they had only the most superficial acquaintance, and — Oh, dear! but of course she hadn't meant *Nigel* . . .

Amalfi had shed her hauteur and awarded Lash a forgiving

smile, Eduardo had ceased to simmer, and Lorraine had stopped looking vague and distrait and had begun to sparkle and laugh, and dispense her own particular and potent brand of charm to such good effect that her guests, with the exception of her daughter, had finally departed to bed in the best of tempers.

A bat flitted past the open window and Dany flinched, and was startled to find that so trivial a thing could have the power to make her heart leap and her breath catch. Especially when there was nothing to be afraid of any longer — except the discovery of her identity, which was inevitable anyway. And yet she was still afraid ...

The night was very quiet and the house very still, and now that the lights had gone out the garden was blue and black and silver only. There were no glints of gold except where the warm reflected glow from her own window touched the top of a jacaranda, and a small orange square, barely visible through the intervening trees, that showed that Lash Holden, in the little guest-house on the seaward corner of the boundary wall, was still awake.

A nightjar cried harshly in the garden below, and Dany's taut nerves leapt to the sudden sound, and she turned impatiently away from the window and looked about her at the strange white-walled room whose high ceiling was almost twenty feet above her head. A room built tall and cool for some lovely lady of the harem in the years before Sultan Saïd had deeded the House of Shade to his friend, Emory Frost — rover, adventurer, black-sheep and soldier-of-fortune.

What had the house seen during its long life? Had there been, as Millicent Bates suggested, 'shady doings' there, and did the rooms remember them? Dany found herself turning quickly to look behind her, as she had done once before in another bedroom in the Airlane in London. But there was nothing behind her except a small cream-and-gilt writing-table on which someone had placed Miss Ada Kitchell's portable typewriter and a solitary book: a

164

solid tome of Victorian vintage that did not look as though it would make entertaining reading.

Dany reached out and picked it up, to discover that it was a musty volume bound in leather that heat and many monsoons had patched with mildew. But despite its age the title was still clearly legible: *The House of Shade* by Barclay Frost.

Dany smiled, remembering Tyson's strictures on the author's style, and dipping into it she found that her step-father's criticisms were fully justified. Barclay's prose was insufferably pedantic, and he had never used one word where half-a-dozen would do instead. Still, it was nice of Lorraine to put it in her room, and she must certainly find time to read some if not all of it.

She was laying it down when she noticed that some inquisitive or would-be helpful servant had opened the typewriter case and had not known how to shut it again. Dany removed the lid in order to set the catches straight, and saw that the machine had also been used, for a fragment of torn cream-laid paper, taken from a shelf on the writing-table, was still in it.

One of the *Kivulimi* servants had obviously been playing with this new and fascinating toy, and Dany could only hope that he had not succeeded in damaging it. She rattled off a line of type that in time-honoured tradition informed all good men that now was the time to come to the aid of the party, and finding that the machine still appeared to function, removed the fragment of paper, dropped it into the waste-paper basket and replaced the cover.

Turning away, she looked at the neatly turned-down bed, but sleep seemed as far from her as ever, and she went instead to the dressing-table, and sitting down in front of it, stared at her face in the glass. Lorraine was right. It was an unattractive hair style and her skin was too warm a tone for red hair.

She removed the spectacles, and reaching for her hairbrush swept the fringe off her forehead, and having brushed out the neat rows of curls that were arranged in bunches on either side of her head, twisted the soft mass into a severe knot at the nape of her neck. Dany's bones were good — as Daniel Ashton's had been — and where a frizzed and fussy style of hair-dressing reduced her to mediocrity, a severe one lent her distinction and a sudden unexpected beauty.

An enormous green and white moth flew in through the open window and added itself to the halo of winged insects that were circling about the electric light, and Dany rose impatiently and, going to the door, snapped off the switch. That should give the tiresome things a chance to find their way out into the moonlight, and she would give them a few minutes to get clear, and then pull the curtains before turning on the light again.

Now that the room was in darkness the night outside seemed almost as bright as day, and she returned to the window to look out once more at the shadowy garden and the wide, shimmering expanse of sea.

Lash's light had vanished and he was presumably asleep. But now that Dany's own light was out she became aware that the window immediately above hers had not yet been darkened, for there was still a warm glow illuminating the jacaranda tree. So Millicent Bates was still awake. And so, it seemed, was somebody else . . .

A pin-point of light was moving through the shadows in the garden below, and for a moment Dany thought it must be a firefly. Then her ear caught the faint crunch of the crushed shell and coral on the winding paths, and she realized that what she could see was the lighted end of a cigarette, and that someone was walking up through the garden towards the house.

The tiny orange spark was momentarily lost to view behind a screen of hibiscus, to reappear again as a man in a dinner jacket came softly up the nearest flight of steps on to the terrace, and turning along it, vanished round the far corner of the house.

He had looked up at Dany's window as he reached the top

166

of the steps, and as the moonlight fell on his face she had seen the anxious frown between his brows, and had resisted an impulse to lean out and assure him that she was all right. Though why she should suppose that Larry Dowling was in any way interested in her safety she did not know. It was far more likely that he had merely been strolling in the garden at this late hour because he, like herself, did not feel sleepy.

From somewhere down among the shadowy trees the nightjar cried again. But this time the harsh sound did not make her start, for the thought that Larry was somewhere nearby, and would be spending the night under the same roof, was an astonishingly comforting one. So comforting, that tension and disquiet fell away from her, and all at once she was pleasantly drowsy. She could go to bed now. And to sleep.

Dany's room was the end one on the first floor, above the dining-room and at the top of one of the four flights of stairs that curved upward from the courtyard. A door at one end of her bedroom led at right-angles into a small bathroom that faced west, with beyond it another and larger bathroom belonging to another and larger bedroom that had been given to Gussie Bingham. On the opposite side of her room, and looking out on the same view, was a morning room, and beyond that again a bedroom and a bathroom, the duplicate of her own, which was occupied by Amalfi Gordon.

All the remaining rooms on the first floor — those on the other two sides of the courtyard — were taken up by Tyson and Lorraine, while Nigel, Eduardo, Larry Dowling and Millicent Bates had rooms on the top floor.

'Perhaps not *quite* the thing to do, popping Bates up among all the bachelors,' Lorraine had said. 'But anyone who has ever seen Millicent arrayed for bed — or merely seen Millicent! — would realize that no bachelor is ever likely to cast her so much as a speculative glance, poor girl, so I expect it's all right. I was going to put Ada Kitchell up there — the real one. But

167

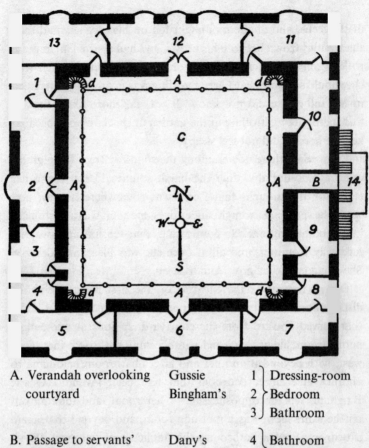

A. Verandah overlooking courtyard

B. Passage to servants' staircase

C. Courtyard

d. Staircase leading up to top floor and down to courtyard

o Pillars at verandah edge

Gussie Bingham's

Dany's

Amalfi's

1 } Dressing-room
2 } Bedroom
3 } Bathroom

4 } Bathroom
5 } Bedroom
6 Morning-room

7 } Bedroom
8 } Bathroom

9
10 } Rooms occupied
11 } by Tyson and
12 } Lorraine
13

14 Servants' staircase

that nice Dowling man can have her room instead. He's rather a pet, isn't he?'

Dany caught herself listening for the sound of Larry Dowling's feet on the stone staircase outside her room. But the walls of the House of Shade had been solidly constructed to withstand high temperatures, marauding pirates and tropical hurricanes, and the heavy wooden doors were old and carved and almost sound-proof. She did not know if Larry had returned to his own room or not, but concluded that he must have done so by now, and realized that he would probably have gone up by the servants' staircase on the far side of the house.

A little breeze blew in from the sea, ruffling the leaves in the garden below, and she heard for the first time the song of tropic islands and coral coasts: a sound that is as haunting and as unforgettable as the sigh of wind through pine trees. The dry, whispering rustle of coconut palms.

It was a soothing and pleasant sound and a relief from the stillness and silence that had preceded it, and Dany leant out over the window-sill, listening to it, until another sound made her turn. A curious scraping sound that seemed to come either from the verandah or from the room above her. Probably Millicent dragging a suitcase out from under the bed. Or Larry Dowling, scraping his feet on the stone stair. The breeze blew coolly through the hot room, billowing the mosquito curtains and bringing with it all the lovely scents of the tropic night, and presently Dany heard the clock strike the half hour. Half past twelve. It really was quite time that she got to bed.

She pulled the curtains, shutting out the moonlight and the moths, and had turned to grope her way across the room towards the light-switches by the door when she heard another sound. A curious harsh cry that was followed by a dull thud, and that seemed to come from just outside her door.

Dany stood still, listening, all her drowsiness gone and her pulses once again leaping in panic; until an obvious explanation

169

occurred to her, and she relaxed again. It had only been a nightjar crying in the courtyard, and the wind must have overturned a top-heavy creeper-filled urn at the verandah edge. She smiled ruefully at her own fears, and walking forward in the darkness, felt for the switch.

The light clicked on and the room became safe and bright and comfortable, and there were no shadows. But the breeze had passed and the night was still again, and in that stillness she heard once again, and more distinctly, the sound that she had previously thought might be Millicent moving a suitcase: a soft, slow, unidentified sound that suggested stone moving on stone, and that seemed to come not so much from the room above her as from the verandah outside. It did not last for more than ten counted seconds, but this time it brought a sudden picture into Dany's mind: a picture of someone who was hurt, trying to crawl up the stairs. That cry she had heard — it had not been made by a nightjar, and of course the breeze could not have knocked over one of those heavy stone urns! It had been someone crying out and falling. Larry! ... Supposing it were Larry, tiptoeing up the stairs in the dark so as not to wake her, and losing his footing——

Dany listened at the door, but could hear no further sound. Had Larry been trying to drag himself up the stairs with a sprained ankle, or was he still lying out there in the dark verandah, winded or in pain?

Forgetting caution, she turned the key and jerked open the door.

The moon was not high enough to shine into the well of the courtyard, and Dany could see nothing but darkness except where the light streaming out from her open doorway made a narrow yellow pathway across the coconut matting, and silhouetted a flower-filled stone jar and a single slender pillar against the black emptiness beyond.

There was no chink of light from any other of the many doors that faced each other across the central courtyard, and the night was once again so still that the plop of a goldfish rising at a moth in the pool below was clearly audible in the silence.

Dany spoke in a whisper, afraid of rousing the sleeping house. 'Larry! — Larry, are you there? Is anyone there?'

The whisper made a soft sibilant echo under the high dark roof of the verandah, but no one answered her, and nothing moved. Not even the fish in the pool.

Then another breath of breeze stirred the creepers and flowering shrubs in the stone jars, and as Dany's eyes became accustomed to the darkness the tall lines of pillars with their rounded arches, the dark squares of the doors in the long white-washed wall and the outlines of the stone jars became visible, like a negative in a bath of developing solution. She could make out the long empty stretch of the verandah to her right, but to the left, where it turned sharply at right-angles, the stairs leading to the floor above made a pool of blackness.

She set the door wide and took a hesitant step forward, peering into the shadows. Surely there was something there ...? Someone. An untidy heap, sprawled in the dense shadow below the curve of the stone stairs and so nearly the colour of the matting as to be almost invisible.

Dany ran forward, and stooping above it touched a tousled head that appeared to be twisted at an odd angle. But it was not Larry Dowling. Who then? She caught at the slack shoulders, desperately tugging the heavy shape nearer to the light from the open doorway, and then remembered that the switches of the verandah lights were on the wall near the staircase, and ran to them.

A switch clicked under her shaking fingers, and a sixty-watt bulb enclosed in a hanging lamp of oriental design dispersed the shadows, throwing elaborate fretted patterns across the white wall and the coconut matting. And on Millicent Bates, dressed in pyjamas and an oatmeal-coloured dressing-gown, lying face downwards and very still on the verandah floor.

171

'Miss Bates!' implored Dany, kneeling beside her and endeavouring to turn her over. 'Miss Bates, are you hurt?'

The foolish question echoed hollowly along the silent verandahs as Millicent Bates's head lolled back from Dany's supporting arm. The breeze had set the lantern swaying, and the fretted lozenges of light shifted and swung and gave an illusion of movement to Millicent's wide, staring eyes. But there was no movement in the dead weight of her slack, heavy body. No movement anywhere except for the swinging, soundless lozenges of light and the flutter of a crumpled piece of paper that stirred in the breeze, flapping like a large pale-coloured moth on the matting.

She's hurt, thought Dany stupidly. Badly hurt ... or she's knocked the wind out of herself. No ... no it can't be just that ... Concussion. Miss Bates had fallen and stunned herself. Those shallow steps with their low, decorative, ridiculously inadequate balustrades—— She must have been coming down them in the dark to see if Gussie were settled in for the night, and slipped and fallen.

Of all the silly things to do, thought Dany frantically. In the *dark*!

The paper fluttered again with a small sound that made her start violently, and she snatched at it, and thrusting it into her pocket, laid Millicent's inert weight back on to the matting, and stood up: trembling but no longer frightened. She must fetch help at once — Gussie Bingham. Tyson——

She ran to Gussie's door and hammered on it, and receiving no answer tried the handle and found that Gussie too had taken the precaution of locking herself in that night. Dany beat on the door and called her by name, and the silent courtyard picked up the sound and echoed it along the lines of arches: 'Mrs Bingham —! *Mrs Bingham ... Mrs Bingham ...*'

A door opened on the adjoining verandah, framing Tyson in a bright square of light.

'What in the name of Beelzebub is the meaning of this infernal

172

din?' roared Tyson, adding his quota to it. 'Who's there? What's up?'

'It's Miss Bates,' called Dany. 'Tyson, *do* come! She's fallen off the staircase, and I think she's concussed herself or — or something. And I can't lift her. She's too heavy.'

The door beside her was thrown open and Gussie Bingham was there, wrapped in a violet silk kimono patterned with wistaria, and with her curling pins inadequately concealed by a turban of lilac tulle.

'Miss Kitchell! Did you want me? What on earth is the matter? Why, Tyson——!'

Tyson charged past her, clad in nothing but a scanty loin cloth of some gaily patterned cotton material, and switching on lights as he went.

Other lights flooded the top-floor verandahs and other heads appeared, peering downwards: Nigel's, Eduardo's, Larry Dowling's...

Lorraine ran along the verandah, her little bare feet thrust into absurd feathered mules whose high heels clicked as she ran, and her diaphanous nightgown barely concealed by an equally diaphanous négligée.

But there was nothing that anyone could do. Millicent Bates was dead. She had fallen from somewhere near the top of the staircase on to the stone floor of the verandah, and broken her neck.

14

'I've always said those stairs were dangerous,' shuddered Lorraine, white-faced and shivering. 'Those silly little edges. They aren't rails at all! But I still don't see how she could have done it, even in the dark. You'd think anyone would be *extra* careful in the dark, wouldn't you?'

'I suppose she must have felt faint,' said Tyson. 'In fact that was probably what she was coming down for. To get some aspirin or something off Gussie. Gussie's got their medicine chest in her room.'

'But wouldn't you think she'd have had the sense to just sit down if she felt faint? Really, people are *too* stupid!'

It was obvious from Lorraine's tone that, horrified as she was, she considered Millicent Bates to have been guilty of thoroughly inconsiderate behaviour, and now that the first shock of discovery was over, her emotions leant more to anger than grief.

It was over an hour since Dany had aroused the sleeping household, and they were all in the drawing-room waiting for the arrival of the doctor, an ambulance and the police. All except Gussie — who had succumbed to a fit of hysterics and was now in bed having been given two sedatives and a hot-water bottle — and Nigel Ponting, who had driven in to the town to fetch the doctor and inform the police.

They had carried Millicent's body into Dany's room because it happened to be the nearest, and left it on Dany's bed, where it lay alone, clad in sternly utilitarian pyjamas and an elderly woollen dressing-gown, staring open-mouthed at the ceiling.

174

Lash had been awakened by the car being backed out of the garage and the flick of headlights across the wall of his room, and seeing the house ablaze with lights, he had put on a dressing-gown and come across to make inquiries.

Amalfi, who had slept through the initial uproar and had been aroused by Gussie's shrieks, had joined the horrified house-party just as Tyson and Larry Dowling were carrying Millicent's limp body into Dany's room. She had behaved with admirable calm, and it was she who had succeeded in putting a stop to Gussie's hysterics by the simple expedient of picking up the jug of drinking water that stood on Dany's bedside table, and flinging the contents in Mrs Bingham's scarlet, screaming face.

Amalfi was now sitting on the sofa, wearing a most becoming confection of peach-coloured satin and lace and looking as poised and sleek and *soignée* as though this was some normal social occasion. She was talking to Lash and sipping black coffee that Lorraine had made in a Cona, but if her composure was genuine, she appeared to be the only one in the room to possess it.

Lash was not even making a pretence of listening to her. He was looking troubled and out of temper, and was apparently more interested in the pattern of the carpet than in anything else, though he occasionally lifted his gaze from it to direct a look of active irritation at Tyson Frost, who was prowling restlessly about the room, looking like some strayed beachcomber from the South Pacific.

Lash, glancing at him and wishing he would stay still, decided that although hair on the chest might be the hallmark of a he-man, too much of it merely suggested that Darwin had been dead right when he attributed the origin of the human species to the ape. There was little to choose between Tyson's torso and a door-mat, and his caged-lion prowl was beginning to get on Lash's nerves. If only the man would sit still for five minutes——! And if only Amalfi would stop talking for ten. His gaze shifted briefly to Dany, and he frowned.

175

Dany was the only one in the room who was fully dressed, and Lash, noting the fact, and the time, was unreasonably disturbed. Two a.m. And they had all gone off to their several rooms shortly before half past eleven. Yet Dany alone had obviously not been in bed, for she was not only wearing the dress she had worn earlier that evening, but she was still wearing stockings. Which made it seem unlikely that she had merely hurriedly pulled on the dress in preference to coming down in a bathrobe as the others had done. He noticed that she was surreptitiously studying Larry Dowling, and his frown became a scowl.

Dany herself, sitting huddled in the depths of a big armchair and feeling cold and very tired, was wondering how Larry had managed to get back into the house and up to his room in time to change into the pyjamas and dressing-gown he now wore, when she had seen him on the terrace below her window, wearing a dinner jacket, only a short time before she had heard Millicent fall. Or had the interval been longer than she had imagined? How long had she stood near the window looking out into the moonlight after he had left the terrace? Surely not more than ten minutes. Yet Larry certainly had the appearance of one who has been awakened out of a sound sleep, for his hair was rumpled and he yawned at intervals. But despite the yawns there was nothing sleepy about those quiet, observant eyes, and Dany did not believe that he felt in the least drowsy.

Eduardo di Chiago, darkly handsome in scarlet silk pyjamas and a spectacular monogrammed and coroneted dressing-gown, was gallantly assisting Lorraine with the coffee. But he too was noticeably distrait and apt to jump when spoken to, and, like Lash, was obviously finding his host's relentless pacing an acute nervous irritant.

Lorraine, noticing it, said appealingly: 'Tyson darling, *do* sit down! You're making us all nervous. Why don't we all go back to bed?'

'Speaking for myself,' said Tyson, 'because I should have to get up again the minute the doctor and the police arrive. However, there's no reason why the rest of you should stay around. The only people they're likely to want to see are myself and Miss — er — Miss——'

'Kitchell,' supplied Lash with something of a snap.

Tyson turned to scowl at him and said: 'At least there's nothing to stop *you* getting back to bed, so don't let us keep you up. You weren't even here when it happened, and I don't know what the hell you're doing over here anyway.'

'Neither do I,' said Lash morosely. But he made no attempt to move, and once again he looked at Dany. A long, thoughtful and faintly uneasy look.

Amalfi, observing it, turned to follow the direction of his gaze, and her eyes narrowed while her charming, curving mouth was suddenly less charming as the red lips tightened into a line that was almost hard. She had not looked at Dany directly during the last hour, but she looked now.

Dany was sitting in a huddled and childish attitude that should have been ungraceful, but was not, for it revealed the fact that her figure was slim and her legs were long and lovely. She had done something, too, to her hair. Brushed it back and got rid of those distressing curls — and discarded her spectacles. Without them she looked absurdly young. Young enough to make Amalfi disquietingly conscious of her own age, and a crease furrowed her white forehead. She turned back sharply to look at Lash, but Lash was studying the carpet again and appeared to be immersed in his own thoughts which, judging from his expression, were not pleasant.

Eduardo too had looked at Dany: and from Dany to Amalfi Gordon. And his dark eyes were all at once intensely alert and curiously wary. He said abruptly, as though replying to Tyson's question:

'Then I think I go to my bed. You are right. No one will wish to ask me questions, and I feel that it may be I intrude.

177

This Miss Bates — she has been known to you for many years, perhaps? *Allora* — it is very sad for you. I feel for you so much. You excuse me, Lorraine?'

He kissed her hand, and then Amalfi's — though with less than his usual lover-like gallantry — and having conveyed his sympathy to Tyson in an eloquent look, returned to his own room. But no one else appeared to feel called upon to follow his example; not even Larry Dowling, who could certainly not have considered himself an old friend of the family: and they were all still there when at long last Nigel returned with the doctor and an Indian Chief Inspector of Police.

The proceedings after that had been mercifully brief. The doctor's verdict had confirmed their own, and it was only too easy to see how the accident had occurred.

Miss Bates, descending the staircase in the dark, had either felt faint or misjudged a step and stumbled, and falling over the edge of the balustrade on to the verandah below had broken her neck. It was as simple, and as shocking, as that.

Tyson had done most of the talking and shown them where the body had lain, and Dany had not been called upon to say very much. The doctor had seen Gussie and prescribed rest and, if necessary, another sedative, and he and the Inspector, having assisted in carrying Millicent's body to the waiting ambulance, had expressed their sympathy and left.

The moon was down and in the east the sky was already beginning to grow pale with the first far-away hint of dawn when Dany climbed in under her mosquito-net at last. Her sheets were crumpled and her pillow still bore the impression of Millicent Bates' head. But no one had thought to suggest that she sleep anywhere else, and she was too tired to care very much that she must sleep where Millicent's dead body had lain. Too tired to care very much about anything ...

She slept so soundly that she did not hear the gentle tap of the house-servant who attempted to bring her a tea tray at eight o'clock, or, an hour later, Lorraine's voice outside her locked door, inquiring if she were awake yet. And it was, finally, Lash who awakened her.

He banged on her bedroom door and went on banging with increasing loudness until she opened it, and when he saw her there, drowsy and bewildered, he said with inexplicable fervour: 'Thank God for that!'

'For what?' asked Dany, blinking at him. 'Is anything the matter?'

'Apparently not,' said Lash, who was looking oddly white and strained. 'But when you didn't come down, and Lorraine said your door was locked and she could get no answer out of you, I thought maybe I'd better come up and make sure.'

'Of what?' inquired Dany, puzzled.

'That you were really only asleep. I guess that lousy business last night was an accident all right, but all the same——'

'*Miss Bates*——!' gasped Dany, recollection hitting her like a blow in the face. 'I — I'd forgotten. She — Oh, Lash! Oh *poor* Miss Bates. Poor Mrs Bingham ... Is she all right?'

'Mrs Bingham? I guess so. She seems to have recovered enough to eat a fairly hearty breakfast, judging from the tray that went up. How about you? Are you thinking of coming down any time?'

'Of course. Is it late?'

'Just after ten.'

'Ten! Good heavens!'

The door slammed in his face, and a silvery voice from half-way down the verandah said: 'Serenading your secretary, Lash darling?'

Amalfi walked towards him and smiled sweetly up into his face; but above the lovely laughing curve of her mouth her green eyes were cold and steady and held no trace of amusement, and looking down into them Lash was conscious of a sudden sharp sense of shock, as though he had walked unwarily into some solid object in the dark.

179

He had not known that Amalfi could look like that while smiling like that, and it left him feeling uneasy and strangely unsure of himself. He said defensively, answering her question: 'Strictly in the way of business.'

'Really?' Amalfi's voice was as warmly sweet as her smile. 'And is a lace and nylon wrap her normal working dress? What fun you business men must have!'

She laughed her lovely laugh, and Lash was startled to find himself angry in a way that he had never been angry before.

He looked at Amalfi for a long moment; seeing her as someone he did not know at all, and noticing many things that he had never noticed before: the years that had been so skilfully held at bay; the ice that could glitter in those cool, mermaid eyes and the malice that could speak in that warm caressing voice. The steel that lay concealed behind that charming, irresponsible, childish sweetness . . .

Amalfi's long lashes fluttered and dropped, and when they lifted again her eyes were softly appealing and her voice coaxed. 'I'm dreadfully jealous, darling!'

'Are you?' said Lash grimly. 'It must make a nice change.' He turned away from her and went down the curving stair to the courtyard without troubling to see whether she were following or not.

Mr Cardew of the police, his peaceful Sabbath rudely interrupted, called again that morning at the House of Shade, and Tyson took him up to see the scene of the accident.

Mr Cardew commented unfavourably on the extremely inadequate balustrades, pronounced the staircases to be dangerous and suggested that iron rails of a reasonable height should be added at the earliest possible moment, and returned to the city taking Tyson, Dany and Gussie Bingham with him, where there had been certain depressing formalities to be gone through in connection with the death of Millicent Bates.

His office was in a tall, square building, four storeys high and

180

facing the sea, with magnificent carved doors and a clock tower. The Bet-el-Ajaib, the 'House of Wonders'; once a palace built by the famous Sultan, Seyyid Barghash-bin-Saïd, and now doing duty as the Secretariat.

The House of Wonders had been built many years later than the House of Shade, and though on a far larger scale, its design was similar: the rooms with their tiers of verandahs being built about a central courtyard. Except that here the courtyard was not open to the sky, but closed over with a glass roof in the manner of a railway station.

Dany had left Tyson and his sister talking to Mr Cardew, and had gone out to stand on the steps and look out towards the harbour where the clove ship for Pemba lay at anchor, and to gaze at the three ancient guns that stood before the Bet-el-Ajaib: cannon that were stamped with the arms of Portugal, and were part of the booty taken by the Persians at the fall of Ormuz.

She had been tracing the worn inscriptions on the old sun-baked metal when a shadow fell across the cannon, and she looked up to see the Arab who had been on the Nairobi plane with them on the previous day, and whom Nigel had introduced as Seyyid Omar-bin-Sultan.

Seyyid Omar's excellent teeth flashed white in his olive-skinned face, and he bowed and said: 'Good morning, Miss Kitchell. How pleasant to meet you again so soon. You have started your sight-seeing already, I see. Are you admiring our guns? They are very old. Perhaps four hundred years and more.'

'Yes, I know,' said Dany. 'I read about them before I came here. What does that inscription on them say? It's Arabic, isn't it?'

'Persian,' said Seyyid Omar; and traced the graceful characters with one slim brown finger ...

'In the Name of God and by the Grace of Mahomed and Ali, convey to the True Believers who have assembled together for

181

war, the Good Tiding of Success and Victory ... During the reign of Shah Abbas, Sajawi, King of the Earth and of Time, whose Power is ever increasing ...'

His finger slowed and stopped, and he did not read the rest of the long inscription, but looking down at it, repeated in a low voice that held a curious thrill of awe (and perhaps of envy?) that magnificent, arrogant title: *'King of the Earth, and of Time ...'*

'That's wonderful,' said Dany, charmed by the cadence of the words. 'Thank you.'

Seyyid Omar dropped his hand swiftly and smiled at her, and his voice was casual and polite again.

'Yes, that is a fine title, is it not? But there are none to hold it now. Our great days have gone — and our court poets — and who knows when they will return again? But what are you doing alone here, Miss Kitchell? Do you go sight-seeing by yourself?'

'No. I'm afraid I'm not sight-seeing this morning. We — that is Mr Frost and Mrs Bingham and myself, had to come in on — on business.'

'Oh?' Seyyid Omar's expressive brows lifted. 'That sounds dull. I had hoped that your first day in Zanzibar would be more entertaining. I wish that I might offer to show you something of the town, but I myself am also here to keep a business appointment. With the police.'

'The police?' Dany looked startled. 'Why — why so are we. With Mr Cardew.'

'Ah! You too. It is because of the death of an acquaintance of mine, I think? Salim Abeid, who died at Mombasa Airport yesterday. Well, I do not expect that you can give them any more assistance than I can.'

Salim Abeid ... Dany heard the name with a sense of shock, for Millicent's death had pushed that other tragedy into the back of her mind. But now she was reminded of it again; and reminded too that she had seen Salim Abeid talking to this man in the shadow of a wing of the Nairobi West Airport barely an hour before he had died.

'Probably a political murder,' Tyson had said. Jembe had made many enemies among the aristocracy and the rich land-owners — such men, presumably, as Seyyid Omar-bin-Sultan. And Seyyid Omar had been on the same plane ...

The midday sun that beat down upon the entrance to the House of Wonders was very hot, but a little cold shiver prickled down Dany's spine, and she remembered innumerable stories that she had read of the cruelty of the East: stories stretching from the Arabian Nights down to the recent atrocities of the Mau Mau.

The Isle of Cloves, as its history showed, was not unacquainted with violence and cruelty, and the murder of a rabble-rouser would probably be considered as of little account today as the death of a dozen slaves in the days when the dhows of the slave traders had moored where the little Pemba-bound steamer now lay at anchor, and their crews had tossed out the corpses from among their human cargoes on to those same beaches.

Dany shivered, and Seyyid Omar, observing it, said solicitously: 'It has troubled you. I am sorry that your first morning in our island should be spoiled by such a thing: the death of a man you had probably not even met. Though I believe he was a fellow-passenger of yours from London, was he not?'

The question was asked quite casually and as though it were a matter of no account, but he waited for an answer.

Dany said: 'Yes. But I didn't actually meet him.'

'But Mr Dowling did,' said Seyyid Omar gently. 'And of course your — host's secretary had met him before. Mr Ponting. I am surprised that Mr Cardew should not have wished to see them, rather than you and Mrs Bingham.'

'Oh, but we aren't here about that,' Dany hastened to assure him. 'There was a dreadful accident at *Kivulimi* last night. Mrs

Bingham's companion, Miss Bates, fell from one of the staircases in the dark, and broke her neck.'

'You mean — she is dead?' inquired Seyyid Omar sharply.

'Yes.'

The monosyllable had a flat finality, and suddenly Millicent was dead. Really dead. Until then it had been unreal: a tale that someone had told her and which she had not quite believed. But now it was true . . .

She heard Seyyid Omar draw in his breath with a little hiss between his teeth. 'That is terrible! I am sorry. I am most sorry. This has been a sad arrival for you indeed. An ill-omened one. I can only hope that it will not give you a dislike of our island and make you wish to leave.'

Dany had no time for a reply, for at that moment Tyson and his sister joined them, and Seyyid Omar offered condolences and sympathy.

They stood in the white glare of the sunlight against a tropical background of flame trees, hard shadows and sauntering white-robed men with ebony faces, and spoke of Millicent: Tyson, burly, bearded and frankly impatient; Gussie looking suddenly ten years older — a lined, shocked, shrunken shadow of the assured and talkative matron of yesterday; Dany with her dyed hair and spectacles, and Seyyid Omar-bin-Sultan, suitably concerned and gravely sympathetic. *Requiem for a British Spinster* . . .

Seyyid Omar refused an invitation to accompany them to the English Club for lunch, and Tyson, Gussie and Dany returned to the car, and were driven through the narrow streets to a tall old building that fronted the sea and managed to epitomize all that is conveyed by the words 'Outposts of Empire'.

'The doors of all these houses are so lovely,' said Dany, pausing to look back along the white-walled street down which they had come. 'All that carving, and those huge brass spikes.'

'Those were to keep the war elephants from battering in the doors,' said Tyson. 'Useful, as well as ornamental.'

'*Elephants?* What nonsense! You couldn't possibly squeeze an elephant into one of these streets, let alone turn it end on to a door!'

'Yes, there is that,' said Tyson. 'But it's a pretty story all the same. And that really is why Arab doors had those spikes on them once. The days of the war elephants have gone, but the design has persisted. And you're right about the streets. Hell to drive through. In most of 'em, if a car is coming one way and a kitten the other, one of them is going to have to stop. And as this is Zanzibar, it's the car that would give way to the kitten. A pleasant crowd. A very pleasant crowd.'

Nigel joined them at the Club, and they ate a sturdy British meal that made no concessions to the climate, sitting in a huge, echoing, sparsely populated dining-room under the ceaseless whirr of electric fans.

Neither Gussie nor Tyson had much to say, and it fell to Nigel and Dany to sustain some semblance of conversation. But as Nigel was as voluble as ever, Dany's share was mercifully limited to adding an occasional yes or no at reasonable intervals.

Her mind was on other things than Roman society scandals, and she did not perceive their trend until Nigel said: '——the old Marchesa, that's Eduardo's grandmother, pulled *every* string within reach — and has she a reach! And so of course that was *that* as far as poor Eddie was concerned. *Too* frustrating for him. And then darling Lorraine asks him to look up Elf in London, and *here* we go again! Another *grande passion* that is doomed to crack on the same old rocks. Too awful for *both* of them, when you come to think of it.'

'Why?' inquired Dany perfunctorily.

'Oh, but my *dear*! It's obvious. Poor, poor Elf — so romantic and unbusiness-like! Throwing away the substance for an *utter* shadow; did she but know. There she was, all set to bridge the dollar gap by rushing Holden Jnr to the nearest registrar, when who should happen along but Eduardo. All Latin charm, a

185

Marquis to boot, and apparently *solid* with lire. *Naturally* the poor sweet began to waver. Well, I mean — there *is* a certain glamour about being able to embroider authentic little coronets on one's smalls, and plain "Mrs Holden" doesn't carry *quite* the same simple charm as "the Signora Marchesa di Chiago". Provided the lire and the lovely green-backs balance, of course! But then they don't. Someone really ought to break it to darling Elf.'

'Someone has,' said Tyson briefly, entering the conversation for the first time.

Nigel registered surprise. 'You? Now that *is* a relief — though I did begin to wonder last night if someone hadn't perhaps dropped the *merest* hint. I hope you mean to do the same for poor Eddie. Just a whisper of warning?'

'Eddie,' said Tyson shortly, 'can look after himself.'

Gussie helped herself to a solid wedge of suet pudding, and said: 'What are you two talking about? Warn who about what?'

'Eduardo;' said Nigel, 'about our dear Amalfi. That she may look *stimulatingly* solvent, but that it's all done by mirrors. Or should one be *really* catty, and say *paste*? Excellent imitations of course — she had them made in Paris. But I happen to know that she popped the diamonds and all Chubby's emeralds. The family were furious — my dear, *furious*! But of course there was nothing they could do about it. And after all, one *does* sympathize with the poor sweet. She had every reason to believe that she'd be left madly well off, and it must have been too infuriating to find an absolute regiment of assorted relatives all queueing up for their cut — and getting it! *Too* soul-curdling. One wonders if it was *worth* it? No thanks, I don't feel I could *face* suet pudding. I think I'll try the cheese——'

Millicent was buried late that afternoon, and the entire house-party attended, with the exception of Amalfi, who complained of a headache, and added that in any case she was allergic to funerals.

186

It was a brief enough service; and to Dany, at least, a tragic one. Not because she had taken any special liking to Miss Bates, who had been almost a stranger to her, but because she could not forget that Millicent Bates had despised all things Oriental and had so disliked the East. Yet now she would never leave it. Alien and alone she must lie in this hot foreign soil, within sound of the surf and the trade winds and the rustling palms, until the Day of Judgement. Poor Miss Bates, who had been so deeply rooted in the life of one small English market town, and who had not wanted to come to Zanzibar.

15

It was a silent and distinctly subdued party who assembled for dinner that night, and afterwards they had gone out to sit on the terrace and made desultory conversation, and no one had suggested dancing.

Amalfi appeared to have recovered from her headache, and in deference to the memory of Miss Bates she wore a deceptively simple dress of black chiffon which lent her a frail and wistful look and made her white skin appear even whiter by contrast.

Both Lorraine and Gussie also wore black. Presumably for the same reason. But as Dany did not possess a black dress (Aunt Harriet having held pronounced views on the unsuitability of black for the young), she had put on the same grey magnolia-appliquéd one that she had worn the previous evening. And it was while Abdurahman, the head houseboy, was clearing away the coffee cups and liqueur glasses, and Nigel was languidly inquiring whether anyone felt like a game of bridge, that she thrust an idle hand into one of the wide pockets that decorated the skirt and touched a crumpled piece of paper.

Dany drew it out and regarded it with faint surprise, wondering how it had got there. It was a half sheet of writing paper, roughly torn along one edge, and flattening out its creases she held it so that the moonlight fell full on it, and read the few typewritten words it bore without at first comprehending their meaning.

May I please speak to you. I am in great trouble, and need advice. Could you be very kind and make it after half-past twelve, as it is rather a private matter, and I do not want other people to know.

188

My room is underneath yours, and I will wait up. Please come.
A.K.

What on earth——? thought Dany, looking at it with wrinkled brows. She turned it over, but there was no more of it. The writer had presumably meant to add something else to it, but had thought better of it and thrown it away. But how had it got into her pocket, and when?

And then, as suddenly and as shockingly as though someone had treated her as Amalfi had treated Gussie's hysterics and thrown a pint of ice-cold water in her face, she remembered——

It was the piece of paper that had fluttered against her skirt when she had knelt above Millicent's body last night, and which she had snatched up and stuffed into her pocket without thinking. But it was more than that. It was proof of murder.

A fragment of conversation from the previous evening repeated itself in her brain as though it were a gramophone playing a record: *'A third what?' 'Murder of course, darling. Things always go in threes ...'* They had gone in threes. There had been a third murder. And an attempt at a fourth — her own. For the note was neither unfinished nor unsigned. It had been written on her typewriter — Miss Kitchell's typewriter — and signed with her initials: Miss Kitchell's initials. And if it had been found——

A clammy mixture of nausea and cold fear engulfed Dany, drowning out the moonlight and the sound of the casual, idle voices. She was caught in a horrible, clinging spider-web, and however much she twisted and turned she could not escape, because there would always be another strand waiting for her ready to wind softly and terrifyingly about her until at last she would be bound and helpless.

Hysteria rose in her, prompting her to leap to her feet and scream and scream, as Gussie had done. To run across the terrace and through the moonlight and out into the white dusty road, and to go on running until she dropped. She fought it down, driving her fingernails into her palms and biting her lip until

189

the blood came. And then a hand came out of the fog and closed over hers. A flesh and blood hand that was firm and real in the midst of miasma and unreality, and that steadied the spinning world and brought it back to some sort of sanity.

The fog cleared and the moonlight was bright again and Lash was standing in front of her; his body a barrier between her and the seven other people on the terrace.

He said: 'Come and take a walk down to the beach. I haven't had the chance of a word with you all day, and there are one or two things that I'd like to go over. You'll excuse us, Lorraine?'

He did not wait for permission, but jerking Dany to her feet he drew her arm through his, and holding it hard against him walked her away across the terrace and down the steps into the ink-black shadows of the tree-filled garden, where he began to talk of business matters and of names that meant nothing to her; continuing to do so as they passed along the shadowy, flower-scented paths, and leaving the garden by a door in the seaward wall, walked down a steep, rocky path to the shore.

The beach was deserted, and nothing moved on it save the quiet tide and a host of ghostly little sand crabs that scuttled to and fro as silently as moths. There were rocks at each end of it: tall rocks of wind-carved, water-worn coral that stood dark against the moon-washed sky and threw sharp-edged shadows on the white sand. But Lash avoided them, and keeping to the open beach stopped near the edge of the tide, where no one could approach unseen and they could not be overheard.

Releasing his grip on Dany's arm he turned her so that she faced him, but he did not lower his voice, or make any attempt to change its pitch, and anyone watching him from the shadows would have supposed him to be merely continuing the conversation he had started in the garden.

'What happened, honey? What was on that paper? Someone write you an anonymous letter?'

190

Dany held it out to him without words, and saw his face set into harsh and unfamiliar lines as he read it.

After a moment or two he said quite softly: 'Did someone put this in your pocket?'

'No,' said Dany in a whisper. 'I found it last night. It was on the verandah ... by ... near Miss Bates. She must have been holding it when ... I put it in my pocket, and I didn't think of it again until — until just now when I felt it, and took it out, and ... read it.'

Lash was silent for a long time, looking at the piece of paper in his hand, and at last Dany said: 'It does mean — what I think it means, doesn't it?'

'Yes,' said Lash, still softly, and without pretending to misunderstand her: his voice strangely at variance with the ugly grimness of his face and his taut hands.

'What are we going to do? Are you — are you going to tell the police?'

'I don't know. I shall have to figure it out. What did you do with that typewriter? Where is it?'

'In my room.'

'Then this probably wasn't written on it; which may help.'

'But it was,' said Dany with a catch in her voice. 'I thought one of the servants must have been playing with it — the lid wasn't on properly, and there was a bit of paper in it: the other half of that.'

'When was this?' asked Lash sharply.

'Last night, when I went up to bed.'

'Did you touch it?'

'Yes. I tried the typewriter to see if it was all right, and it was, and I took the paper out. It's in the waste-paper basket.'

Lash let out his breath in a little sigh. 'So your fingerprints will be on it. And they're on this too. A nice, neat, slick little fool-proof frame-up! Dear God, what have I let you in for?'

He crushed the piece of paper savagely in one clenched hand

191

and turned to stare blindly out at the shimmering sea, and Dany saw the muscles along his jaw twitch and tighten. He said, half under his breath and as though he were speaking to himself: 'I ought to have taken you straight to the police — back in London. It might have been a little sticky, but no more than that. Instead of which I have to let you in for a piece of crazy, drunken lunacy that——'

He made a violent despairing gesture, and Dany said quickly: 'Don't, Lash! It wasn't your fault. It was mine for not realizing that you—— Oh, what does it matter? We can go to the police now.'

Lash turned quickly to face her, his eyes blank with bitterness. 'No, we can't. That's the hell of it. We shall have to let the Bates woman's death stay on the books as an accident. There's no other way out.'

'But Lash——'

'There's no "but" about it!' interrupted Lash savagely. 'I may have been behaving like a certifiable moron of late, but I'm still capable of adding two and two together and coming up with the correct answer. That dame was killed because she talked too much; and but for the mercy of Providence, this bit of paper would have been found on her or near her. You'd have been asked to explain it — and a few other things as well! Such as how did the other half of it get into your room if you didn't write it, and what the heck were you doing fully dressed at least an hour after everyone else was in bed? What *were* you doing, by the way? *Were* you waiting for her?'

'Lash!' Dany flinched as though he had struck her.

'I didn't mean "Did you kill her?"' said Lash impatiently. 'Or even "Did you type that note?" Of course you didn't. But did she say anything about dropping in to see you?'

'No.'

'Then why hadn't you been to bed? What had you been doing?'

'Nothing. I just didn't feel sleepy; that was all. I suppose I

192

didn't want to put the light out, and so I kept putting off going to bed. And then I heard a nightjar again, but it wasn't a nightjar——'

Dany shivered, remembering that sound, and said with an effort: 'It was Miss Bates. She must have cried out as she fell. And then I heard a thud ...'

She told him about that, and about finding Millicent's body and the scrap of paper, and about Larry Dowling, who had been walking in the garden so short a time before.

'Dowling,' said Lash slowly.

He appeared to be turning something over in his mind, and then he shook his head, and abandoning Larry Dowling, said: 'Didn't you hear any other sound at all? No footsteps? Nothing? If someone waited for her to come down those stairs, and then pushed her off them, you'd surely have heard footsteps.'

'No, I didn't. I didn't hear anything else. Just a sort of screech and a thud: I told you. There wasn't any other ... No. No, I'm wrong. There was another sound. A queer soft grating sort of noise like——' She wrinkled her brows, trying to recall what it was like and put it into words, but gave it up. 'I don't know. But it wasn't footsteps.'

Lash dismissed it with a shrug. 'Let it go. But the fact remains that you were up and dressed, and it wouldn't have looked too good if that note had been found, because it would have helped back up the theory that you wrote it. Which wouldn't have been a criminal thing to have done, and would only have meant that you'd asked Miss Bates to come to see you, and that she'd slipped and fallen while she was on her way down. But the moment you denied having written it the thing would have begun to look screwy, and the chances are that you wouldn't have been believed. They'd have wanted to know why you were denying it when all the evidence supported it; and the next thing you know they'd have found out that you are no more Miss Kitchell than I am, and that you'd skipped out of England on a false passport to avoid a murder rap. It wouldn't have sounded so good, and though maybe you could have talked your way out of one of those situations, I doubt if you could talk yourself out of both. Which is why that accident last night is going to have to stay just the way it is — an accident! Anything else is too darned dangerous. And now the sooner we get rid of this particular piece of poison, the better.'

He took a cigarette lighter out of his pocket, snapped it open and held one corner of the crumpled type-written note to the flame, and Dany said on a gasp: 'Lash you can't — it's evidence!'

'Sure. But it won't be in a minute. And without it that other bit of paper in your room won't mean a thing, and there'll be nothing to connect you with Miss Bates.'

He watched the small scrap of paper that had lured Millicent to her death blacken and curl and burst into flame, and when he could hold it no longer he dropped it and ground the burnt fragments into the sand with his heel. He was silent for a moment or two, scowling down at the small dark depression that his heel had made, and then he said slowly: 'I wish I could take you out of here, but I can't. If we make a break for it, it would only look worse. And yet it's a risk either way. Listen, Dany, I want you to promise me something.'

'What?' inquired Dany in an uncertain voice.

'That you won't ever leave your room at night, for any reason at all. That you'll lock yourself in, and if anyone taps on your door and pushes a note under it asking you to go anywhere, even if it's signed by your mother and written in her own hand-writing, you won't even touch it. Give it to me in the morning. And don't go off on any *tête-à-tête* expeditions with anyone — unless it's me! Get it?'

He smiled at her, but it was a smile that did not reach his eyes, and Dany said with a catch in her voice: 'But why should anyone want to harm me? Or try to pin things on me? It was

194

different before — when I had that map or clue or whatever it was. But now it's been stolen. Whoever wanted it has got it. Why doesn't it all stop? Why did anyone have to murder Miss Bates?'

Lash said: 'Because she insisted on telling us that she was in the neighbourhood of this solicitor's house around the time that the guy who rubbed him out would have been on his way in to do the job. That same guy happens to know that you were around too; and he's giving you a strong hint not to talk, or it will be the worse for you! Either that, or he's laying on a useful scapegoat in case he should ever need one. A hell of a lot of guys will do a hell of a lot of lousy things for the sake of three million — take it from me! That's why you're going to watch your step from now on. And I *mean* watch it! We ought to have the cops down on us in a day or two, and after that it's their headache.'

Dany twisted her hands together and said on a sob: 'Lash — I'm frightened.'

'You're not the only one!' retorted Lash with strong feeling. 'I've never been so scared in all my life. I do not relish the idea that one of that bunch back there on the terrace makes a hobby of murder, and I wish I had a gun.'

'But it can't be one of us! It can't be!'

'Don't be silly, Dany. It can't be anyone else. It's one of six people. You, me, Amalfi, Gussie Bingham, the Latin lover or Larry Dowling. Take your choice!'

Dany shivered and Lash reached out suddenly and pulled her into his arms, holding her against him and ruffling the outrageous red curls with his free hand. He said: 'I know, honey. But it'll all be the same in a hundred years.'

Dany made a sobbing and unintelligible remark into his shoulder, and he put his hand under her chin and lifted it. 'What was that one? I didn't get it.'

'I said "be c-careful of my s-spectacles".'

'I never liked them anyway,' said Lash, removing them and kissing her lightly. At least, that is what he had meant it to be, but it did not turn out like that. It began lightly enough, but ended very differently, and when at last he lifted his head he was astounded to find himself feeling breathless and shaken.

'That your first kiss?' he inquired, holding her away from him.

'Yes,' said Dany dazedly; her face bemused and beautiful in the white moonlight. 'How did you know?'

'I get around,' said Lash dryly. 'Well, it's going to be the last for tonight, because if I do that again there's no knowing where we'll end up.'

He stooped and retrieved the spectacles that had fallen unheeded to the ground, and having dusted the sand off them, replaced them carefully.

'And that'll be all for today, Miss Kitchell. I guess we'd better get back to the house and see you safely locked in for the night. And with reference to that last item on the agenda, you might consider letting me have a copy of it tomorrow — in triplicate.'

He walked her back towards the house across the white beach and through the door into the garden, where they encountered Larry Dowling loitering in the shadows by the edge of a shallow pool set about with stone birds and spider lilies. They might have passed without knowing that he was there, except that a reflection moved slightly in the water, and there was a faint smell of cigarette smoke.

Lash had stopped and said: 'di Chiago?' and Larry had moved out into the moonlight and said: 'No. But that was quick of you. It's one of his cigarettes. Can't say I like 'em much: give me gaspers every time. Nice on the beach?'

'Yes, thanks,' said Lash curtly. 'You on your way there?'

'No. Just strolling around,' said Larry. 'Just strolling around.'

Lash said: 'Don't let us stop you,' and went on up the path that led to the terrace.

There were only two people on the terrace: Amalfi and

Eduardo, who appeared to be quarrelling. They broke off on hearing footsteps, and Amalfi said with an edge to her voice: 'Oh, it's you. I hope you had a nice brisk businesslike session and got everything straightened out?'

'We did,' said Lash amiably. 'Thanks for asking.'

Amalfi laughed. 'Gussie was right: you're nothing but an old slave-driver. I really do believe that "Business First" is your motto.'

'The Americans!' said Eduardo. 'So efficient, so ruthless — so eye-on-the-ball. It is wonderful.'

Amalfi said hastily: 'Lorrie said to say good night to you, Lash; she and Gussie both thought they could do with an early night. She wanted to know if you'd like to go along to the fish market tomorrow morning. Gussie wants to see it. She says if she mopes around here she'll go mad, and Lorrie said that if you'd like to tag along you'll have to have breakfast at eight, and there'll be a car going in immediately afterwards. However, I told her I didn't think it sounded at all in your line.'

'Then you thought wrong,' said Lash, still amiably. 'I like fish. Where's Tyson? Is he making an early night of it too?'

'No. He and Nigel are as bad as you. They're doing a bit of work for a change.'

'It won't hurt 'em,' said Lash, and turned to Dany. 'That reminds me: I've got one or two things to do myself. I guess I'd better borrow your typewriter, Ada. I'll go right on up with you now and get it, if that's all right with you?'

'Yes, of course,' said Dany.

She moved towards the door, and Lash was following her when Amalfi spoke softly, addressing no one in particular: 'I do hope this means that Ada's mumps are better?'

16

'I have always considered,' remarked Nigel, holding a delicately scented handkerchief to his nose, 'that a fishmonger's emporium ranks slightly above a morgue, and only a point below a butcher's shop and an abattoir. All those slippery white stomachs and cold coddy eyes glaring at one. *Utterly* emetic. But just look at these colours! *Pure* Roerich. *Do* let's have some of those turquoise-blue fish with coral spots — or what about these heavenly shocking pink ones? You know, this might almost reconcile one to doing the weekly shopping.'

'But can one really *eat* the things?' inquired Gussie, apprehensively eyeing the fish in question. 'Lorraine, you're *surely* not going to buy those pink creatures?'

'Changu, Gussie. They're delicious. Wait until you taste them!'

'Well, if you say so,' said Gussie in a fading voice.

The fish market was a riot of noise and colour, and the variegated and vividly patterned clothing worn by the housewives of a dozen different nationalities was rivalled in both colour and design by the wares they were bargaining for.

It was as though the exotic contents of a tropical aquarium had been emptied onto the crude trestle tables, the floor and the wooden-sided pens and tubs: fish of every conceivable shape and colour, the beautiful jostling the sinister — such things as sting rays, hammer-headed sharks, cuttle fish and octopuses.

Competing with it in the matter of colour, while greatly improving on it in the way of smell, were the stalls of the open market where fruit and grain and vegetables were sold. A glowing,

198

aromatic medley of oranges, limes, bananas, coconuts, cloves and chillies; yams, pawpaws, sweet potatoes, piles of green vegetables and flat wicker baskets full of assorted grains.

'What's that you've been buying?' inquired Lash, coming across Dany standing before a fruit stall with her hands full of greenish-yellow objects.

'Mangoes. I said I only wanted one — just to try. But it seems they don't sell them in ones. Only by the basket, and I couldn't possibly cope with that many. But luckily Seyyid Omar came along, and he—— You do know each other, don't you? This is Seyyid Omar-bin-Sultan; he was on the plane with us.'

'Yeah, I remember,' said Lash, shaking hands. 'I'm very pleased to know you. I'm Lash Holden. I don't think we actually met.'

'You're an American?' said Seyyid Omar.

'That's right. The Country of the Future.'

'Of the present, surely?' corrected Seyyid Omar with a faint smile and a slight emphasis on the noun.

'Maybe,' said Lash lightly, and turned to regard Dany with some suspicion. 'Say, you aren't going to start in eating those things right here, are you?'

'Where else?'

'Well, in your bath, I guess. It looks a messy business. And anyway, you can't possibly eat six mangoes.'

'Just watch me.'

'Not on your sweet life!' said Lash; and arbitrarily confiscated her booty.

Seyyid Omar laughed and said: 'It is plain that Miss Kitchell has not yet tried to eat a mango. A plate and a knife are a help. Will you allow me to lend you one? My house is only a short way from here, and I know that my wife would be very pleased to meet you. If you would accompany me, you may eat your mangoes in more comfort.'

Dany threw a quick look at Lash, and Seyyid Omar, intercepting it, made him a slight smiling bow that included him in the invitation.

'Sure,' said Lash slowly. 'We'd be very pleased to. Here — would you mind holding these for a minute?'

He unloaded the mangoes on Seyyid Omar and strode off across between the stalls to where Nigel was assisting Lorraine in the selection of pineapples, and returned a minute or two later to say that that was O.K. and that the others would be going on to the English Club later in the morning, and would meet them there.

'I will drive you over,' promised Seyyid Omar, and led the way out of the market and towards the harbour.

Seyyid Omar's house was in a narrow street that was a cavern of cool shadows slashed by an occasional hot, hard shaft of sunlight: a huge old Arab house, four storeys high and colour-washed in saffron and blue.

A magnificent brass-studded door with elaborately carved lintels and architraves opened into a stone-paved hall and a central courtyard surrounded by rising tiers of pillared verandahs: a house that was almost a duplicate of Tyson's, though larger.

Seyyid Omar led the way up two flights of stairs to a room on the second floor, where there were latticed windows looking out over the old stone-built town of Zanzibar to where the open sea lay blue and dazzling in the morning sunlight.

A white-robed servant brought sherbet, fruit and cigarettes, and their host's pretty wife instructed Dany in the best way — or the least messy one — of eating a mango.

Seyyide Zuhra-binti-Salem was on first sight a character straight out of the Arabian Nights: Scheherazade herself, or one of Bluebeard's lovely wives. A slender, charming, dark-eyed young woman with blue-black hair and a complexion of pale ivory. It was something of a shock to discover that this enchanting creature not only spoke six languages besides her own, but was entitled, if she so wished, to write the letters B.A. after her name.

It altered all Dany's preconceived notions on the subject of 'ladies of the harem' to find that the young wife of an Arab in Zanzibar was infinitely better educated than herself, or, for that matter, than the majority of European women with whom she had so far come into contact.

It proved to be an entertaining, stimulating and surprising visit; in more ways than one. Time slipped past unnoticed while Zuhra laughed and talked of Oxford and Paris and the Sorbonne, and her husband told them enthralling tales of the island, and volunteered to take them that very afternoon, in the cool of the day, to see the underground wells and the ruins of the haunted palace of Dunga.

Conversation was easy and animated until the subject of the two tragedies that had marred the arrival of Lorraine's guests was raised. It was Lash who had introduced it, and his inquiry as to whether there had been any further developments in relation to the death of Salim Abeid was greeted by an odd little pause. Not long enough to be uncomfortable, but nevertheless definite enough to break the pleasant ease that had prevailed during the last hour and a half.

'Ah,' said Seyyid Omar thoughtfully. 'Jembe — "the thin man".'

He did not reply to the question, but asked one of his own. 'Did you know him?'

'No,' said Lash. 'But he was on the same plane out from London. I understand he was kind of well known in your island. A public character.'

'He wished to be one,' said Seyyid Omar dryly. 'That is not quite the same thing.'

'I take it you knew him?'

'Yes. Slightly.'

Seyyid Omar's expressive brown hands sketched a small deprecatory gesture as though he would have preferred to end the conversation, but Lash did not choose to take the hint. He said: 'Tell us about him. Would you have said that he was a man who made enemies?'

'He was a hireling of Moscow — and of Egypt,' said Zuhra gently.

She disregarded another faint gesture of her husband's as Lash had done, and said: 'Oh, he did not call himself that. He called himself a Democrat — which is Soviet double-talk for the same thing. He wished to found a Single Party in Zanzibar. In other words, a dictatorship. With himself, of course, as the dictator. It was very simple. He had a certain following, for there are, everywhere, dissatisfied, embittered or envious people who get pleasure out of tearing down what they cannot build. And also poor people and unfortunate people and ignorant people, who should be pitied and helped, not exploited — but who are so easy to exploit. Here in Zanzibar we have, perhaps, less of such people than in other places; but enough to cause trouble. He will be no loss.'

Lash said casually, watching the smoke of his cigarette: 'I guess it must have been a political murder. Sounds that way.'

Seyyid Omar shrugged. 'Perhaps. It is always a possibility.'

'But you don't believe it,' said Lash. 'Now I wonder why?'

'I did not say so.'

Lash gave him a slanting look. 'Not in words. Why don't you believe it?'

Seyyid Omar laughed and threw up his hands. 'You are very persistent Mr Holden. Why does the death of Jembe interest you?'

'I guess because it interests your local police to such an extent that I have been requested to stay in Zanzibar for a few days. Just while they make some inquiries. I don't know what that suggests to you, but it suggests quite a few things to me.'

Seyyid Omar rose to replenish Dany's glass, and said lightly: 'Yes, I had heard. I too had an — interview with Mr Cardew yesterday. They seem to think that someone must have stopped to speak to Jembe at the airport, and dropped a pellet in his coffee. Myself, I think it would have taken a brave man or an exceedingly rash one, or else a very stupid one, to do such a thing. Think of the risks of being seen! I cannot believe it was as clumsy as that.' He paused to stub out his cigarette, and added: 'Mr Cardew also told me about the unfortunate tragedy that occurred on the night of your arrival. It must have been very distressing for all of you.'

His face expressed nothing more than polite concern, but there was something in the tone of his voice that made Dany wonder if his linking of those two deaths had been deliberate, and she was conscious of a sudden and urgent sense of unease: as though someone had whispered a warning that she had been unable to catch.

'Nigel Ponting told me in the market this morning,' said Seyyid Omar, 'that she had been with Mr Frost's sister for many years — this Miss Bates. That is sad for Mrs Bingham; to lose a friend and a confidante. Nigel has not been so long with Mr Frost; a few years only, I think; but he could probably tell you more about Jembe than I could. You should ask him. If he does not know he will at least invent something interesting.'

Lash grinned. 'Yeah. You're probably right there. Nigel's a mine of gossip. He ought to be run as a syndicated column. But it's your opinion I'm interested in, not his. You belong here.'

'But is it not one of your sayings that the onlooker sees most of the game?' said Seyyid Omar with a slight smile.

'Meaning that you yourself are right out there with the team?' inquired Lash.

Seyyid Omar laughed and helped himself to another cigarette. He said reflectively, reaching for the match box: 'If you really wish for my opinion, I do not think that Jembe's group were either large enough or important enough to put any other party to the trouble of poisoning him. His was merely a splinter group, and though noisy, a thing of no real weight.'

'Not even worth anyone's while to nip in the bud?' suggested Lash. 'Vested interests, large land-owners and the ruling classes are never very anxious to see the seeds of revolution get sprouting.'

'That is true, of course. But then they never believe it can come to anything. Never. And so they do not even trouble to reach for the weed-killer!'

'You're probably right there,' said Lash. 'Which leaves us with what?'

'For a possible motive for the murder of a man like Jembe?' said Seyyid Omar, striking a match. 'Who can say? Except that as a grave risk was taken, it must have been a strong one. Hate possibly: if it were deep enough and sharp enough. Or money, if it were a large enough sum.'

'Say — three million?' suggested Lash gently.

Seyyid Omar was suddenly very still. So still that he did not seem to breathe, or be aware that he still held a lighted match between his fingers.

It burned down, and he dropped it with a quick gasp of pain and put his foot on the tiny glowing fragment, and Dany stood up hurriedly and said a little breathlessly: 'It must be getting very late. I'm sure we ought to go. What time is it?'

'Just on twelve,' said Lash, rising. 'Yes, I guess we'd better be going. Well, thanks a lot, both of you, for a most enjoyable morning. It's been a great pleasure meeting you, and I hope we'll see more of you. A lot more.'

'I shall call for you this afternoon,' said Seyyid Omar, recovering himself. 'To take you to the wells. And now, if you must go, my car will be waiting below, and the driver will take you to the Club. You will forgive me for not taking you there myself, but I have some things to attend to.'

They took their leave of Zuhra, promising to come again, and went out into the high, shadowed verandah, closing the door behind them. There were no stone jars full of shrubs and creepers here, but in the courtyard below there was a tulip tree and a

204

fountain, and Dany looking down from the verandah edge said: 'Are all the big houses in Zanzibar built like this?'

'To this design?' asked Seyyid Omar. 'No. Very few of them. But it is not surprising that you should ask that, for this house and the one you are living in now were built for the same man, and almost certainly by the same builder. They are probably the oldest houses in Zanzibar. He was a bad character, that old gentleman, but plagued with many wives, so perhaps much may be forgiven him! He came to a bad end, but a richly deserved one — "hoist with his own petard", I think you would say.'

'How?' inquired Dany, intrigued. 'What happened to him?'

'He fell into a trap that he had often laid for others. I will show you. But you must not tell, for it is a secret that very few know. Is that agreed?'

'Yes, of course. It sounds very exciting.'

'I think you will find it so. And instructive.'

Seyyid Omar turned and looked over his shoulder down the length of the verandah, and then down over the balustrade at the storey below. But though they could hear voices and laughter, for the moment there was no one in sight, and he said: 'Quick — while there is no one here.'

He led the way swiftly to the top of the staircase that curved down to the verandah below — a duplicate of the stairs in the House of Shade — and telling them to watch, went to a nearby pillar and stooping down moved something near its base.

There was a slow, soft grating sound; the sound of stone moving on stone; and two of the wide, shallow steps drew back into the wall, leaving a gaping space below the first step so that they were looking down on the stone floor of the verandah, sixteen feet below.

Dany gave a long, helpless gasp that was almost a scream, and Lash caught her by the arm and jerked her back as though he were afraid that she might have walked forward.

Seyyid Omar stooped again, and once more they heard that

soft, rasping scrape, and the yawning gap closed as smoothly as it had opened. The steps were in place once more: solid and seemingly safe, and with nothing to mark them from any other steps.

'It is very ingenious, is it not?' inquired Seyyid Omar softly. 'More so than you would think. Naturally I cannot show you, as it is too dangerous, but when it is open, the first step will tilt when a foot is placed upon it: to ensure that the victim will fall head first, you understand. When that happens the steps go back of their own accord — it is all an ingenious matter of weights and balances — and if it is not done, then one can replace it oneself, as I did. I was sure that you would be interested.'

Lash swung round to stare at him, his mouth a tight line and his grey eyes dangerous, but Seyyid Omar returned his look blandly; the pleasant host, drawing attention to an unusual feature of his house for the entertainment of his guests.

'You will understand,' he said with a smile and a shrug, 'why I do not show many people this. It is always so much safer to keep one's own counsel, do you not think? Shall we go down? You need not be afraid. It is quite safe now.'

He led the way, talking polite trivialities, down the curving stairs to the ground floor and out into the street where a huge white car and an ebony-coloured chauffeur waited to drive them to the English Club.

It was a short enough drive, and during it neither Lash nor Dany spoke, or even looked at each other, and it was not until they were standing in the cool deserted hall of the Club that Lash said tersely: 'Did you move her?'

'Yes. I — I didn't think of that before, but she must have been lying under the staircase when I found her. It was dark and I tried to drag her towards my room. That was why it looked as if — as if——'

'As if she'd fallen over the edge,' finished Lash. 'Well, there's the proof, if we needed it. But at least it couldn't have been

206

pinned on you. You couldn't possibly have known about that devilish booby-trap.'

'Yes, I could,' said Dany, her voice a dry whisper. 'Because I'm Tyson Frost's step-daughter, and it would be difficult to prove that I didn't know. You see, it's sure to be in the book.'

'What book?'

'*The House of Shade*. The one Tyson's uncle wrote. Tyson was talking about it at dinner that night, and he said that there were several copies in the house. There's one in my room. It may have been put there on purpose, so that it would look——'

'Business again?' inquired a charming voice from the staircase, and Amalfi was there: wearing a preposterous rainbow-coloured hat of fringed straw, bought at some shop in Portuguese Street and looking, on Amalfi's golden head, as decorative and enchanting a piece of nonsense as ever came out of Paris.

'No,' said Lash shortly. 'Pleasure. I hope we haven't kept you all waiting?'

'For *hours*, darling! We've all been drinking pints and pints of Pimms. Except Larry, who is being all British-to-the-Backbone on luke-warm beer. Did your fascinating Arab friend introduce you to all the luscious lovelies of his harem? Or don't they have them any more? Nigel says he has a quite ravishing wife, and Eddie's simply pining to meet her. But as it seems that she's got a classical degree, I feel he'd better keep away and keep his illusions.'

Amalfi turned and led the way up to a large high-ceilinged room where the rest of the *Kivulimi* house-party were sitting under whirling electric fans, moodily sipping iced drinks and making no attempt at conversation.

Gussie greeted them with a sombre look and Lorraine with a vague smile, and Nigel said crossly: 'Had I known that you intended to spend the *entire* morning "fraternizing with indigenous personnel" as I believe it is termed among your countrymen, I should have gone home and sent the car back for you. *I* happen

207

to have work to do, even though some people have not. I hope we can go now?'

He sulked the whole way home, but both Dany and Lash had too much on their minds to notice the fact, and Larry Dowling, who was the fourth passenger in their car, took one long reflective look at Dany and also relapsed into silence.

They found Tyson in good spirits but still as averse as ever to discussing any form of business, and on hearing that Lash and Dany were accompanying Seyyid Omar on a sight-seeing expedition that afternoon, he instantly announced that it was a damned good idea and that they could all go: it would give him a pleasant spell of peace and quiet.

'Working, darling?' inquired Lorraine solicitously.

'No. Sleeping! And I shall do it a damn sight better without people chattering and nattering all over the house. Last time Gussie was taken to the wells she was eight — and screamed the place down, as far as I remember! Time she saw 'em again.'

So they had all gone. Lash, Dany and Gussie Bingham in Seyyid Omar's great white car, and Nigel, Amalfi and Larry Dowling in one of the *Kivulimi* cars driven by Eduardo.

They stopped by the roadside in a forest of palms to drink coconut milk from the ripe nuts; explored a copra factory and saw a clove plantation; and leaving the cars in a small dusty side road, followed a narrow, winding track across a no-man's land of scrub and rocks and dried grasses, and came suddenly upon a hole in the ground where a flight of worn stone steps led down into darkness.

'I don't think I like the look of it all,' said Gussie, shuddering and clutching nervously at Dany's arm. 'Suppose we fall into the water and drown in the dark? Hasn't anyone got a torch?'

No one had. But there were matches and cigarette lighters, and Seyyid Omar assured them that there was not the least danger of anyone drowning, and that women from the little village where they had left the cars came here daily to draw water.

208

The steps led down into a huge underground cave where the light barely penetrated and smooth water-worn rocks sloped sharply downwards towards, not wells, but a spring of water or an underground stream that came up out of the darkness and disappeared again into a black rock tunnel.

Holding cautiously to each other so as not to slip and fall on the rocks, they ventured down to the edge of the spring, their voices echoing strangely through the shadowy vault, and Seyyid Omar told them that the water was supposed to be the continuation of a stream that fed one of the great lakes in Africa, and flowing on far under the sea bed, bubbled up briefly here in Zanzibar; to vanish again into the rock and the Indian Ocean.

'I'm sure it's wildly interesting,' said Amalfi, 'but let's go, shall we? I think it's dark and spooky and altogether rather gruesome, and personally, the sooner I get out of the place the better. What happens if the roof falls in?'

There was an unexpected note of shrillness in her voice, and instantly everyone looked up at the dark curve of rock overhead, and moved closer to each other, their feet slipping on the steep rock-face.

Eduardo said soothingly: 'The roof will not fall in, *cara*. It is only a big cave. There are thousands of such places all over the world. But if it does not please you, we will go at once.'

'Yes, do let's,' said Gussie, shuddering. 'It's giving me claustrophobia.'

Within a few minutes they were out in the open air again. But it was not until two hours later, as the cars drew up before the gateway of the House of Shade, that Dany discovered that the white suede bag that she had carried had been neatly slit open with a sharp knife or a razor blade, and everything in it had gone.

17

'I will see that it is reported at once to the police,' said Seyyid Omar.

He had invited Dany, Lash and Gussie to dine with him at a restaurant in the town, but Gussie having refused on the plea of tiredness they had dropped her at the House of Shade, and driven back to Zanzibar city under a green and lavender sky that was already freckled with pale stars.

'No, for goodness sake, don't!' said Dany hastily. 'The police have had enough of us. Besides, it isn't worth making a fuss about. There was nothing of any value in it. Only a handkerchief and a pair of sunglasses, and a powder compact and a lipstick. That sort of thing. And possibly about eightpence in English pennies!'

'It must have been lifted by one of those picturesque characters in the village near the wells,' said Lash. 'Darned disappointing for him. Though I guess his lady friends will get a load of fun out of smearing themselves with lipstick. It's a shame about the bag, though. I'll get you another one tomorrow. Souvenir of Zanzibar.'

The city by night was very different from what it had been in the heat of the day, for the cooler air had brought all Zanzibar out of doors, and there were gay crowds strolling under the trees in the public gardens and along the sea front, while every roof-top and *baraza* appeared to have its family party.

Music and laughter, the tuneful cry of the coconut seller, and a continual rub-a-dub-dub of drums made a gay, enchanting medley of sound, mingled with the more normal noises of any Eastern city.

'Is it some special day?' asked Dany. 'A feast day, or something?'

'No. What makes you think that?'

'Everyone seems so gay. Listen — can't you hear them? They all sound very happy.'

'It is a happy island,' said Seyyid Omar, smiling. 'And when we feel gay we laugh — or sing; or play the *kinanda* — the mandolin. Or beat a drum. And, as you hear, we feel gay very often. It is a thing worth keeping, I think. Yes — very well worth keeping. But there are times when I become afraid.'

Lash turned his head and regarded him attentively. 'Afraid of what?'

Seyyid Omar slowed the car to a stop under the scented canopy of an Indian cork tree that leaned above a high, white-washed wall, and sat back, resting his slim brown hands upon the wheel: his face faintly illuminated by the dash-board lights.

He said slowly: 'I will be frank with you, Mr Holden. I think that you know something about a sum of money: a very large sum of money that many people have searched for for a great many years, though few have really believed in its existence. That vast legendary treasure that Seyyid Saïd, the first Sultan, was rumoured to have buried at Bet-el-Ras.'

Neither Lash nor Dany made any answer, and Seyyid Omar presumably translated that silence as admission, for after a momentary pause he said: 'I myself did not believe that it had ever existed or was more than a tale or legend. But not so long ago there arose a rumour; a whisper that it was fact and not fiction.'

He shifted a little; a small uneasy movement, and his hands tightened on the wheel. 'There are certain people in this island who need money, a large sum of money, to buy power at the next election. We have an old proverb that says "I will change

211

my religion and the colour of my coat, but thou must pay," and there are, alas, always votes — too many votes! — that can be bought for cash where they cannot be acquired from conviction. For money will always speak with a louder voice than any politician. One of those who wished to buy power travelled out with you from London, and is now dead. Jembe. But there are others, and they still need money.'

He was silent for a moment or two, and then he gave a quick shrug of his shoulders and drew a cigarette-case from his pocket.

'You do not smoke, I think, Miss Kitchell? You will not mind if we do?'

He offered the case to Lash with a pleasant smile and as the car filled with the fragrant smell of Turkish tobacco, leant back against the seat as though the conversation had been concluded and he had no more to say.

Lash said lightly: 'Then I guess a lot of guys are all set for a sad let-down. Why are you telling us this?'

Seyyid Omar laughed. 'You are not really stupid, Mr Holden, are you.'

It was an assertion, and not a query, and Lash said: 'Not that stupid, anyway! But I don't see what this has got to do with me, or with Miss Kitchell.'

'Don't you? Well, perhaps you are right. All the same, it is just as well to be warned.'

'Warned?' Lash's voice had a sudden sharp edge to it, and Dany felt his lounging body stiffen. 'That's quite often a fighting word where I come from. What exactly are you warning us about? Or have I got it wrong and is this a threat?'

'Ah, no!' Seyyid Omar held up a deprecatory hand. 'You misunderstand me. Why should I threaten? I am merely offering advice.'

'O.K., let's have it.'

'If there is any truth in this legend of the hidden treasure, and should — anyone, have any knowledge of where it may be

212

found, it would, I think, be wise for that person to take such knowledge to His Highness the Sultan, whom God preserve. Or to the police.'

'Why? Because to possess that knowledge is dangerous?'

'That, of course. To be the possessor of such knowledge might prove very dangerous indeed. But there is a much more important, though less personal reason for speaking of it. To prevent it falling into the wrong hands. Such a sum of money can be a dangerous thing when used for evil. And it would be used for evil. Of that you can be sure. There is a curse on it.'

Lash said impatiently: 'You don't mean to tell me that you believe that old wives' tale?'

Seyyid Omar looked at him and laughed. 'So you have heard of it? Yes, I believe it, though you will not. But then you are a young man, Mr Holden, and from a very young country. You still have a great many things to learn — particularly about the East. One of them can be summed up best in words that have been worn threadbare from use, but which cannot be improved upon: "There are more things in heaven and earth," Mr Holden, "than are dreamed of in your philosophy"!'

He turned to Dany with an apologetic smile and said: 'I am sorry, Miss Kitchell. This cannot interest you. We will go on to my Club, where we will talk and drink and you will meet my friends. They will be far more entertaining than I.'

He refused to say anything further on the subject or to answer any questions, and took them to the Arab Club, where they sat out under the stars and spent a pleasant hour. And afterwards they dined on strange foods in a little restaurant in a quiet back street, and then drove to the sea front outside the Sultan's palace, to listen, in company with a light-hearted collection of His Highness's subjects, to the Sultan's band playing — of all things — excerpts from Gilbert and Sullivan and *The Belle of New York*.

The lights were still on and the house-party still up when they arrived back at the House of Shade, for it was barely half past ten. But Seyyid Omar would not come in with them, and watching the tail-lights of his car dwindle and fade Lash had said thoughtfully: 'That guy knows a heck of a lot more than he's telling. A heck of a lot! The question is, who is he really pitching for? Is he on the side of the angels, as he makes out, or is that just a bluff? He wouldn't be the first well-heeled *aristo* to go back on his class and join the fellow-travellers!'

Dany said in a low voice: 'He was talking to that man Jembe at the airport in Nairobi. I saw them.'

'When? Where? You didn't tell me.'

'I didn't think of it. There have been so many other things. Worse things.'

She told him then, and Lash said meditatively: '*Hmm* ... It sounds a screwy set-up all round. Maybe he did the job himself. Slipped this Jembe a slug of cyanide because he's after the number one spot in the Dictator Stakes himself. He may fancy himself as the local Hitler. The Führer of Zanzibar.'

'*"King of the Earth and of Time",*' quoted Dany under her breath.

'What's that?'

Dany flushed and apologized. 'I'm sorry. I was thinking of something. A Persian inscription that he translated for me yesterday. I can imagine him dreaming of being that sort of king — and of restoring that sort of kingdom.'

'And wanting the cash to start it off with. Maybe.'

'But it can't be him. At least, he can't be the one who stole that letter or map or whatever it was off me, because then he'd know where the stuff was, and he doesn't. But he may think I've still got it. Perhaps he even thought I might carry it about with me. I never thought of that!'

'Thought of what? What are you talking about?'

'My bag. You said it must have been slit open by one of the Arabs in the village, but it wasn't. I've been thinking about it, and none of them came within yards of me.'

214

Lash gave a short laugh and said: 'Listen, honey. If you're thinking that anyone can drive a car with one hand, and at the speed that guy drove, while slitting a passenger's purse and abstracting its contents with the other, you're nuts! And anyway, you weren't even sitting next to him this afternoon. Gussie was.'

'I didn't mean it was done in the car,' said Dany impatiently. 'I told you, I've been thinking. It was all right just before we got to the cave, because I put my sunglasses into it, and I remember stuffing them down on one side of the handkerchief.'

'So what?'

'So there was only one place where anyone could have cut that bag open without my knowing it. In the cave. It was dark in there, and we were all huddled together and grabbing at each other to keep from falling. But there wasn't anyone else down there except — except us.'

Lash stopped abruptly in a patch of pale moonlight and said: 'Are you sure? That it couldn't have happened anywhere else?'

'Yes. Quite sure. That's why I didn't say anything more about it. I was sorry that I'd said anything at all, but I was so surprised when I saw it that the words jumped out. But when I'd thought a bit I realized that it could only have been done while we were in the cave, and that no one who was there would do it just to steal a compact and a lipstick and perhaps a little money. So it must have been someone who wanted something special, and thought that I might carry it with me. It *must* have been!'

'Yes,' said Lash slowly. 'The same bunch again. Six of us who were on the London to Nairobi run, and two who were on the last lap to Zanzibar. Gussie and Elf and Larry Dowling; Nigel and Eduardo and our smooth Arab pal. None of them in the least likely to go in for lifting lipsticks and petty cash. I guess you're right. Someone thinks you've still got it.'

It was a verdict that was to receive swift confirmation.

The remainder of the house-party were playing *vingt-et-un* in the dining-room, but Lash excused himself from joining them

and went off to the guest-house, and Dany went up to bed —
to discover that in her absence someone had searched her bedroom
as thoroughly, though far less untidily, as her room at the Airlane.

Every drawer and cupboard had been gone through, and even
the sheets and blankets had been taken off her bed and replaced;
though not very neatly. A box of face powder had been probed
with a pair of nail scissors and a jar of cleansing cream with
a nail file: face tissues had been pulled out of their container
and roughly stuffed back again, stockings unrolled and a locked
suitcase forced.

'But I haven't *got* it!' said Dany, speaking aloud into the silence
as though she were addressing that unknown searcher. The sound
of her own voice startled her even more than the evidence of
her disarranged possessions, and she turned and ran from the
room.

The lights were ablaze in every verandah and in the courtyard,
and there were no shadows on the staircases: but she tested every
step, her hand pressed to the wall and her heart in her mouth.
She could hear voices and laughter from behind the closed door
of the dining-room, and she tiptoed past it and out into the quiet
garden.

The moonlight and black shadows were not as frightening as
the house had been, and she ran lightly along the twisting paths
between the flower-beds and the scented bushes of roses, jasmine
and Lady-of-the-Night, and skirting the shallow pool with its
stone birds, reached the steep flight of narrow steps that led up
to the guest-house on the wall.

The lights were on but Lash did not answer her knock, and
she opened the door and went in. The little sitting-room appeared
to be empty, and supposing Lash to be in the bedroom she was
about to call out to him when a sound made her turn sharply.

Lash was standing on the narrow stone window ledge, holding
on by the frame, and she could only see his legs and part of
his body. The rest of him was outside the window, and he appeared

216

to be attempting to pick a spray of the purple bougainvillaea that hung down over the wall of the house.

He swung himself in again and jumped down on to the floor, brushing dead leaves out of his hair, and said: 'For the love of Mike! — what are you doing here?'

Dany, who had been about to ask almost the same question, abandoned it in favour of more urgent matters. She said breathlessly: 'My room's been searched again. Every bit of it. Like last time, only——'

'Same here,' said Lash briefly. 'Take a look around.'

Dany looked about her and became aware of much the same mild disorder as her own room had contained, and stooping with a cry of dismay she picked up a white fluffy ruin that lay half concealed under the edge of the divan. The late Asbestos; that washable and unburnable cat, his stuffing ruthlessly removed and his green glass eyes stonily reproachful.

'All flesh is grass,' said Lash. 'And all cat's too, judging from the look of it. Yes, someone's frisked this joint in a conscientious manner.'

'Did he get in by the window?'

'I don't know. All I know is that he hasn't missed much. Even my soap has been broken in half to make sure that I hadn't hidden anything in it. Most of the stuff has been put back in place; but not, as you see, very tidily. Here, stand yourself a slug of your step-father's Scotch. At least that has been left alone — I hope!'

He poured out some of the whisky from the bottle that Tyson had left there on the morning of their arrival, and having smelt it, tasted it with extreme caution.

'Seems O.K. No cyanide. At least, not noticeably so. I'd better try it out for effect first. Here's to the witch doctor, deceased, who put a curse on that cash deposit. He certainly knew his onions!'

He drank, and having put down the glass turned to look out

through the open window for a moment or two, and then said: 'Well, I guess this puts one suspect out of court. Pal Omar couldn't have pulled this one. He was with us the whole evening, so he's out. It was one of the others. If only we could find out who knew the trick of that staircase it would help a lot, but there would appear to be at least four copies of that damned book in the house, and you were right about it. It's all there: tucked away back in a musty maze of architectural drawings. It took some finding, but I ran it to earth. Anyone could have stumbled across it and put it to good use.'

He sat down on the window-seat, his reflective gaze still on the moonlit seascape outside, and said slowly: 'I'd like to know more about this Larry Dowling. A lot more. And I'm willing to bet that the cops will too, just as soon as Tyson's letter turns up at Scotland Yard and they move in on us.'

Dany said flatly: 'It isn't Larry. It couldn't possibly be Larry.'

'Why not? There's something phoney about that guy. I've known a good few newspapermen in my time, and he doesn't ring true.'

'But he's not a newspaperman! He's a feature writer. And——'

'What's that got to do with it? He's after a story — Tyson's. So why doesn't he get on with it? If he's done any writing since he arrived, I'm Ernest Hemingway! Then there's Gussie ...'

Dany subsided suddenly on the divan, nursing the wreck of Asbestos. She said tiredly: 'Yes. I thought of her too. Because she would have known so many things that — that whoever it is must have known. But I don't believe it. I just can't see her climbing fire-escapes and things like that. And she was fond of Millicent.'

'How do you know that? None of us can really know anything much about anyone else. We can only go by what we see. I guess I thought I knew plenty about Elf. I meant to marry her, heaven help me! — and me, I'm an Old World throw-back to my respected Scotch ancestors when it comes to saying "I do." It's not going

to mean to me "Until Alimony and the Other Man doth us part".
No, I thought I knew more about Elf than any of the other guys
had done: that none of them had understood her as I did —
all the old routine. That'll show you!'

His laugh held more than a trace of bitterness, and turning
his shoulder to the window and the moonlight, he said: 'Millicent
Bates may have been rubbed out because she was the active
partner in some little scheme of Gussie's. She may have done
that job in London, then caught on to it later that Gussie had
shot the family lawyer, and taken a poor view of it. And then
there's the Latin lover . . .'

Lash rose and poured himself another drink, and broke off
to remark conversationally: 'Your step-father is one hell of a
host. He thinks of everything. Gin, soda-water syphon, bitters,
Scotch. Look at 'em all! Say, who does he think I am? It's a
libel. Have one?'

Dany shook her head, and he brought his drink across and
sat down in an arm-chair facing her; holding the glass between
both hands and looking down into the golden liquid intently,
as though it were a crystal ball in which he could see the future
— or the past.

'The Signore Marchese di Chiago,' said Lash softly. 'Apart
from racing cars he has quite a reputation as a fast guy. And
a weakness for blondes. He's known Tyson, and your mother,
for a good many years, and this isn't his first visit to Zanzibar.
He's stayed in this house before. And if there's anything in gossip
— largely Nigel's I'll admit! — he's had several affairs of the
heart that his family have managed to bring to a grinding halt
just short of the altar, and it's a cinch that they'll queer this
one too if they can. But maybe this time it's gone deeper. Maybe
he's got to have Elf, come hell or high water. She can have that
effect on some people. There was one guy — Douglas something
— who took a header out of a top storey window when Elf
threw him over. But Eduardo isn't the kind that likes taking

"No" for an answer. He comes from a country where a male with a title gets all the breaks, and if he wanted anything badly enough I guess he wouldn't stop at much to get it. But Elf is a strictly cash proposition — from both angles. His and hers. No lire — no Elf. Maybe we haven't paid enough attention to Eduardo and his fiery Southern blood.'

Lash gave the contents of his glass some more practical attention, and lit a cigarette, and Dany watched him anxiously. She wished that she did not feel so frightened, and that she could look at it all as Lash appeared to be doing: as an interesting problem of the 'Who's Got the Button?' variety. But looking about the small room with its silent evidence of an unknown searcher, she was aware of nothing but an acute sense of danger.

This was neither a game nor a nightmare from which she would awake. It was real. It was the springing of a trap that had been set over ninety years ago, and which had caught her when she had called on a prim, elderly, country solicitor to fetch a letter written by a man who had died back in the last century.

Lash said thoughtfully: 'It could be Tyson,' and she came back to the present with a sharp jerk.

'*Tyson?* What are you talking about?'

'This——' said Lash, gesturing with his cigarette at the ill-concealed disorder of the room. 'That——' he indicated the sad remains of Asbestos. 'And your room too. He may have wanted to satisfy himself that one of us hadn't double-crossed him. If you remember, he did once suggest that you might have held on to the contents of that envelope yourself. It could be Tyson. Or Ponting. In fact, why not Ponting? He was in Nairobi. You know, that's quite an idea — except that I guess he'd have made a far neater job of it if this had been his lily-fingered handiwork! He could have been pressed for time, of course, but somehow I can't see that elegant, willowy tulip leaving the place in this sort of mess. If dear Nigel had been conducting "Operation Frisk" I've a strong feeling that we wouldn't have known that anything had been touched. And yet it's got to be someone in the house, who knew that we wouldn't be back for quite a while, and—— Say! Wait a minute!'

He put his glass down and came suddenly to his feet. 'Why didn't I think of that?'

'Of what?' demanded Dany, her voice sharp with anxiety.

'Seyyid Omar! He knew damned well just how long we'd be away. He could even be the original weevil in the woodwork. Yes ... why not? He's a big shot in this island. He'd be the only one who could easily plant his servants — or even his relatives — in the house. And who would know?'

Lash took a quick turn about the room and came back to stand in front of Dany.

'Now look. Supposing he got all his information from a servant in this house — that silent, slippered guy who slides in and out with the coffee and takes the letters to the post. Suppose he can read English after all, and that he read Tyson's letters to this Honeywood, and possibly Lorraine's to you as well, and passed on the information? Omar doesn't go after Emory's letter himself, but he sends a stooge — Jembe — who gets rid of Honeywood but fails to get the goods. Jembe has another try at finding it when he frisks your room at the Airlane, and so he——'

'Steals my passport,' put in Dany. 'But that *can't* be right! What would be the point of stopping me leaving the country?'

'Ah, I've thought of that one: it occurred to me once before. So that you'd mail it. The letter. Who's to say they haven't got a pal planted in the post office here, as well as in the house? It wouldn't be difficult if you were Seyyid Omar. For anyone else, yes. But not for him.'

'I don't think——' began Dany doubtfully.

'No one's asking you to! I'm developing a theory. Now, this Jembe finds that you are on the plane after all — thinly disguised by dyed hair and glasses. So what does he do? He has another shot at stealing the thing in Nairobi, fluffs it, and has to report

221

failure to the boss — our friend Omar, who meets him at Nairobi West. You actually saw 'em talking.'

Dany said: 'Yes. But why should Seyyid Omar want to poison him? It doesn't make sense!'

'I'm not so sure. After all, you've arrived and you've still got the goods. Jembe has shot his bolt and is of no further use — and probably knows too much anyway! So the best thing is to get rid of him and leave the rest to one of these poker-faced guys in white night-gowns who seem to be all over the house, and who would probably skin their grandmothers alive for ten dollars down and ten to follow. For all we know any one of them may easily turn out to have majored in modern languages and picked up a coupla degrees on the side. Who's to tell?'

Dany said: 'Yes ... I suppose so. But you've forgotten something. There are two quite different people in all this. The one — or the ones — who are still trying to find that letter and who think I've still got it, and the one who *has* got it. If Seyyid Omar hasn't got it, who has?'

Lash's face changed and became wholly expressionless. He looked down at the cigarette he held, and after a moment he flipped it away through the open window and said lightly:

'Yes — who? Certainly not our friend the Seyyid, if he was the guy who picked your pocket in the cave and so neatly got us out of the way while one of his tarbooshed minions went through our rooms.'

Dany said: 'But if you really think he's the one behind all this, why did he show us how Miss Bates was killed?'

'To scare us, I guess. Make us lose our nerve — and our heads.'

Lash finished his drink and tossing the empty glass on the sofa, said: 'I think a short talk with your step-father is indicated. I don't think he's got any idea of what a hornet's nest he stirred up, and I intend to bring it home to him — if I have to use a sledge-hammer to do it!'

He looked down at Dany's white face and smiled a little

crookedly. 'It's a helluva mess, honey, but you don't have to lose your nerve.'

'I haven't any left to lose!' admitted Dany ruefully. 'Not an atom!'

Lash laughed and reached down his hands to pull her to her feet.

'Nuts, Miss Kitchell! Momentarily mislaid, perhaps, but never lost. And I don't know if that aunt of yours ever warned you against visiting in bachelor's apartments at this hour of night, but I believe it is frowned upon in the more prudish circles of society. So in about two minutes time I am going to take you back to your room.'

Five minutes later he said reflectively: 'You know something? — This looks as though it might become a habit.'

It was, in fact, just over fifteen minutes later that he finally escorted Dany back to the house.

18

There had been no chance for any private talk with Tyson on the following day, for he had slept late, and then in response to a message delivered to the house, had gone off deep-sea fishing with a friend: a visiting peer who had arrived unexpectedly, and only that morning, in a private yacht.

'Really, *too* exasperating!' complained Nigel. 'We have a positive plethora of work on hand, but will he get down to it? — will he hell! The *rudest* wires from the publisher: one can only hope that the operators can't read English. And he *swore* he'd have a talk with Larry this morning. Have you been able to pin him down to anything yet, Holden?'

'Nope,' said Lash lazily, and turned over on his stomach.

They had all been bathing, and were now basking on the hot white sand on the beach below the house, acquiring what they hoped would be an even tan and not a savage case of sunburn.

'Who's been sending rude cables?' inquired Lash. 'Sounds like my respected Pop.'

'No. Our British publishers. So *testy*,' said Nigel.

Gussie looked up from anointing her legs with sun-tan oil and said: 'I thought you were supposed to be doing some sort of deal with Tyson about the Emory Frost papers, Mr Holden. A business-with-pleasure visit. Though I'm afraid it can't have been very pleasant to ... Oh, dear, I didn't mean to be tactless.'

'You weren't,' Lash assured her. 'And you're dead right about those papers. I am hoping to persuade your brother to sign on the dotted line. If I can get him to sit still that long. But

224

he's a difficult man to pin down, and right now I feel too idle to chase after him.'

'Where's your American hustle?' demanded Gussie with a bright smile.

Lash yawned. 'I guess I shed it somewhere short of Naples — along with my raincoat. Right now I prefer basking to business. But don't worry: I'll get round to it sometime — no kidding. What are we doing the rest of today?'

'Nothing,' said Nigel firmly.

'Swell. That sounds right up my street.'

'Nonsense!' said Gussie briskly. 'We're all going shopping and sight-seeing in the town. It's all arranged. And then we're having tea at the hotel, and Lorraine said something about a moonlight picnic somewhere along the shore.'

'Holy Moses!' murmured Lash devoutly.

'Didn't you, Lorraine?' said Gussie, ignoring the interruption.

'Yes, Gussie dear. But only for anyone who wants to do any of it. You don't have to, you know.'

'I can see no point in coming to a place like Zanzibar if one is going to lie about and sleep all day. One can do that at home.'

'But not on lovely white beaches in the sun,' murmured Amalfi. 'Nigel, why is this sand white instead of yellow?'

'Coral, you pretty ignoramus. And pumice I expect. You know, I found out something totally fascinating the other day. Do you know where all those silly little pumice-stones that you find all along the beaches come from? Krakatoa!'

'And where,' said Eduardo, 'is Krakatoa?'

Nigel shuddered and put a hand over his eyes. 'The educational standards of the drinking classes would appear to be universally and *utterly* inadequate. Krakatoa, my decadent barbarian, was a volcano in the Sunda Straits — that's between Java and Sumatra in case you didn't know — which blew itself to bits in 1883 with a bang that no A-bomb will ever equal. And these are the bits. They bobbed along in the currents and got stranded here.

225

I can't say I ever used pumice-stone before, but I do now. It *enchants* me to feel that I'm scraping off my ink stains with Krakatoa!'

Eduardo said: 'You ought to write a guide book, you clever little thing, you. Me, I never read them.'

'You, you never read anything if you can help it!' said Nigel crossly.

'Now that is really *very* unjust of you, Mr Ponting,' put in Gussie, wagging an admonitory finger at him. 'And the Marchese was only joking. Why, he was reading all about the house on the very first afternoon we were here. My grandfather's book: *The House of Shade*. Weren't you, now?'

'Was I?' said Eduardo with a shrug of his bronzed shoulders. 'I do not remember. Perhaps I may have picked it up to glance at it. If I did I am quite sure I must have put it down again very, very quickly!'

'Not at all! You are too modest. You were so absorbed in it that you did not even hear me come into the library; and I assure you that there is *nothing* to be ashamed of in being a book-worm. I love a good book myself.'

'The point,' said Nigel, 'is that *The House of Shade* is probably the worst book ever written, and certainly the dullest, and one doubts if any book-lover, worm or otherwise, could bore their way past page two.'

'Then why,' demanded Amalfi petulantly, 'are we boring on about it now? Are you by any chance conducting this shopping and sight-seeing tour this afternoon, Nigel?'

'I am happy to be able to answer promptly,' said Nigel. '*No!* Why? Were you intending to join it?'

'I think so. As long as we don't start until half-past three or fourish. There was a shop in Portuguese Street that had the most divine Indian jewellery, and the man said he'd get in some more to show us today. So Eddie and I rather thought that we'd go along and take another look.'

'Not forgetting Eddie's cheque book,' said Nigel waspishly.

'Nigel darling, you *are* being cross and catty this morning!' complained Lorraine plaintively. 'What's the matter? It's such a lovely day, yet everyone seems to be jumpy and on edge instead of just relaxing peacefully.'

'We are relaxing peacefully,' said Lash, with his eyes shut. 'Just take a look at us.'

'No, you're not. You may look as though you are, but I can feel the atmosphere simply buzzing with jangled nerve ends. I suppose it's all this business of Honeywood and Jembe. And then poor Millicent——'

Gussie Bingham rose abruptly, and snatching up towel, sun-tan oil and sunshade, walked quickly away across the beach and up the short rocky path that led to the door into the garden.

Amalfi sat up, and removing her sun-glasses, said: 'Now you've upset your dear sister-in-law. Too bad. Lorrie darling, be a sweetie and *don't* let's get back onto that subject again.'

'But why be ostriches,' demanded Lorraine, aggrieved.

'Why not? I've nothing against ostriches. In fact I'm all for them if they prefer burying their heads in the sand to poking their beaks into drearily depressing subjects. Are you really taking us in to Zanzibar this afternoon?'

'Yes, if you like. It's Gussie really. She seems to want to keep doing something: so as not to have to think about Millicent, I suppose. Gussie hates being upset. As we're going in, you can all go and sign your names in the visitors' book at the Palace and the Residency. It's rather the done thing.'

'You have my permission to forge mine,' said Lash.

'I shall do no such thing. You'll do it yourself — and like it!'

'O.K., O.K.,' said Lash pacifically. 'Anything you say. I'll go.'

They had all gone. With the exception of Nigel who insisted that he had work to do, and Dany, who had unexpectedly fallen asleep in a hammock in the garden.

227

'Let her sleep,' said Lorraine, restraining Lash who would have woken her. 'It will do her more good than trailing her around Zanzibar city in this heat, and she doesn't look as though she's had much sleep of late. Nigel can keep an eye on her. She'll be all right. No, Lash! — I won't have her wakened.'

She had spoken with unexpected decision, and taking Lash firmly by the arm, had gone out to the car.

Lorraine had had few opportunities to see her daughter in private after the day of her arrival, for Tyson had warned her against treating Dany with more intimacy than would be due to the secretary of one of her guests. But she had seen her alone in the earlier part of the afternoon, and in the garden: Dany having gone out after luncheon to sit in the hammock, and Lorraine happening to catch sight of her on her way to pick some roses as a peace-offering for Gussie.

'Darling how nice to get you by yourself for a bit,' said Lorraine, abandoning the roses and joining her daughter on the hammock. 'It's so tiresome, never being able to talk to you without looking over my shoulder. I'm afraid all this is being simply horrid for you, baby, but Tyson says it will only be for a day or two, and then the police will sort it all out and we needn't go on pretending that you are the Kitchell woman. Thank goodness!'

She sighed and swung the hammock with one foot, and after a silent interval began a little diffidently: 'Darling ... about Lash——' And then did not seem to know how to go on.

Dany said, startled: 'What about him?'

'You rather like him, don't you, darling?'

Dany blushed to the roots of that distressing dyed hair, and Lorraine, observing the unfortunate colour effect, said abstractedly: 'No — quite the wrong shade for you. It *is* a pity.'

'Mother, what are you talking about?' demanded Dany.

Lorraine threw a hunted look over her shoulder. 'Darling, *don't*! Suppose anyone were to hear you?'

228

'There isn't anyone anywhere near,' said Dany. 'What were you saying about Lash?'

'Well — I felt perhaps I ought to say something, because it did rather occur to me that you perhaps liked him more than — let's say, than a secretary should. And after all, he is rather an attractive creature, and . . .'

She made a slight helpless gesture with one hand, and once again did not finish the sentence.

'And what?' said Dany defensively.

'Well, darling, I happened to go out on to the terrace last night to fetch a magazine I'd left there, and I saw you two coming back to the house. You looked very — friendly.'

Dany said nothing, and Lorraine gave a small unhappy sigh. 'I'm afraid I'm a useless parent,' she said. 'The trouble is, I don't seem to know how to behave like one. But I do feel that as a parent I ought to say something. About Lash, I mean. You do know that he was to have married Elf — Mrs Gordon — don't you?'

'Yes. You told me in your letter. And so did he.'

'Oh, well; that's something.' Lorraine sounded relieved. 'But darling, you will be a little careful, won't you? You see, you've met so few men so far. That's been my fault, I suppose: I've been horribly selfish and not really remembered how quickly time goes. I was always going to be a good mother one day, but you always seemed such a baby. And now suddenly you've grown up. But you don't want to go losing your heart to the first attractive man you meet. In fact it's the greatest possible mistake! It's not that I've got anything against Lash, but . . .'

'Which means that you have,' said Dany coldly.

'No, I haven't, baby. Really. It's just that Tyson says he's had a lot of girls, and — well, he simply *adored* Elf, and men do do such silly things on the rebound: snatch at admiration from the nearest person who offers it, to bolster up their wounded egos. It doesn't mean anything. I like Lash, but he's as wild as a hawk

229

and I'm not sure I'd trust him as far as I could throw a grand piano. Elf can manage that type; but when one is young and romantic and naïve, one is apt to take things — and people — at their face value. So — so you will just think a bit, won't you, darling? I mean, you don't have to believe everything he says, just because he's gay and good looking and has a fair share of charm. Take it all——'

'With a pinch of salt?' interrupted Dany bitterly. 'I know!'

'I was going to say "in your stride",' said Lorraine reproachfully. 'But salt will do. After all, it improves so many things, doesn't it darling? Oh — here comes Larry. He's rather a charmer, isn't he. I'm glad we asked him to stay — though Tyson's being a bit sour about him. He says we ought to watch out, because Larry's the type that all women trust on sight and end up falling for, and that all the best bigamists and confidence tricksters have been that kind of man. You know, it's astonishing how catty men can be about each other when — Hullo, Larry. Are you looking for anyone?'

'No,' said Larry, smiling. 'Just looking around. This is a fascinating old place you've got here, Mrs Frost. That wall at the end of the garden is a good ten feet thick if it's an inch. There must have been guard rooms or stables in it once. Were they bricked up?'

'I expect so,' said Lorraine vaguely. 'If you're interested, I'm sure you'll find all about it in old Barclay's book. Are you going to the city with us later on?'

'Certainly; if you'll take me. Is there any chance of your husband joining us?'

'He's meeting us at the hotel for tea,' said Lorraine, rising. She turned and smiled at Dany. 'I'll leave you in possession of the hammock, Miss Kitchell. You ought to put your feet up and have a rest. We shan't be leaving for at least an hour.'

She took Larry Dowling away with her down the winding path between the orange trees and the roses, and Dany watched them go and thought of Lash; and of what he had said only last night about Amalfi Gordon. He had not sounded as though he were still in love with her. But had it just been bitterness and sour grapes?

You don't have to believe everything he says ...

Was she just 'young and romantic and naïve'? An inexperienced school-girl, taking things and people at their face value? How was one to know? How did one ever learn? The hard way? Had Lash only made love to her because he was snatching at the nearest bit of admiration to soothe his sore ego? Trying to show Amalfi that he did not care?

For the better part of an hour Dany lay in the hammock, staring up at the blue chips of sky through the thick scented canopy of leaves and flowers over her head, her mind so fully occupied with personal problems that she never once thought of Mr Honeywood, or of Jembe, or of Millicent Bates — or of murder. And then, without warning, sleep reached out a light finger and touched her eyes, and she did not even hear Lorraine and Lash when they came in search of her.

It was close on five o'clock when she awoke, and the shadows had lengthened in the garden and the heat had gone from the day. The house was very quiet, but she found Nigel in the drawing-room, sipping China tea and reading a week-old London newspaper.

He dropped the paper on the floor and came to his feet when he saw her, but Dany, glancing down, found her eye caught by familiar words: 'Man Murdered in Market-Lydon.'

Nigel, following the direction of her gaze, laughed and said: 'You have caught me red-handed, Miss Kitchell — soaking myself in crime on the sly. I blush for it. *Too* fish-and-chip. But to tell you the honest truth, after all that sordid chit-chat the other night I felt quite intrigued. That Bates woman went on and *on* about it, until one couldn't help wondering what she was getting at: if *anything*, of course! But one felt, somehow, that there *was*

231

something ... Do sit down and have some tea. Indian or China? The China is divine. Tyson has it sent direct from some aromatic old Mandarin friend in Canton.'

Dany accepted a cup of pale yellowish-green liquid that smelt of dried flowers, and listened a little abstractedly to Nigel's light, melodious voice lilting on and on in a nonstop monologue. It was, she discovered, quite easy to listen to Nigel and think of something else. And then, with shocking suddenness, she was jerked out of her detachment.

'Now *do* tell me,' said Nigel, 'who you *really* are? I won't tell a *soul*. Of course one can *guess*. But it *has* been intriguing me so. Deliciously mystifying!'

Dany gaped at him and dropped her cup.

'Tiens! Tiens!' said Mr Ponting, leaping gracefully to his feet and repairing the damage. 'I *am* sorry. Entirely my fault. But honestly, *dear* Miss Whoeveritis, you simply *couldn't* be Ada Kitchell — not by any stretch of the most *elastic* imagination. And you have no *idea* how flexible mine is!'

Dany said stonily: 'Why couldn't I be?'

'Well darling – your *voice*! Utterly Nancy Mitford. Not a whisper of the New World in it. And what woman *ever* wore spectacles if she didn't need them? Why, those are just plain glass! And — well, not to labour the point, a little blonde bird told me that *actually* there is a rumour flying about to the effect that poor Ada is at this moment incarcerated in the Islington Isolation Hospital with mumps.'

'Mrs Gordon!' said Dany involuntarily. 'I might have known it!'

'Well, frankly, darling, I *do* think that you might. However, don't let it worry you. It probably isn't true, and anyway I won't breathe a syllable. Now do tell me: I'm *dying* to know. *Why?* And of course, *Who?* ... though of course one can make a very accurate little guess at *that* one, can't one?'

'I don't know. Can one?'

'But of course! There is really nothing subtle about our sweet

232

Lorraine, and when she hurries about the house removing every single photograph of her darling daughter, one *does* tend to ask oneself a few shy little questions. Not that there were *many* photographs. Lorraine is not what one would term *madly* maternal. But there were just one or two. And where are they now? "Gone with the wind that blew through Georgia?" But she forgot that there is a liberally illustrated volume lying around, all about explorations in Central somewhere, which includes a handsome photograph of her first husband; and I fear I was inquisitive enough to take a tiny peek. You really are very like your father, you know. The resemblance was quite remarkable as *soon* as one saw you without those spectacles and that distressing fringe. You forgot them the other night.'

Dany got up and went over to the window, and stood with her back to the room, tugging nervously at the edge of the curtain and staring blindly out at the garden. Her first feeling of panic had subsided, and now she was only conscious of a lessening of tension and a certain degree of relief. Being Miss Kitchell was a strain, and it was going to be very restful to be Dany Ashton again, and to stop pretending — and being frightened. But she wished that Lorraine were here. Or Tyson, or Lash. Someone to advise her as to what she should say and how much she could say.

Had everyone seen through her? Had they all guessed? Not the passport officials at all events! and they were the only ones who really mattered — except for Larry Dowling, who must not guess.

She said: 'Has Mrs Gordon told everyone?'

'About Ada? Oh, I don't think so. She may have whispered something into Eduardo's lovely brown ear, but he won't be in the least interested; and I'm quite *sure* she wouldn't tell anyone else. Not Gussie anyway. And *certainly* not our intrusive Mr Dowling.'

Dany turned quickly. 'Why do you say that? Are you sure?'

'That she wouldn't have twittered to Larry? But my dear, of course not! the man writes for the newspapers, and if he got his predatory little pen on to this, Tyson and your lovely Mum would be distinctly testy, and Amalfi wouldn't like being shown the door at all. You're quite, *quite* safe there. At least, for the time being. I suppose it's all bound to come out sometime or other, but, with any luck, after our scribbling little friend has got his interview — and enough material to libel the lot of us — and left.'

The thought of Mr Larry Dowling appeared to divert Nigel's interest into other channels, for he frowned and said: 'I simply cannot understand what Tyson is playing at. Why doesn't he give the man an interview and a basin full of facts, and send him off? Why ask him to the house and keep him hanging about? — putting him off, and putting him off. Really, *very* vexing. I wish you'd tell me what he's up to. I suppose you know?'

'I don't know anything about Mr Dowling,' said Dany hastily, evading the question.

'And how much do you know about Mr Holden, I wonder?' said Nigel, and gave a malicious, knowing little giggle. His face was both mocking and sly, and Dany said hotly: 'What do you mean?'

Nigel looked at her with his head on one side like some large, sleek, wary bird — a secretary bird. Then he put a finger to his lips and rose swiftly and silently and went quickly and very quietly to the door that led into the hall, and jerked it open.

The whole manoeuvre bore such an exaggerated air of secrecy and stealth that Dany quite expected to see a crouching figure disclosed, kneeling with its ear to the keyhole. But the hall was empty, and having satisfied himself that there was no one there or in the courtyard, Nigel returned to his chair looking slightly self-conscious.

'Forgive the amateur theatricals, but I would *so* much prefer not to be overheard. I take it that you don't really know much about the merry Mr Holden? apart from the usual things — the fact that he was head over heels about the bewitching Amalfi, and got pipped at the post by Eduardo (there ought to be a law

234

against these Latins, don't you agree?). But otherwise, has he spilled the beans? Are you, in the distressing jargon of the age, "hep"?'

Dany said uncertainly: 'I don't know what you mean.'

'Don't you? Hasn't it ever struck you that there is something a little — odd about Lash Holden?'

'No. Why "odd"?'

'Well, "peculiar" if you prefer the word. And don't start jumping down my throat, I beg! As you see, I have been the *soul* of tact, and refrained from probing into *why* you feel it necessary to masquerade as his secretary. But hasn't it ever struck you as odd how *very* conveniently he always turns up at just exactly the right moment? Just like one of those *painfully* competent G-men. Or would it be more accurate to say, like some really expert card-sharp at work? It all looks *so* casual and simple; "Hey presto! — and here's the Ace of Spades; now how on *earth* did it turn up there? *What* an astounding piece of luck!" But is it?'

Dany came back to her chair, but she did not sit down: she held on to the back of it and stared at Nigel, white-faced:

'What are you trying to say?'

'Nothing, darling. I'm merely trying to *hint*. So much safer I always think, don't you? You see, Lashmer Holden, Senior, is a very old friend of Tyson's — an intimate friend, one might say. There isn't anything about Tyson or his house or his affairs that he doesn't know, and he also has the reputation of being one of those forthright characters whose motto is "Never Give a Sucker an Even Break".'

He saw Dany start, and said: 'Why the surprise? What have I said?'

'N-nothing,' stammered Dany. 'It was just that—— What were you saying about Lash's father?'

'Only that Pop Holden is what is technically termed a tough egg. He sticks at nothing and he has of late been edging on to queer street.'

'On to——?'

'Queer Street, darling. Don't be all *ingénue*. I believe he only just squeezed out of being indicted before some committee on a charge of un-American activities. Toying with the Commies. Nothing was ever *proved* you know, so of course one is being *dangerously* libellous even to whisper it. But everyone knew; and I believe it cost him simply thousands of dollars in bribes and what-have-you to keep it out of the courts. We were over there just when it was boiling up, and I believe he tried to borrow off Tyson. *Most* embarrassing. That was why one couldn't help wondering if Tyson hadn't rather naughtily refused to play, and so Junior decided to put the screw on. Very filial, if he did.'

Dany frowned and looked bewildered: 'I really don't know what you're talking about, Nigel, and I think you'd better stop.'

'Blackmail, darling,' explained Nigel, ignoring the request. 'Is that his little game? Has he involved the Daughter-of-the-House in some complicated piece of jiggery-pokery, and is he now telling Step-pop to pay up, or he spills it all to the Press? Tyson's really *very* well supplied with stocks and shares and lovely money, and quite *devoted* to your charming Mum. He'd probably pay and pay. Could it be that, I wonder?'

'No, it couldn't!' said Dany stormily. 'I've never heard such ridiculous nonsense! There isn't a word of truth in it!'

'Now, now, *now*, darling——! Don't get so excitable. You're as bad as Eduardo. Oh well — it was just an idea. But one couldn't help wondering if he didn't have *some* little game on. One is sorry for him, of course. The family name teetering on the edge of the dustbin, the family fortune down the drain, and the glamorous girl-friend (who between you and me must have got wind of the cash deficiency!) abandoning ship for a coroneted Italian cutter. But what is he here for? Just what is he after? That's what I'd like to know. Call me inquisitive if you like — and how right you will be!'

Dany said stiffly: 'You know quite well why he is here.'

236

'Oh, but you're wrong. I don't. Has he joined the G-men or the F.B.I. perhaps? Is he, if one may be forgiven a winsome little pun, playing International M.I. Fives? Americans are becoming *painfully* Middle-East conscious these days. They can think of nothing else but Spheres of Influence and Rocket Bases. (And women of course — there's still simply *nothing* like a dame! Especially if she looks like Elf!) Or is he playing some sly little game of his own, and if so, what?'

Dany's hands tightened on the chair-back and she said furiously: 'You know perfectly well why he came here! He came to discuss the publication of the Emory Frost papers — and — and for a honeymoon in Zanzibar.'

'That's what *he* says. But the whole question of the Frost papers was discussed *ad nauseam* with his dear Papa less than six months ago in the States. Of course they hadn't been released from the lock-up then, and they might not have been worth publishing. But a couple of letters would have settled the matter. He wasn't invited here, you know. He suggested it himself. And who ever heard of anyone combining a honeymoon with business? Even the most dollar-adoring Yank would shy like a steer at that one. They may worship cash (and who doesn't!) but they are also simply *saturated* with sentiment about such things as Momma and Marriage Bells. That's what makes it all *so* intriguing. Surely you can see that?'

'No!' said Dany stormily. 'I can't. I think you've just got a — a fertile imagination.'

'My dear, *too* right! And at the moment it is positively *fecund.* The wildest conjectures came sprouting out of the soil as soon as I saw the dear boy turning up here minus a honeymoon and plus the phoniest American secretary that it would be possible to conceive in a month of provincial repertory matinees! One was *instantly* reminded of Crippen.'

'*Crippen*? Why? How ...' Dany suddenly discovered that the chair-back was an inadequate support, and releasing it, sat down in the chair instead with a feeling that her legs were made of something that closely resembled half-cooked macaroni.

'*Surely* you've heard of Dr Crippen, dear? He brought off quite a tidy little murder, and then lost his head and skipped out of the country with his secretary, who was faintly disguised as a boy. It popped into my head almost as soon as I saw you. Well, perhaps not *quite* as soon as that, but as soon as I began to feel curious. I confess I was *thrilled*. Delicious shivers all up and down the spine! I said to myself "Now is he escaping from the law, and *where* has he buried the body of poor Ada — the real one?" But that of course was before I'd read the papers.'

Dany said in a brittle, breathless voice: 'What do you mean by that?'

Nigel gave his little tittering laugh and looked down at the newspaper that lay on the floor beside his chair, and then up again at Dany:

'Suppose you tell me that one?'

Dany said jerkily: 'I don't see why I should, but — but I will. If you want to know, Mr Holden happened to be staying at the same hotel as I was in London——'

'So convenient,' murmured Nigel.

'Do you want me to go on?'

'But of course, darling. I am *enthralled*. And I promise I won't interrupt again.'

'His secretary, Miss Kitchell, had developed mumps, and I had — had lost my passport, and hadn't time to get another before the plane left. So he suggested I should use hers. For — for a lark.'

'"Ha-ha"!' said Nigel. *'What* a cut-up the boy is! He must have lots in common with those Northern 'varsity students who think up all the sparkling and sophisticated pranks for the installation of a new Rector. But seriously, darling — *did* she have mumps? Or was it just sleight of hand?'

'I don't——' began Dany.

238

'The Ace of Spades,' explained Mr Ponting with a trace of impatience. ' "Hey presto — why, what a bit of luck!" That sort of trick. So simple really; if you know how it's done.'

'But there wasn't any trick about it,' protested Dany. 'Of course she had mumps.'

'How do you know? Because you are a nice, unsophisticated Innocent who believes everything she is told?'

The words were an echo of something else that Dany had heard that day. Lorraine had said almost the same thing. And she too had been talking about Lash——

Nigel said: 'So easy to say something like that. And almost as easy, one imagines, to see that you lose your passport! You did say that you'd lost it, didn't you? How — if one may ask another intrusive little question? It isn't a thing one just casually drops on the nearest counter, or leaves in the loo.'

'Well, it was — I mean, I . . .'

Nigel tittered again. 'You seem confused. But it was probably all too simple. Like the card trick. You palm one passport, and Hey presto! — here's another! What a happy coincidence. See?'

'No, I don't! And I don't believe a word of it. And anyway, why should Lash — Mr Holden — do anything like that? Why bother to bring me here when I was coming anyway?'

Nigel shrugged his shoulders and flung out his hands in an affected gesture: 'Well, darling — I did advance a little theory about that, didn't I? But as you trampled on the poor thing most harshly, I won't risk making it again. Perhaps he just wanted to keep you under his eye. And why not, indeed? Though I must admit that as the honeymoon was off it was perhaps a teeny bit tactless of him to tag along after his ex-love and the new Italian model, and one would have imagined that he would cancel the trip. Oh, well, I expect it will all be as clear as Vichy water one of these days — and equally innocuous. It's much more fun wondering, isn't it? I adore mysteries! Have another cup of tea?'

He peered into the tea-pot, clicked his tongue regretfully and

239

announced that there wasn't any and that the hot water was cold. 'Just as well, really, as it's almost drinking time. I'd no *idea* it was so late and I'm dining out tonight with some enchanting Parsees. They serve the most delicious curries, which one can never resist but which play havoc with the digestive juices. Still, better that than eating a picnic meal by moonlight, which is sheer hell. Sandy sausages and mosquito-repellent getting into every glass. I *do* pity you all.'

He rose gracefully. 'Will you forgive me if I leave you to entertain yourself a bit while I hurry off and change? And don't worry, dear Miss Kitchell. Your guilty secret is *quite* safe with me. I promise I won't even drop the teeniest hint to anyone. Cross my heart!'

He retrieved the fallen newspaper, folded it carefully, and tucking it under his arm, tripped away, leaving Dany alone in the empty drawing-room with the tea cups and some most unpleasant thoughts.

19

Lash. *No . . . It isn't possible!* But it was. Unthinkable, but not impossible.

Lash . . . She must speak to him. She would ask him . . .

You don't have to believe everything he says.

But she had believed everything. Why? . . . Because he was Lash, and she had fallen in love with him. Because he was almost the first attractive man she had ever met, and any girl in love for the first time is convinced that this is the real thing — this is for ever. And find that it is neither.

'That your first kiss?' 'Yes, how did you know?' *'I've been around.'*

She hadn't stopped to analyse the significance of that reply, but she did now. It meant that he had made love to a good many other girls: and kissed a good many women. He would know just how to handle them. How to string them along.

She would, she realized, have been perfectly prepared to believe that anyone else might commit murder: Gussie, Seyyid Omar, Eduardo di Chiago, Amalfi Gordon and perhaps even Larry. But not Lash.

She had worked out ways and means and theories, and had heard Lash do so, in the case of other suspects: but it had never occurred to her for one moment that Lash himself might be one. And yet he was surely the most obvious one. He had even pointed it out himself — and she had rejected it: brushed it aside instantly and with impatience.

Was that why he had done so? To ensure that she would reject

241

it? A form of bluff? And yet — he could have done every-thing ...

Dany dropped her head into her hands, pressing them over her eyes and trying to think back. To think clearly.

His father knew Tyson probably better than anyone else, and Tyson might well have written to him about the discovery he had made among the Frost papers, and also told him what he intended to do. Lash could have gone down to see Mr Honeywood, and been seen by Millicent, who would not have recognized him, or he her — until later.

He had booked a room at the same hotel as Dany, and the rest would have been easy enough to contrive. He might even have been on the fire-escape or the balcony outside her room, and seen her leave it, and walked quietly across the room, and shut the door behind her. Then, taking her own key off the dressing-table, left by the window and come up the stairs, pretending to be the worse for drink.

He would have had plenty of time to search her room while she was waiting in his, and, when he could not find what he was after, to remove her passport and plant that gun. And now that she came to think of it, he had turned up right on cue, when she found it. *'Hey presto and here's the Ace of Spades! now how on earth did it turn up here?' That sort of trick!* ... And it had been Lash's idea that she come with him in the place of Miss Kitchell.

Had Miss Kitchell really had mumps? Or had she merely been informed at the eleventh hour that her presence was not required — because her passport was?

But there had been that night in Nairobi, and the man who had meant to chloroform her. That could not possibly have been Lash. He had been sound asleep on the sofa. No, the whole thing was nonsense! A wild figment of Nigel's jackdaw imagina-tion, that did not stand up to a moment's sober examination.

But ... but there were two people who wanted that letter.

242

Or two groups of people. One who was still looking for it, and the one who had it. The sealed envelope that bore Emory Frost's initials had been taken out of her coat pocket, the seal broken and the letter abstracted. And it could only have been done by one person — Lash Holden.

'No — no — *no!*' said Dany, aloud and desperately. 'He wouldn't. He didn't. I don't believe it and I won't believe it!'

Who else? whispered a small, remorseless voice in her brain. How else? You don't have to believe everything he says . . .

Dany stood up quickly and began to walk up and down the darkening room, arguing with herself: trying to remember; trying to persuade herself that someone else could have taken it. But there was no way out. No loophole of escape. It had to be Lash.

It was just conceivably possible that a skilful pickpocket could have stolen the whole thing; chiffon scarf and all. But to take it out, remove the letter and return it, was utterly impossible. But Lash could have done it with ease. Either while she was in her bath that morning, or when she had given him her coat to hold on the plane.

'No!' said Dany again, speaking pleadingly into the unheeding silence. But even as she denied it she knew that the answer was 'yes', for she had remembered something else——

Lash standing on the window-sill of his room last night, reaching up into the mass of bougainvillaea that grew above it. Lash's face when she had said: 'If Seyyid Omar hasn't got it, who has?' His face had changed and become blank and expressionless, and he had looked away from her and would not meet her eyes. Yes, Lash had got the letter. She was suddenly and wearily sure of it. He had probably carried it in his pocket, and been startled by the realization that pockets can be picked, when he had seen her ruined handbag, and had decided to find a better hiding place for it.

What did he want it for? If, as Seyyid Omar had said,

243

there were men in Zanzibar whose ultimate object was a dictatorship under Soviet domination, was Lash a Secret Service man whose task was to prevent this? Or did he want Seyyid Saïd's treasure for himself?

Jembe ... Millicent Bates ... It could have been Jembe who had meant to search her room at Nairobi, and Lash could have known it, or guessed it. Millicent had said that she never forgot a face, and Lash had said that she had died because she talked too much. Lash's father almost certainly possessed a copy of *The House of Shade*, and the note that had lured Millicent to her death had been written on Ada Kitchell's typewriter.

'A rakish heel who could hook the average woman with the ease of a confidence trickster getting to work on a frustrated small-town spinster ...' Someone had said that — about Lash. Was she, Dany, a frustrated small-town spinster? Lorraine too had suggested that she was young and inexperienced and naïve — and too romantic! — and Nigel had begged her not to be so *ingénue*. So perhaps she was all those things.

A tear crept down Dany's white cheek and she brushed it away impatiently. Crying would not help her, but there was at least one thing that would. She could make sure. She could go to the guest-house and look for Emory Frost's letter. Not now, because it was getting late and the others would be back soon. But as soon as another opportunity offered and she was certain of Lash being out of the way.

The cars returned not five minutes later, and as Dany had no desire to see or speak to anyone at the moment, she ran up to her room and locked the door, and only opened it when Lorraine knocked on it to ask if she were all right, and had she had a good sleep?

'You know, darling,' said Lorraine worriedly, observing her daughter with some anxiety, 'you're looking very washed out. Or perhaps it's that hair. I really do think we should——'

'Mother,' interrupted Dany tersely, 'did Tyson ever write to

Lash's father about that letter of Emory Frost's? The one I fetched from Mr Honeywood?'

'Darling, I've no idea. He may have done — they've always been such bosom buddies. Why?'

'Nothing,' said Dany quickly. 'I only wondered if — if anyone else knew about it.'

'I don't think so. Except of course that someone must have known, mustn't they? Really, it's all very worrying and upsetting, and I often wish — Oh, well — don't let's talk about it.'

She sat down on the dressing-table stool, and looking at her charming reflection said: 'I look a mess. I wonder if there's time for a bath before we start off on this picnic? No, I suppose not. We didn't mean to be back so late, but Tyson brought a friend of Elf's along to the hotel. It seems he flew to Mombasa only the day after you, and joined George Wallingborne's yacht, and they got here late last night. Tyson's been out fishing with them. A man called Yardley, Sir Ambrose Yardley. And if you ask me, he's only come here because of Elf. He should have been doing something or other in Khartoum, but he only stayed there about a day and a half, and followed her down here. I suppose I should have asked him back to the house: he was angling for it. But Eduardo was being rather rude and silly about the whole thing, and I really felt that I could not cope with any more dramas. And anyway, we're all lunching with them tomorrow.'

She dabbed her face absently with some of Dany's powder, rubbed it off again, and rose with a sigh.

'Don't put on anything too nice darling, because we're having a picnic supper on the beach. Tyson's idea. He's gone all Boy Scout and wants to build a drift-wood fire and fry sausages. *Ugh!* I can't think of anything much less alluring, but he's feeling energetic and all hearty-and-outdoor. Don't be too long, will you baby?'

The sky was rose-pink and apricot with sunset and the house was full of shadows by the time Dany returned to the drawing-room. She had expected to find the entire house-party assembled there, but there were only two people in the room: two people standing so close together that for a moment, in the dim light, they had looked like one.

They moved quickly away from each other as they heard the soft sound of Dany's sandalled feet on the thin Oriental rugs, and Amalfi Gordon came towards her, her face and her slender figure dark against the wash of sunset that burned beyond the french windows. She passed Dany without speaking, and went out of the room and across the darkening hall, her high heels clicking on the polished stone.

Lash said: 'Why the old-fashioned look, bambina? Did you think you'd walked in on a Grand Reconciliation scene? Because if you did, you've got it wrong. I'm not as polygamous as I look.'

Dany said coldly: 'I can't see that it is anything to do with me if you feel like hugging Mrs Gordon.'

'Now wait a minute! I was not hugging her!'

'No? Well that's what it looked like to me. Where has everyone else got to?'

'I don't know, and I can't say I care. Tell me what you've been doing with yourself all the afternoon? I didn't like the idea of leaving you on your own, but Lorraine said to let you sleep, and that Nigel would keep an eye on you. Did he?'

'Yes,' said Dany briefly.

She turned to leave the room and Lash came quickly after her and caught her arm. 'What's the matter, honey? You aren't really sore at me, are you? Look, I can explain——'

'Can you?' said Dany bleakly. 'But then I don't have to believe your explanations, do I?'

Lash's fingers tightened painfully on her arm and he jerked her round to face him, and then released her abruptly as someone came quietly through the open door behind her.

'Hullo,' said Larry Dowling, his casual, pleasant voice in marked contrast to the quietness with which he had moved. 'Am I late? Where is everyone?'

246

'In the garden, I guess. Why don't you go and look for them?' snapped Lash.

'Yes, let's,' said Dany thankfully. 'I'll come with you, Larry.'

She caught at his arm and they went out past Lash through the french windows and on to the terrace, where they were joined a few minutes later by Gussie and Tyson.

Dany had hoped to find some opportunity to speak privately to her step-father, but it was obvious that she was not going to get it tonight. Tyson had spent a strenuous day fishing and drinking, but it did not appear to have exhausted his energy. He herded his guests down to the shore and along the wet sands in the last of the sunset, and having selected a suitable spot in a little bay less than a quarter of a mile from the *Kivulimi* beach, set them to collect drift-wood for a fire.

'He gets these hearty fits at intervals,' explained Lorraine in a resigned aside. 'Very exhausting while they last, but fortunately they don't last long. You shall all have a lovely smoked salmon and caviar meal tomorrow to make up for it. But I do think this view is rather heavenly, don't you? Look at those fantastic rocks. And that dhow out there — isn't it enchanting? I wonder where it's bound for? Hejaz or Samakhand ...'

Gussie said tartly: 'They'd have some difficulty in navigating her there, unless she's amphibious!'

'Oh, I didn't mean literally. Her cargo, perhaps. But those are such lovely names.'

As the sunset faded and the sky turned from pink to lilac, lavender and green, the firelight gained strength and lit up the weird shapes of the coral rocks and the fronds of pandanus as though they had been stage scenery. And presently the moon rose, lifting into the quiet sky like some enchanted Chinese lantern and filling the night with magic.

The sausages, as Nigel had predicted, were both sandy and underdone; but honour and Tyson being satisfied, Lorraine had produced an excellent selection of cold foods that had been carried

247

down to the beach by one of the house-servants. And later, when the remains had been carried back again, they played what she called 'suitable moonlight music' on a portable gramophone, and explored along the shore.

Tyson and Lash went off armed with flashlights and fish spears to peer into the rock pools further down the beach, and Dany, watching them go, suddenly made up her mind that this was as good an opportunity as any to visit the guest-house. They would obviously be occupied for at least half an hour, and it would not take her much more than ten minutes to get back to the house, where there would be only the servants, who at this hour would have retired to their own quarters. She would be back again before anyone had troubled to notice that she had gone, and she could not endure the thought of another night — or even another hour — without knowing.

Gussie was discussing cookery with Lorraine, while Larry Dowling was lying on his stomach on the sand and putting records on the gramophone, and Amalfi and Eduardo had strolled away along the beach in the wake of Lash and Tyson. It would be quite easy.

Dany stood up, brushing off sand, and went across to murmur in her mother's ear, and Lorraine said vaguely: 'Yes, of course. But why not just behind a rock, darling? There are lots about.'

Dany withdrew, flushed and indignant, and once out of range of the dying firelight began to walk quickly, hurrying without running, until at last she reached the rocks that bounded one end of the *Kivulimi* beach, where she paused briefly to look back. But she could no longer see the glow of the drift-wood fire or any of her fellow picnickers, and the only thing that moved in the moonlit world were the ghostly little crabs, the lazy, lapping tide, a soft breeze and the lateen sail of an idling dhow.

Once on the far side of the rocks the *Kivulimi* beach lay before her, quiet and deserted, and Dany ran across the white, open sand and up the short rock path to the door in the garden wall.

The heavy wooden door with its flaking paint and iron nail heads creaked as it opened, and the sound was suddenly daunting. Dany stood still under the stone archway, listening intently, but she could hear nothing more than the soft breathing of a little breeze that whispered among the leaves of the garden and rustled the palm fronds.

There were no lights on in the house, but the white-washed walls and the window-panes caught and reflected the moonlight so that it gave the impression of being brightly lit and awake and watchful. An impression so strong that for a moment Dany found herself wondering if it was still looking seaward, as it had in a past century, for the sails of ships — merchant ships, pirate ships, whaling ships, ships from Oman and the dhows of the slave traders. *Then I'll go sailing far, off to Zanzibar . . .*

Dany caught her breath in a small sob, and looking resolutely away, turned to follow a path between the orange trees, skirting the pool and keeping parallel to the wall until she reached the flight of steps that led up to the guest-house.

The top of the wall was bright with moonlight, but the steps were in black shadow, and Dany was half-way up them when she heard the gate creak again.

She froze where she stood; listening with every nerve strained and alert for the soft crunch of crushed shell and coral that would tell her that she had been followed. But it did not come, and as the gentle breeze lifted the fringe on her forehead she remembered that she had left the gate open, and the breeze would have swung it on its hinges. And turning again she ran up the remaining steps, careless of noise and only aware of the necessity for speed.

The guest-house too was in darkness, and Dany turned the handle of the door, and pushing it open, felt for the switch.

The light seemed startlingly garish after the cool white night outside, and she turned it off again; realizing that she did not

249

need it, for it was not here that she meant to search. She did not even glance about the room, but went straight to the window and looked out and up.

The bougainvillaea swung down from the roof edge in a mass of blossom whose colour had been almost lost in the moonlight, and it was not going to be nearly as easy as she had thought to stand on the narrow window-ledge and reach up.

The wall itself was built up on a little rocky cliff, and there was a drop of at least thirty feet from the window-ledge on to more rocks. Looking down on them Dany felt a cold qualm of vertigo, but it was too late to draw back, and she might not get a chance like this again.

She set her teeth, and having climbed cautiously on to the narrow ledge, holding desperately to the wooden frame, found that the worst part was turning round to face the wall. But once that was accomplished the worst was over, and with her back to the horrifying drop below her she found that she could look up into the mass of creeper above her with comparative ease.

She reached up and felt among the leaves, but could find nothing; and then her wrist touched a round edge of stone. There was a gutter some distance above the window; a narrow curve of stone, choked with dust and dead leaves and jutting out a few inches from the wall in the shadow of the overhanging creeper.

Dany found that she could just reach into it, and probing with shrinking fingers, fearful of snakes or spiders, she touched something that was not a dead leaf. And knew with a dreadful, sinking despair that she had been right. It was Lash who had taken the letter.

She drew it out from its hiding place and looked at it in the moonlight. A man's white linen handkerchief wrapped neatly about something that could only be a small folded piece of paper.

She felt a little sick and oddly light-headed, and for a moment she swayed against the wall, pressing her cheek against the rough stone, and afraid of falling. Her left hand, gripping the window-

250

pane, felt cramped and numb, and she knew that she must make the effort to get down and back into the room while she had the power to do so. She could not stand here, silhouetted against the lamp light, where anyone passing on the beach below could look up and see her.

She bent her head and her knees, and sliding her left hand down the frame, stepped down on to the low window-seat.

And it was only then, looking down at her scarlet linen sandals on the gaily coloured cretonne cover of the window-seat, that she remembered that she had turned out the light only a few minutes ago. But it was on now.

Dany stood quite still: unable to move or breathe. Unable even to lift her head.

Then someone had seen her leave, and had followed her. Someone had come up the steps and into the guest-house; but standing on the window-ledge with the rustling of the creeper in her ears she had not heard them. And in the shock of finding the thing that Lash had hidden she had not even noticed that the light had been switched on, or known that someone was standing in the doorway, watching her ...

She lifted her head very slowly and stiffly, as though fear had frozen her muscles, and looked into the cold eyes that were watching her from across the room.

20

'There now! I *knew* you'd lead me to it if I gave you the chance,' said Nigel Ponting in a self-congratulatory tone. 'Really, *too* simple.'

He tripped across the room and held out a thin, elegant hand. A hand as curved and predatory as the claw of a bird of prey.

'That's a good girl.'

He twitched the handkerchief from between her nerveless fingers and unwrapped it, disclosing a small folded square of yellowed paper which he opened and favoured with a smiling, comprehensive glance. 'Yes, indeed. The goods — as advertised. How very satisfactory! And now, darling, if you'll just stay right where you are——'

Dany shrank back and clutched at the sides of the window as he came towards her. 'Nigel — what are you going to do? You can't tell them! Not yet. He — there must be some explanation. He must be — be in the F.B.I., or something like that. You said so yourself! He *couldn't* be a murderer. He couldn't! Don't tell anyone. Give him a chance to explain first. Or — or to get away ...'

'What *are* you babbling about, dear girl?' inquired Nigel. 'Don't tell who what? Give who a chance to explain?'

'Lash. Oh, I know he took it, and I suppose it looks bad, but it can't be. And even if it were, I don't want the police to get him, whatever he's done! Nigel, please——!'

Nigel stared at her for a long moment, and then burst out laughing. 'My dear girl——! Oh, this is *too* delicious! Do you mean to say that you still haven't got it? Well, well! don't they teach

252

you anything at these expensive schools? Perhaps it's a pity to disillusion you. But why not? It isn't your American dreamboat whom the police would want to interview. Alas, no. It would be yours truly — Nigel P.'

'*You?* But you can't — It couldn't be——'

'Oh, but it could. It was! I read that peculiar document of Emory Frost's (your respected step-father is not aware that I possess a duplicate key to his locked box!) and also the letters to Honeywood. Even — I blush for it — your mother's to you. It was all laughably simple. Then all I had to do was to ask for a holiday, slip off to Kenya, and get a dear friend to flip me across to Egypt where there are simply *dozens* of nasty men who will do anything to annoy the Great White Raj.'

'Egypt——' repeated Dany in a dazed, foolish whisper. 'But Mr Honeywood wasn't——'

'*Tch! Tch!*' said Nigel reprovingly. 'You don't really suppose I stayed there, do you? No, they merely fixed me up with the necessary papers and popped me on to the plane for Naples, where I was met by a fascinating character; quite unscrupulous and *madly* talented. He used to be top make-up man in a film company before the war — and *what* a loss to the trade! You simply wouldn't have recognized me boarding the London plane a couple of hours later. I made a ravishing Signora. Too *chic!* I wasn't *nearly* so alluring on the return journey; but perhaps just as well, as we had some *rather* impressionable Oriental potentates on board. Direct to Cairo that time: and by a different line of course — you've no idea how efficient the whole set-up is! The staff work was quite beyond praise. As slick as a Sputnik. One was *most* impressed.'

A sudden hysterical wave of relief swept over Dany, drowning all other considerations. 'Then it wasn't Lash! It was you — it was you!'

Her knees buckled under her and she collapsed on to the window-seat, weak with tears and laughter.

'Of course it was,' said Nigel with a trace of impatience. 'Who else would be likely to know everything that went on in this house? And the whole affair would have gone off swimmingly if only you'd done what you were told. Really, *very* tiresome of you! I had it all worked out. Honeywood knew me, and he'd have had the packet ready and handed it over like a lamb when I explained that Tyson had sent me for it because you couldn't come. But you had to change the time and go and see the old fool in the morning instead, and mess everything up. So vexing and unnecessary.'

He frowned at the recollection, and then his face cleared and he laughed. 'Ah well——! "All's well that ends well". And now, darling, as we haven't got all night——'

Dany scrubbed her eyes with the back of her hand and looked up. And then, suddenly, terror was back. A crawling, icy terror that widened her eyes until they were dark pools in her white face.

She had been too stunned by shock and relief to take in more than a fraction of what Nigel had said, but now, staring up at him, she realized that he had been saying things that he would never have said unless ... unless ...

Her mouth was so dry that it was an effort to speak at all, and when the words came they were only a harsh whisper:

'What ... are you going ... to do?'

'Only give you one little push,' said Nigel gaily. 'It's a thirty-foot drop, and on to rocks, so it ought to do even better than that cunning little staircase trick. And Holden will be able to tell them just exactly how it happened. You were standing on the sill to reach into his private *cache* and you must have slipped and fallen. Like this——'

His hands caught her, forcing her back over the low sill, and then the dreadful numbness left her and she began to fight, twisting and clawing. But the ledge was low and her back was to the uncurtained window, and there was nothing to grasp at but wood and stone.

Her finger-nails scraped and broke and her screams were no more than harsh, gasping breaths: she was no match for Nigel's five-foot-nine of lean bone and muscle, and those thin white hands, that had once felt so limp, were astonishingly strong and curiously smooth — as though they were encased in silk. They gripped her shoulders, pulled her forward and then jerked her head back violently against one side of the window embrasure so that it hit the stone and stunned her.

A savage pain seemed to slice its way through her skull: coloured lights shot before her eyes, and the strength went out of her. She heard Nigel's little giggling laugh, but it seemed to come from a long way off, and to be cut off suddenly and sharply. And then the grip on her shoulders relaxed and she was falling . . . Falling down miles of echoing darkness from the window . . . No, not the window . . . Down a well. An underground well. Deep and cold and black, where there was black deep water in which she would drown . . .

The water filled her eyes and nose and mouth, choking her, and something burned her throat and choked her afresh. She struck out wildly, struggling to swim and to keep her head above water, and her hand touched something and clutched at it frantically.

A voice that hurt her head abominably said: '*Hi!* — look out! Let go of my ear!' And she opened her eyes with an enormous effort and found herself looking up at Larry Dowling.

Mr Dowling, who also appeared to have been in swimming, was tenderly massaging the side of his head and holding a dripping water jug, the contents of which he had evidently poured lavishly over Dany.

She stared up at him, blinking the water out of her eyes and wondering why he was there and where she was. Nothing

255

made any sense except that, somehow, he had saved her from drowning.

'Are you all right?' inquired Larry Dowling anxiously.

Dany attempted to give the matter her consideration, and after a moment said childishly: 'I'm wet.'

'I'll say you are!' said Mr Dowling fervently, taking the words in an uncomplimentary sense. 'You must be mad! Going off like that on your own when——'

'You're wet too. Did you jump in with all your clothes on?'

'I fell into that bloody bird-bath — that's why I didn't get here a lot sooner. I'm sorry about that. But at least you're not dead. It was a near thing though — *phew*!'

He took out a sopping handkerchief and mopped his wet forehead and Dany said: 'I think I'm going to be sick.'

'Here——! don't do that,' said Mr Dowling, alarmed. 'Try another swig of this.'

He reached for a bottle that had been standing on the floor beside him, and lifting Dany's head poured a liberal quantity of some fiery liquid down her throat.

Dany gasped and choked, but the stuff warmed her stomach and helped to dull the excruciating pain in her head. Larry Dowling, having laid her back, took a long pull at the bottle himself and said: 'Gosh, I needed that!'

He put it down, and lifting Dany, carried her over to the divan and lowered her on to it carefully. 'Are you feeling any better?'

'I don't know. What happened? Was I going to drown?'

'Drown? No. He was stuffing you through the window, and in one more minute—— However, don't let's think of that. Can you stand up?'

'Who was stuffing me through a window? I don't know what you're — *Nigel*!'

Dany attempted to rise and once again a blinding wave of pain and nausea lashed out at her.

256

'Here, take it easy,' urged Larry Dowling anxiously. He sat down beside her and put a dripping arm about her, supporting her.

Dany leant against his wet shoulder and said without opening her eyes: 'Where is he?'

'Over there,' said Larry briefly. 'It's all right. He won't move for hours — if ever. I cracked him over the head with a bottle of gin.'

Dany forced open her eyes again and saw for the first time that Nigel's limp body was lying face downwards on the floor near the window. She could not see his face, but there was a lump on the back of his head the size of a healthy orange, and his hands were joined behind him by links of metal.

She said slowly and stupidly: 'Handcuffs. Where did you get them?'

Larry Dowling looked slightly embarrassed. 'As a matter of fact, I thought at one time I'd have to use them on you.'

'On *me*?'

'Yes. I've been tailing you for days, young woman. And a tedious dance you've led me. You actually bumped into me once in London — rushing out of the dining-room at the Airlane. I was afraid you might recognize me next day, but you didn't.'

'*Tailing* me? To get a story? But you're——'

'Only a simple cop, I'm afraid. I'm sorry if it's a disappointment to you. We were going to grab you in London, and then, what with one thing and another, it seemed a better scheme to see where you went and what you led us to. The M.I.5 boys had a few ideas of their own on the whole situation, and wanted us to play it their way. So we radioed all the proper people to let you through on that borrowed passport, and I was sent along to find out what I could.'

'Oh,' said Dany; and added after a pause for thought: 'Lash isn't going to like that.'

'Lash has got a lot of explaining to do,' said Larry Dowling.

257

'I have, have I?' said a furious voice from the doorway. 'Well let me tell you that it's nothing to the explaining you're going to have to do!'

Dany said: 'Lash—— Oh, Lash!'

'I'll deal with you later,' said Lash savagely. 'When I've taken care of this double-crossing ten-cent Romeo of yours!'

He covered the distance between them in two hasty strides, and before the startled Mr Dowling had even grasped the implications of his remarks he had thrust Dany to one side, gripped her rescuer by the collar, jerked him to his feet and slugged him scientifically on the jaw.

Mr Dowling went down for the count and Dany started to laugh, burst into overwrought tears, and quite suddenly slid off the divan on to the floor in a dead faint. Making it three in all.

Lorraine was saying: '. . . raw beef steak. It's the only thing. I put it on Tyson once when he got into an argument with some men in San Francisco, and it worked *wonders*. Didn't it, darling?'

'Yes,' said a resonant voice. 'I ate it. And where do you think you're going to get raw beef steak at this hour of the night, I'd like to know?'

Dany winced and opened her eyes. She was lying in her own bedroom and there seemed to be a lot of people in it. Lorraine, Tyson, Gussie Bingham . . . She tried to turn her head, but finding that it was too painful, gave up the attempt and lay still.

At least she was not wet any longer, for someone had removed her drenched clothes and put her into a nightgown. She wondered if anyone had removed Larry's, which had been a good deal wetter, and she must have made an attempt to inquire, for suddenly they were all leaning over her, looking at her anxiously, and Lorraine was saying: 'Darling, how do you feel?'

Tyson said: 'Now don't go trying to sit up. Much better to lie still. Get some brandy into her.'

'I think Mr Holden gave her some,' said Gussie.

'Nonsense! How could he? She wasn't conscious. Here, Dany——'

Dany attempted a feeble protest, but to no avail, and Tyson, having dealt efficiently with the matter, laid her back on the pillows and said bracingly: 'Now you'll feel better!'

'Do you, baby?' inquired Lorraine anxiously, holding both her hands. 'Lash has taken one of the cars in to fetch a doctor and the police and medicines and things, and they'll be here soon, and then you'll be all right.'

Dany said: 'I'm all right now. Where's Larry? He saved me.'

'I know, darling. *Bless* him! If it hadn't been for him—— Oh, don't let's think of it. It's too awful!'

'It was Nigel.'

'Yes, darling. We know.'

'Ought to have known from the beginning,' growled Tyson, sitting down moodily on the end of her bed. 'No one else could have possibly known every dam' thing there was to be known. I suppose he took the letters off Abdurahman and said he'd post 'em. And he'd met old Honeywood, so he thought it would be quite easy. Turn up just before you, get the letter and then shoot him. And while you were being held up and questioned he'd be off and away.'

'But *how*?' said Gussie. 'How could he possibly be in England? He was in Kenya!'

Tyson said: 'Obviously he flew out. If you're in that camp, nothing is too difficult.'

'In what camp? What are you talking about?'

'The Reds, of course. Dowling is being a bit cagey about it, but it's obvious that the police, or M.I.5, or some of those cloak-and-dagger boys, had a line on him. And on this Zanzibar business.'

'What Zanzibar business?'

'An under-cover revolutionary movement that has recently

been started in this island. Dowling says that Nigel's always been in it up to his neck. He's one of the really fervent kind, and those are always more dangerous than the ones who are merely after the cash rewards. He was behind Jembe's party: working to turn the island into a hot little Soviet stronghold. Get rid of British influence, then the Sultan, start a "Democratic" republic — and up with the red flag! And the next step would have been to slap an iron curtain round it, and use it as a spring-board for all sorts of merry Russian ballets. But they needed money to buy votes and supporters and get the thing really moving, and when that paper of old Emory's turned up it seemed they'd got it.'

'But they hadn't got it!' protested Gussie.

'Don't be unintelligent, Gussie! They meant to get it. They thought it was more or less in the bag. All they had to do was to get that envelope off Honeywood. And since Nigel was the obvious person to get it, they arranged to send him home and get him back again — presumably by means of some flourishing and very well organized under-cover route. And then Dany spoilt the whole show by jumping the gun.'

Gussie said: 'It's all very confusing. And I still don't understand what this Jembe was doing in England, anyway.'

'At a guess, because the Reds have never learnt to trust one another a yard, and I imagine that he was sent to keep an eye on Nigel. But Nigel failed to get the goods off Honeywood, so he put Jembe on to trying to find it — that is the supposition, anyway — and to planting that gun and pinching her passport for good measure. To ensure that the police would be kept busy suspecting her for a bit, so that she'd probably end by posting off the letter.'

'*Too* silly,' said Lorraine. 'Once he knew she had it, he ought to have just let her bring it out with her, and found some way of getting it off her here.'

'Ah, but he couldn't travel out with her — and Jembe could!

Nigel would have had to nip back to Kenya in order to meet the plane at Nairobi, and I imagine he didn't trust Jembe. Probably thought that if Jembe got his hooks on it, while on his own, he'd stick to it and leave the Revolution to chase itself round the block. Dowling says that Jembe was obviously trailing Dany too, and so knew quite well who she was, and it seems that either he or Nigel had another crack at getting the letter in Nairobi. As a result of which, that blasted young idiot, Lash, got the wind up and swiped it.'

'Why?' croaked Dany.

'Oh, hullo kid. You feeling better? Have some more brandy,' said Tyson. 'Do you good.'

'Do you really think she ought to, darling? inquired Lorraine anxiously.

'Why not? Look how much better she's looking already. Drink it up, child.'

Dany drank, blinked, and said: 'Why did Lash take it?'

'Because he's an interfering, impertinent, insolent young son-of-a—— Well, let it go. He didn't like the set-up and thought it was a dangerous thing for you to have. Thought you'd be safer without it.'

'Why didn't ... he ... give it ... you,' said Dany slowly and carefully.

'Says he wanted to know a hell of a lot more about things before he did. Didn't trust me or anyone else with a sum like that at stake. Blast his impertinence!'

Gussie said in a hard voice: 'And Millicent? Why does Mr Dowling think that Nigel did that?'

'Probably because he was afraid that she really might have spotted him. He was officially supposed to be in Kenya, so what had he been doing mucking about in Kent? He'd actually read *The House of Shade*, which is more than I have — I've never been able to struggle further than page six — so getting rid of Millicent was easy.'

261

'And I suppose he killed Jembe too,' said Gussie with a shudder.

'Probably. If he talks, we may know. However, Dowling appears to have landed him such a crack that there's an even chance he won't. Can't think why he couldn't have used the siphon. Sheer waste of gin.'

'Tyson, how *can* you!' said Lorraine, releasing her daughter's hands and straightening up indignantly. 'Why, it saved Dany's life!'

'She'd have been saved quite as effectively by soda water,' said Tyson. 'Or better still, a bullet! Can't think why he didn't shoot.'

'Because of Dany, of course! He was afraid he'd hit her. He told you that.'

'So he did. Well, just as well he was there. Very lucky he saw her slip away.'

'Did he know that it was Nigel all the time?' inquired Gussie.

'I don't think so. But he had a few shrewd suspicions. It seems that parts of Kent were fairly misty on the morning that Honeywood was killed, and one or two trains ran late in consequence. Dowling says that Nigel mentioned that mist twice; though as it was only localized, and there was no mention of it on the news or in the papers, how did he know a thing like that — unless he was there? But Dowling didn't know that Nigel was hoping to needle Dany into leading him to Emory's letter, and he very nearly didn't get there in time because——Oh, there you are, Dowling. How's the jaw?'

'Swell,' said Larry Dowling bitterly, '— if I may borrow an Americanism from the donor. By this time tomorrow I shan't even be able to talk.'

'Or see out of your left eye,' said Tyson. 'The boy would appear to pack a punishing left. But I still can't see why he should have thought——'

'Neither can I,' said Larry. 'Considering that I happen to be a

262

loving husband and an indulgent father. How are you feeling, Miss Ashton?'

'Drunk,' said Dany. 'You all will keep on giving me brandy and whisky and things.'

She held out her hands to him. 'I'm sorry about your face, Larry. And — and thank you so very much. For everything.'

Her voice broke and her eyes filled with weak tears, and Larry sat down on the edge of the bed and took her hands in his.

'You haven't anything to thank me for. If I'd had the sense to look where I was going I'd have got that pro-Red so-and-so before he started any rough stuff. But because I didn't, I expect your head is a good deal worse than my jaw; so you're not really even with me yet!'

Gussie, who had been standing by the window, said: 'Here are the cars. This will be the police. Or the doctor.'

'And Holden,' said Larry Dowling, hastily releasing Dany and rising to his feet: 'Time I went. I'm not taking any chances on being found holding your hands again and getting another crack on the jaw. That boy is too impetuous by half. See you tomorrow.'

He went out, leaving the door ajar behind him, and they heard footsteps running up the stairs and then Lash's voice on the verandah outside. 'You here again?'

'And very well chaperoned,' said Larry, 'so you can keep your hands in your pockets! Have you brought the doctor?'

'Of course. I also gave him your letter.'

'Thanks. Where is he now?'

'Ministering to that murderous louse, who has apparently surfaced — worse luck!'

'Good: I'll send him up to see Miss Ashton as soon as he's finished down there.'

Larry's footsteps retreated and Dany sat up dizzily as the door opened and Lash came in.

He paid no attention at all to Lorraine, Gussie or Tyson, but

263

came straight across to the bed and took Dany into his arms.

'Don't mind us,' remarked Tyson caustically.

'I don't,' said Lash, '— much.'

He turned his head to look over his shoulder at Lorraine, and said: 'The doc will be up here as soon as he's through with Ponting, and after that, if I know doctors, he'll throw me out on my ear. So I'd be deeply obliged if you'd all scram.'

'Of course, dear,' said Lorraine. 'Come on Gussie. Tyson——' The door closed behind them.

Dany said: 'Lash, you aren't a G-man, are you? I thought you might be — or a murderer — because you'd taken that letter, and Nigel said—— And I knew I ought to hate you if you were a murderer, but I couldn't — and I'm so glad you're not a G-man! I didn't want you to be, and I'm so sorry. Lash, I'm sorry — so sorry——'

Lash said: 'All right, honey, all right. You're sorry. For Pete's sake, how much brandy did they give you?'

'Lots,' said Dany. 'Lots and lots and lots. Firs' Larry, then you, then Tyson . . . It's good for you. I shouldn't have listened to Nigel. Lash, you will forgive me, won't you? because I couldn't bear it if you didn't . . . I couldn't bear it——'

'This is just about where we came in,' said Lash. 'Only it was me last time. It's a judgement on me! Darling, you're plastered! All right, I'll forgive you — but after this if I ever catch you drinking anything stronger than a chocolate-soda, so help me, I'll take a strap to you! Darling — my darling — *my darling . . .*'

The African police-constable on guard saluted smartly and ushered Mr Dowling into a small ground-floor room leading off the central courtyard, where the window shutters were further reinforced by iron grille work and the doors were stout. A room that was, oddly enough, the self-same one to which Tyson's grandfather, Rory Frost, had brought his share of Sultan Saïd's treasure for temporary safe-keeping on a wild, rainy night over ninety-five years ago. No one now alive was aware of this; yet, strangely, a superstition survived that the room was, for some obscure reason, a place of ill-omen: which perhaps accounted for the fact that until an hour or so ago it has been kept locked and unfurnished.

Now, however, having been hastily denuded of dust and innumerable spiders-webs, it contained a heavy brass bedstead, a couple of cane armchairs loosely covered in faded chintz, a bed-side table, and an ornate, marble-topped Victorian wash-hand-stand complete with an imposing array of flower-patterned china utensils. It also contained — in addition to the doctor — Nigel Ponting and Mr Cardew: the former lying prone upon the bed with his right wrist securely handcuffed to a brass bedpost, while the latter, who had arrived at the House of Shade in response to an urgent telephone call from Larry Dowling, occupied one of the cane chairs, pad and pencil at the ready.

Mr Dowling noted with approval that the doctor had wasted no time. The wet towel that some amateur hand had hastily wound about the secretary's head, in the manner of an untidy turban, had been removed, together with his coat, and a shirt sleeve that had been rolled back disclosed the mark of a recent injection on Nigel's bare arm. An empty syringe lay on the bed-side table, and Nigel's eyes were open. He was muttering to himself, and watching someone whom he could see, but the others could not, moving about the room.

'Is it going to work, Doc?' inquired Superintendent Cardew in an undertone.

'I don't know,' returned the doctor shortly. 'I've never had occasion to use it before. And, if it does, I don't guarantee that you'll get the truth. It's more likely to be a load of old rubbish or else pure fantasy. And, what's more, I'm not at all sure that this business isn't illegal and that I won't wind up finding my-self struck off the Medical Register!'

'Nonsense. Besides, if anyone hears of it — and they won't —

265

you can always say that you were only carrying out the orders of the police, and put the blame on us. We're used to that.'

'And how!' endorsed Larry feelingly. Adding a trifle anxiously that he hoped that the quality and volume of the sound was going to improve, because at present he could not make out a word that the prisoner was saying.

'Give him time,' urged the doctor, busy replacing the discarded turban with an elaborate and highly professional bandage. 'You can't expect that stuff to act with the speed of light.'

Larry sighed, and pulling up the vacant chair, seated himself gingerly in its creaking depths, produced his own notebook and pencil, and sat waiting to take down anything relevant that the prisoner might say.

Mr Ponting continued to mutter unintelligibly and the doctor, having completed the bandage to his satisfaction and felt his patient's pulse again, picked up the syringe and wrapped it in a square of surgical gauze. He was stowing it away in his bag with some ostentation — as if to forestall any request from the guardians of the law for a further injection of the drug he had been asked to administer — when Nigel Ponting began to talk: aloud and clearly . . .

'. . . There is no proof,' declared Nigel, addressing the unseen person whose movements he had been watching, and who was now apparently standing at the foot of the bed. 'I've been too clever for them. There isn't an atom of proof, and they'll never think of looking under Tyson's floorboards for that duplicate key . . . Right under his nose! And of course for any serious work I always took care to wear gloves — that pair of silk ones to match my skin that Don had specially made for me in Cairo. They've proved invaluable. There'll be no prints on the stair mechanism, or anywhere else. They teach you to cover your tracks, as you know. They're very insistent about that. Old Honeywood never noticed the gloves even though it was mid morning. Though of course it was a grey day, and I have to admit that the mist

266

was a bonus — one might almost call it providential — if one believed in Providence, which luckily I don't . . .

'A pity it wasn't thicker . . . If it had been, that Bates woman would never have recognized me — silly bitch! *I never forget a face!* That really was bad luck. Hers not mine. Tiresome, beady-eyed old busy-body! I certainly didn't remember hers. But of course after that I had to get rid of her as quickly as possible . . . I must tell you about that. It was laughably easy and I really do pride myself on it . . . It was a stroke of genius. All I had to do was type an urgent little note on the Ashton girl's typewriter, push it under Bates's door, set the stair trap and wait for her to fall into it. Which of course she did — *plunk*!

'. . . Yes. Terrible about Jembe — I don't know how I'm going to manage without him. I wonder who did it? We shall have to find out. I suppose the police will have searched his luggage. Let's hope he was careful: his type so often aren't . . . too conceited. It's our weakest link. Oh, well, I shall have to find a replacement. It shouldn't be difficult — three million will buy almost anything! . . . We could swing the elections for a fraction of that. It's after we've done it that the trouble will start. I know we need islands and that this one is the best one to begin on . . . but the snag is going to be the Zanzibaris. They're too damned easy-going. They'll have to be educated . . . taught to kill. And to hate. That's the important thing. Hate . . . to hate . . . to hate. And after that . . .'

The harsh, unfamiliar voice, that contained no trace of those high-pitched and carefully cultivated fluting tones that had been part of a successful disguise for so long, talked on and on, while the horrified doctor (who had been more than half inclined to take all he had been told about Ponting with a large helping of salt) frowned and fussed and muttered oaths that were certainly not Hippocratic, and Messrs Cardew and Dowling scribbled swiftly, filling page after page of their official notebooks. Jotting down names that would later be identified and their

267

owners traced, together with dates and details that were to prove damning ...

When at last the hoarse voice slurred to a stop, the doctor — having declared that the performance was over and that the prisoner would now sleep for several hours — departed upstairs to see what he could do for Miss Ashton, and Mr Cardew mopped his brow with a pocket handkerchief and announced that he would be jiggered.

'If you'd told me that, and I hadn't heard it with my own ears, I wouldn't have believed a word of it,' confessed Mr Cardew. 'And, whatever the Doc's reservations are about using that drug, there was nothing phoney about that performance! If ever anything came straight from the horse's mouth, that did! But I didn't follow that stuff about the three million that's going to give Jembe's dupes a walk-over in the elections, and turn Zanzibar into a Communist paradise and a base for Russian spy-rockets and atom-subs and all the rest of it. Whose three million?'

'Tyson's grandfather's,' said Larry. 'The old reprobate reportedly stashed away roughly that amount as his share of Sultan Saïd's treasure, which he and a subsequent Sultan, Majid, somehow got their hooks on. And all this murder and mayhem was apparently sparked off by a map that shows where he hid it. It seems to have turned into a nasty adult version of that popular children's party game, "Hunt-the-slipper", and to date three people — if one can count "the thin man" as one of them — have been murdered for the sake of that map.'

'Who's got it now?'

'Mr Frost, I imagine. Unless it's still on the floor of young Holden's room in the guest annex. I forgot to ask.'

'Do you think they'll find it? — the loot, I mean.'

'I expect so. That is, if it's still there. It may not be. But if it is, at least it won't be going to swell the coffers of some local Dictator and his Commissars, and their home-picked brand of the K.G.B.'

'No, thank God! Well, Dowling, now that that's over, I'll be off to dig the Resident out of bed and see what can be done to ensure that this murderous fellow-traveller gets sent back under guard to stand trial at the Old Bailey. And a very good night to you!' The door banged behind him.

'Some hope!' sighed Larry sadly. And resigned himself to spending what remained of the night in a creaking and far from comfortable cane armchair.

Postscript from 'Kivulimi'.

. . . it sounds to me a very dull place for a honeymoon, baby. Though I do see that you both felt you'd had enough of romantic places for a bit. It's a pity we didn't buy you a mackintosh and some sensible shoes, but anyway, I expect you can get them there, and I'm sure you're both having a heavenly time, even if you are only on parole or bail or something. And by the way, Larry said to remind you that if you don't turn up in London on the right date and the right time he'll have you both arrested and never speak to you again. So you won't go all starry-eyed and forget, will you darling? (Tyson says that if I'm referring to your husband, I mean pie-eyed. But of course I don't.)

I think we've got rid of the police at last, which is a blessing (except for darling Larry. I wish he could have stayed) and we had a bit of drama over Elf. I expect you saw the announcement in the papers. She's going to marry Sir Ambrose Yardley. She says that Tyson advised her to marry someone like that. Very naughty of him, as of course Eduardo was simply heartbroken, and we had the most exhausting scenes — and right on top of everything else: I can't tell you! Still, they've both gone, and if I know Eddie, he's already in love with someone else.

Everything else seems to have been sorted out, except for the Jembe business. I don't suppose we shall ever know about that, but

269

it seems that Nigel didn't do it, and Tyson says he's quite sure that Seyyid Omar did. He was dining with us here the other night and mentioned that Jembe suffered from air sickness, or nerves or something, and that he'd given him something to take for it. And then he looked at Tyson with that bland smile of his and said: 'Like your revered uncle, one does what one can.' And then they both drank Barclay's health. Really — men! How could they? When one thinks of all that lovely money. Oh I forgot you wouldn't know about that — I must tell you——

It wasn't nearly as easy as they thought to find it, the treasure I mean, because of course Tyson's father had bricked up all those walls. (Tyson says he was always messing up the place with improvements.) And when we got there at last, all we found was a rather pompous letter from Barclay. It was a bit difficult to read, as it got damp, but we read it and it seems that the silly old man had come on the gold when he was poking about in the foundations for material for that boring book of his, and believe it or not, he had carried it all out, bit by bit and night after night, and dumped it into the sea from one of those little fishing carracks, about a mile offshore. Really, *darling!*

He said money in a place like Zanzibar was a source of evil, because all it led to was Progress; and he was against progress, because it seldom led to happiness, and more often only meant hideous buildings, ugly factories, dirty railway yards and noisy motor cars, and things like strikes, lockouts and exploitation. He preferred coconuts, cloves and charm.

Tyson says it's rather like a story called 'The Treasure and the Law', but I don't think I can have read it. By the way, he's sending Lash a copy of The House of Shade *as a sort of extra wedding present, and he says if the first one's a boy you'd better call him Barclay, because in his opinion there can't be too many of them.*

Tyson doesn't seem to think much of Progress either. He says it was a good idea, but that it's got out of hand.

Well, darling——